IN THE VALLEY, A SHADOW

In Xypha's Shadow: Book One

Samantha Tano

About the Author

Samantha Tano is a science fiction author based in Rhode Island. She has worked as an award-winning journalist and development editor. She is a proud and vocal transgender woman. Her first novel published in 2024, her micro-fiction has appeared online in *Deep South Magazine*, and she has appeared in *The Boston Globe*. You can find her reading in coffee shops around New England.

Acknowledgments

I must thank a handful of people who helped make this book possible. First, my friends Bailey, M, and Mark provided such insightful feedback when reading the manuscript that I believe made this story better. Alexa Thomas performed a thorough edit, for which I am very grateful. Caitlin Alexander, who created the stunning cover, is truly a master of her craft. And of course, I must thank my beautiful wife, Kelly. Without her love, encouragement, and validation, this never would have been possible.

For Kelly, my regular bird.

1

The Pilot

A village with no name sat upon a mesa. Surrounding that mesa sprawled a canyon, steep-walled channels reached across the high desert in many directions, a river trickled over the sandy bottom. The canyon walls rose no higher than the mesa, and from a distance, the village lights could be seen, as if they sat upon a continuous plain. There weren't more than a dozen buildings, each one was uglier and dirtier than the last: beige plaster with dark mud and old, rotting wood. Beneath some of the plaster-covered walls, however, faint glimmers of sleek steel peeked through. A cluster of lights lifted into the sky beyond the town before turning and heading eastward, up among heavy clouds, pink with the setting sun.

The tallest building, a leaning and broken-down three levels, housed the most raucous bunch of gamblers, fighters, smugglers, thieves, murderers, and pretty much anyone else who didn't want to be found or bothered. Pleasant music drifted from the open windows and echoed in the cold air. Smoke hung thick in the air inside, and a din of voices, music, the angst of losing, and the confidence of winning created a vibration that passed through every being sitting at the many wooden tables beneath lamps hovering in midair.

At one of the tables sat a slim, fair-skinned woman, a blue scarf around her neck, goggles pushed back on her head, her dark hair tied in a ponytail. No one spoke around her, each player deep in thought, staring intently at the cards in their hands. A bearded man, dried food and spit in his beard just below his mouth, sat back, cards partially face down on the table. An old sentient, an android, in a black bowler hat and a fine red vest waited patiently, his eyes glittering within his faceplate, his cards neatly fanned out on the table in front of him.

The woman tapped her cards on the table, knowing what they held, but she counted and recounted the meager pile of crits in front of her. Surely she had not lost *that* much. *Too much? Had they noticed?* She cracked a smile, her sharp blue eyes darting from one player to the next, landing on the man to her left, who had begun to sweat.

With a final tap of her cards on the table, she pushed her remaining crits into the center and leaned back in the chair, which creaked beneath her. "I'm in."

The dirty-faced bearded fellow seemed displeased, which was exactly what she wanted to see, and though he wiped the small twinge from his face almost immediately, almost imperceptibly, she noticed it. Judging by the way he chuckled, he knew she noticed it too, and he tried to play it off, to carry the bluff to its conclusion, even though he knew the game was over.

The others around the table sighed and, one-by-one, they turned their cards over, some with the confidence of their hands. There were a few sneaky Matches; the sentient even had a strong Lunar Rise. He hoped that others were bluffing their strong bets and that the game was his, for he knew the odds well. But Alix had better, and she knew the man who wore his dinner and bad habits on his face had worse.

"Match seven," the bearded man said, turning over his cards. He looked at the sentient smugly. The sentient shook his head and began grinding his metal teeth, suddenly becoming interested in his gold pocket watch.

Alix smiled and cocked her head to the side, slowly turning the cards over to reveal a full Sunrise. The bearded man was furious, and his face flushed redder than the iron-rich soil outside. Alix leaned in, raking in the winnings—how many crits' worth, she had lost count.

"Sorry, fellas, but I guess my losin' streak is over," she said, trying to keep her voice innocent, feigning a bit of surprise, as if she hadn't played them all night.

The bearded man huffed and gulped down the rest of his ale. "Ain't it funny how that happens?"

Alix smiled as she stacked her crits. "Had to happen sometime, I guess."

The man pounded his fist on the table. "You been losing all night, and now here you are, raking in the biggest hand of the game."

"Sometimes, luck is just on your side, pal," Alix said with a calm shrug, straightening another stack of crits.

"Or you're a cheat!" The accusation shot across the table with a crack, and everyone around went silent, looking at him and Alix.

"Frankly, Bandy, I'm offended you think I'd have to cheat to beat you."

Alix smiled, laughing at her own joke. In a loud rush, Bandy kicked back his chair, but before he could reach for the Plasveld-7 Alix noticed him carrying when he first sat down, the barrel of her own Plasveld-7 pointed squarely at his chest. In her left hand, the Plasveld's cylinder glowed blue as the plasma-energized rounds within the six chambers heated and released a subtle buzz. Bandy slowly lifted his hand from his belt, palms out.

The sentient in the bowler tried to mediate. "Let's get back to the game and keep our cool."

"Don't I look cool to you, Willy?" Alix said, turning to the sentient. She turned back to Bandy. "Like I said, I'm offended you think I'd have to cheat to beat you. Took about five minutes to notice your upper lip twitches in the corner when you bluff."

Bandy snarled with brittle confidence. "You ain't the only one in here with plasbolts, darling."

As if on cue, four men came up around their table, their hands at their hips, all looking tough.

"And you aren't the only one with friends," a deep, static voice said in response.

From Alix's left, the sentient at the next table towered over everyone else in the room. His crystalline eyes shimmered a deep blue, sparkling like stars in the Celestinian night. The sleeves of his red shirt were rolled up to his elbows, exposing the silvery, semi-translucent artificial skin over his omniite skeleton. A beaten brown hat, which he pushed up by the brim, sat on his bald head and shadowed his almost-human face. He crossed his arms while everyone else held their hands near to their plasbolts. A deadly silence hung about the room, and the other card players at Alix's table slowly looked at the standoff and began sliding back their chairs, ready to spring away from the upcoming carnage.

Bandy looked at the sentient standing behind Alix. He looked at the plasbolt pointed at his chest before he turned his head to look around and behind him, making sure his friends were still with him.

"So, you can put back *my* money, or—" he said.

"You're not giving orders here," Alix cut him off. "You can either walk out of here or not, simple as that."

Bandy sucked his teeth and chuckled for the last time. Alix narrowed her eyes, and Bandy stupidly went for his plasbolt. Before his fingers could wrap around the grip, two sharp, high-pitched whistles left Alix's Plasveld-7 as she put two rounds in him. Her right hand moved before the second shot hit, and she pointed her second Plasveld across the table, dropping another man. The saloon burst into chaos, and Alix kicked back on the table; her chair fell backward as the table fell forward, creating a makeshift barrier, but it would do little to protect her for long.

"You just lost your winnings," the huge sentient said with a slick smile as he knelt behind the fallen table with Alix.

She smiled wide. "Well get them for me, Felix, dear. I'll take care of these punks."

Alix knocked her goggles down onto her eyes and they lit up immediately. The crowd in the saloon ran outside, stumbling and pushing past one another. The confusion allowed Alix the moment she needed, preventing the other men from getting shots on them. She sprang up and fired in multiple directions, Bandy's remaining companions diving behind overturned tables and over the bar. Her goggles shifted into a different display, allowing her to see through the tables, chairs, and even the bar. With deadly precision, she fired rounds through the metal and wood of the bar, knowing exactly where the men crouched behind it.

Felix laughed as he reached around the table, remaining as low as his huge frame would allow, gathering up as many crits spilled onto the floor as he could. The saloon filled with smoke, the blue streaks of light and heat from plasma-infused rounds creating swirling lines through the smoke. Plasbolts whistled as they fired. Wood splintered and glass shattered.

"Let's go, Felix!" Alix shouted.

They made for the doorway, Alix walking backwards after Felix, her Plasvelds steaming. The ejected energy cells sprang from the cylinders with a sharp zing and clattered to the floor as the plasbolts went quiet.

The hostiles remaining alive inside took the chance to jump up and fire back, and Alix dove out the doorway to find Felix sitting with his back to the wall, cradling his crummy hat like a child—a *very* valuable child. Alix rolled and put her back to the wall on the other side of the door as she holstered her Plasvelds.

"Time to go!"

They both sprang up and ran across the street. Only two men came out of the saloon to continue firing at them, but Alix and Felix had already ducked into an alley to avoid the incoming fire. The village was built with only a few exit points; a stone staircase carved into the mesa wall on the west side was the closest. It descended in a zigzag down the rock, at least twenty meters down. Numerous swiftbikes, stirrols, and even several skimmers waited in the sand and soft gravel of the canyon floor. Standing on the mesa's edge, Alix lifted her goggles onto her head and laughed.

"Well, that didn't turn out like I hoped."

"Yeah, you cut our night short," Felix grumbled. He dumped the contents of his hat in a pouch that he then tucked away in his pocket. "I don't think I managed to get even half of what you were set to win."

Alix cringed.

"Half is better than none, I guess. Let's get out of here before they catch up."

She started down the stairs. Felix skipped several steps at a time as he descended. Towards the bottom, Alix jumped the last short flight altogether, putting a hand on the rock step and jumping over the side, landing softly on her feet. Felix landed with a heavy thud, but no less skillfully. An old man sleeping in a crude dugout carved into the rock awoke at the sounds. Alix waved to the old man, and he tucked his chin to his chest and went back to sleep.

Several tied stirrols grumbled and whined as the two of them passed. Alix and Felix climbed onto two parked swiftbikes and skimmed over a carved pathway up the canyon wall, out onto the wide desert of Celestine's low latitudes. Stars dotted the purple night sky, the dancing lights of ships coming and going, blinks in the atmosphere faded to nothing far away. Alix sighed. It had been six months since she flew and the outlets for paying back her debts at the dock were quickly drying up. The crackdown on unaffiliated pilots had grounded so many. Most couldn't pay the fee to license with the Xypha Corporation that now dominated Celestine, while some, like Alix, simply refused. The cold wind made her eyes water, or so she told herself.

The high desert gave way to a wide, rolling plain of gold and green chis grass. It parted like water before the bikes' force suspenders, which carved a churning wake over the hills in the vast grassy "oceans" of Celestine. As the chis grass ocean came to an end, a great short grass plain lay all around Verisport, chief city and portage of the Isidis Valley. Verisport was a mix of old-fashioned Celestinian settler structures, augmented by scarce omniite parts. Where stone and wood foundations crumbled through the passage of time, the blue shimmer of omniite maintained its strength.

There was no known source of the ore needed to produce the near-indestructible material on Celestine, and thus it all had to be imported, but the people of such a remote world couldn't afford enough to construct whole cities. The original settlers built only one structure of the material, expending nearly every ounce they brought with them. The tower stood above the skyline, reflecting the rising sun, a swirling blue, orange, pink, and purple light, like a drop of oil in water: the great watchtower and control center for the city's spaceport.

Alix and Felix rode through a swarm of tents and shanties outside the city and onto a wide stone pathway that led to the port. It skirted the city proper and up to a great dark wall surrounding the entire complex. A small door in a larger gate opened to them and their bikes passed through, greatly reducing speed as they slowly hovered between a row of walled docking bays.

The complex was laid out in a honeycomb, a large octagonal space filled with smaller octagons within where ships landed. At the center of it all was the tower, rising some three hundred feet in the air from a wide base of angular buildings stacked atop one another. Whether steel or stone, all surfaces within the walls had been stained black and dulled to avoid painful reflection. The tower's dark base thus gave way to a smooth surface, unstained and shimmering even in moonlight. At its pinnacle was the flight control deck, windows looking out in every direction for hundreds of kilometers.

The pathways between the docking bays were still quiet in the early hours of the morning, with only a few workers milling about. A heavy skimmer flew by, loaded with crates. Alix tapped the syncpad on her left forearm as they approached the docking bay door. The screen flashed red, and a slight vibration went through her arm. She let out a frustrated groan and tried the touch sequence a second time: red again. They both sat on their bikes by the door as the dock master approached.

"Good morning, captain," he said.

"My sequence isn't working," Alix replied instead of greeting.

"Ah, yes, I know I disabled it."

He was a lean man in a tight grey slipsuit, the green arc on his breast and the gold bars on his shoulders indicative of his stature. He looked down at his own syncpad on his wrist. "It seems you're behind six-thousand crits."

Alix furrowed her brow. "How much'll get you to open the door?"

The dock master paced and seemed to perform complex calculations in his head.

"Well, I don't know. We're not used to accepting partial payments for such things…"

Felix reached over and held out the pouch of crits from the night before. Alix snapped her head around and glared at him. Felix returned a look that told Alix they had no choice, and she knew it, letting her shoulders dip. The dock master stepped forward and with a gloved finger, moved the crits around in the pouch while it still sat in Felix's large hand.

"Ah! Let's see one thousand three hundred crits?" He looked up from the pouch dissatisfied, but he knew he wasn't getting anything else today. "We look forward to receiving the rest in due time."

Alix rolled her eyes. "Yeah, yeah, thanks."

The dock master took the pouch from Felix, and with a simple swipe on his left arm, opened the door to the docking bay.

"Of course, until such time, your ship must remain grounded. Mag-locks are in place."

Alix sneered. The dock master bowed and walked away quite pleased with himself.

Inside stood a dark, 40-foot light-freighter: the *Shadow*. Alix and Felix stopped their bikes near the bay wall and Alix opened the personnel ramp near the ship's center. The air seals hissed and unlocked. They walked up the ramp and into the main cabin.

"We're not going to be able to stay here," Felix said. "It'll just run up our costs."

Alix could hear the distance in his voice, but he touched familiar surfaces; they were both glad to be home inside the ship.

"Yeah, I know." Alix strained as she removed her shirt, pulling off her goggles with it and letting them both fall onto the floor.

She fell into the cushioned bench that surrounded a vizscreen table against the hull. Her head fell back. Felix stood motionless, staring at her dirty cargo pants and threadbare, off-white tank top.

"I'm sorry," she groaned. She rubbed her face and sat up, pulling the tie out of her hair and shaking it loose. She stood and walked aft into the galley, gently letting her hand rub across Felix's chest as she went by.

"We'll find a place to stay in town, I guess."

She stepped into a passageway, walking by their quarters on her left and a spare crew quarter they used for storage on her right. The head connected to their quarters, but she entered through the door at the end of the passageway. Alix stared into the mirror at her dark and worn face, eyes drooping from a lack of sleep—days without sleep. She kicked off her pants and washed her face. From a small metal compartment, she pulled a small capsule, screwed it into a metal plunger, and injected the hormone mix into her thigh. She tossed the plunger into the metal basin and stared at her dripping face in the mirror again. *Yet another thing that will run out if we don't find work soon.*

The memory came flooding back to her and the face in the mirror staring back seemed to change into her youthful reflection. Blood stained that face, and the shaking and crying came back to her like it was yesterday. The child was only eleven, standing in front of a similar basin full of water and blood. No matter how hard the child scrubbed, the blood wouldn't come off her hands. Back in the now, Alix shook her head and looked down at her hands, calloused and scarred. She closed her eyes hard and took a deep, calming breath.

Alix put on a change of clothes and stuffed what she had left into a rucksack. She went through the rest of the ship and filled the sack with ammunition, rations, tools, and the remaining hormone vials she had. She lugged it over her shoulder and found Felix at a small workbench in the cargo hold. She watched from the catwalk overhead as he powered down several holographic displays and gently placed metal tubes into a cushioned box, closed it. Beneath the bench, Felix had created a false panel in the bulkhead and put the box inside, then replaced the panel.

He had three tubes of the nano hyper-fluids that coursed through his own body. It was the closest thing to blood a sentient had, and theoretically, it never needed replacing. Of course, a sentient could lose enough of the stuff to slow down their inner repair functions or even die. Alix had no idea how long Felix kept the tubes, but he regularly inspected them, making sure things were still functioning properly, that the nanites inside weren't succumbing to the passage of time. He treated them like a relic of another age, and they were so precious to him, she never questioned his motive in keeping them safe.

"Think they'll be safe while we're away?" she said.

"I believe so," he replied, cinching his bag and looking up at her.

The sight of her made him smile.

She blushed and winked at him, though she was trying to keep her composure. Leaving the *Shadow* for who knows how long felt like a death sentence. Without the *Shadow*, she was trapped. She hadn't felt that way in years. The thought brought back memories of childhood, of the Cradle. Shaking her head and wiping an eye, she said, "Well, let's get moving."

"Where to?" Felix asked.

"For now? I need a drink."

Verisport finally woke up for the day. Dusty stone lanes were now filled with skimmers and wagons, people walking, animals trailing behind them, and workers setting up shops, opening windows and doors, moving goods out to the boardwalks along the lanes. There were also people lying against the walls of buildings, still asleep or passed out from their antics the night before. Everywhere, the inhabitants found their voices, shouting over the growing noise.

Alix and Felix hadn't bothered leaving the lane as they left the walls surrounding the port. They weaved around people and vehicles as they walked at a halting pace. A wagon came in off a side street, pulled by two stirrols and driven by two women sitting up on a bench. The woman holding the reins caught Alix's eye. Alix held her hand up to block out the morning sunlight as she looked up at the woman who wore a loose-fitting white shirt, obviously handmade, under a vest with tools sticking out of several pockets on her chest. Her reddish-brown skin glistened in the light, sweat trailing down from her curly hair. Alix could see a smear of black grease on her cheek which the woman had obviously tried in vain to wipe off. Alix looked from the woman's hands up to her green eyes, which looked down, meeting hers. Suddenly, Alix felt embarrassed and dropped her hand, squinting in the light, looking off somewhere else. The woman quickly snapped the reins and the stirrols picked up their pace as the wagon pulled away, though the woman turned and looked back.

"Want me to shout and get her to stop?" Felix said.

He brushed against Alix, a wry smile on his face. Alix punched him in the shoulder, and they continued strolling through the busy streets until they hit the large market square. Multistory wood and stone buildings stood tall, covered with brightly colored awnings, flags, and lines stretched between them for clothes and sheets from the tenements inside. The market was the busiest area of town, one where farmers ranchers all around the valley came to sell fruits, vegetables, crafts, meats, textiles—and buy just as much. A cacophony of noise filled the square, and pleasant aromas of food drifted from cafes and pop-up stands all along the streets and alleys.

They avoided having to cross through the crowd by following a narrow alley on their right, which turned behind buildings and took a few steps down, then turned again, ending in a small door with a ragged sign above it: Docking Bay-94. Unlike many of the market's open-air bars, cafes, and shops, the Docking Bay was all enclosed. It took a few steps down from the front door to get inside, a dark room built into the foundations of another building above. The bar had long been a hangout for pilots, and while it was once a place of relaxation and laughter, it had become tense and quiet since Xypha's arrival.

The saloon was dark regardless of the time of day. The lights flickered, barely staying in the air, bobbing around like they were partaking in Stim's chisik. If someone sat around long enough, one of the lamps would bump into their head. Stim, an old sentient, stood behind the bar drying metal cups with a rag, an apron hanging over his shirt, his metallic legs bare. A handful of regulars were lumped over at the few tables scattered through the room. Alix fell into one of the circular benches cut out from the wall and dropped her head on the table in front of her as Felix squeezed in beside her.

"Howdy, Alix," Stim said in a raspy voice, like two small gears grinding together after decades of poor maintenance. "How are things going?"

"Don't ask me that question," Alix said, her voice muffled against the table.

"That bad, huh? You two still looking for work?"

"Well, I thought I had a line on paying some of my debt to the port, but we, uh, lost it last night."

"How'd that happen?" Stim put the cup he'd been drying on the table in front of her and filled it with a dark chisik he'd made himself. Nobody ever asked questions if it got the job done.

"Thanks," she said, lifting her head and taking a large swig. "Got into a fight."

"You two?" Stim feigned surprise.

"It wasn't my fault!" Alix took a drink and winced as the liquid went down, like drinking hot oil.

"I'm sure," Stim said with a hint of skepticism.

"Did you have work in mind?" Felix interjected. "You asked if we were looking."

"Well, I spoke to Kimi this morning. He's having skimmer trouble. I told him to take it to a scrapper, but he insists it'll still fly. But—"

"Xypha's running local mechanics out of business too," Felix said.

"Just as bad as the pilots have it, I'd guess," Stim said.

"I warned them," Alix finished the drink and playfully pushed the cup closer to Stim with her forefinger until he reluctantly filled it again. "Eight months ago, I told the marshal: you let them in here, and everything will dry up."

"People out here aren't used to dealing with them," Felix said.

"Well, I know you are handy enough, so maybe you can see what Kimi would give you for getting the skimmer up and running again?" Stim suggested.

"Well, first, I gotta figure out what will pay for these drinks," Alix said.

"You can do some dishes next time you're around," Stim laughed and took the cup with him.

Later that day, Alix and Felix entered one of many scrapyards on the eastern edge of town. The scrapper's workshop was open to the street, clanging metal and hissing air bouncing off the walls and buildings opposite the workshop. Heaps of twisted, rusted metal peeked over the metal fence on both sides of the shop. Mangled skimmers, bikes, farming equipment, and all sorts of other smaller machines lay about like skeletons of various shades of grey, blues, browns, and more than any other, red rust. The air smelled of hot plascutter beams, oil, grease, and chemicals. A short person wearing a heavy apron came out of the shop and took off their heavy gloves, brushing back short, greasy hair with a sweaty hand.

"Can I help you?" they asked.

"We're looking for parts to fix a skimmer," Felix said. "I've got a list of what we need."

"Where?" Felix pointed to his head. "Ah. Well, you're free to look through the yard," they said. "Just get me when you find what you need." They started walking back into the shop, then yelled, "And don't steal anything, please!"

Alix looked at Felix and shrugged. The two of them passed through a set of metal gates that barely remained attached to the hinges. A row of skimmers lined against the left wall, sitting on the ground instead of hovering in the air like they would've been if they were operational.

Large piles of scrap metal created a chaotic pattern of footpaths between them. Through the sightline between the mounds to her right, Alix noticed a familiar wagon toward the back of the yard.

"We needed a 762-guage hose, a negative charge generator, and two induction coils," Felix said, as if reading off a list in his hand.

"I got this one." Alix ripped a panel off the side of one skimmer and stuck half her body inside.

She knocked her goggles down over her eyes and they immediately scanned the parts that hadn't been picked clean already. The goggles showed the machinery in wireframe, making it easier to identify each piece in the dark. Her legs hung out the side of the skimmer's body and she pulled herself deeper into the space using two support struts. Alix laughed, recalling a memory of crawling through another ship's inner workings. She had experience crawling through the bowels of ships, some more pleasant than others.

"Remember that time we had to crawl through a Pisces-9 to get Rick out of that slip seal?" she said into the comms channel to Felix.

"*You* crawled through that, and I warned Rick the seal would close on him."

"Right." Alix strained trying to reach the skimmer's coolant hose with her right hand. "When did that idiot ever listen?"

She gripped the hose with one hand and ripped it out with two hard tugs. "I've got the hose, but the rest of this thing has been picked apart."

"I'm only coming up with one induction coil," Felix said.

Alix writhed her way out of the skimmer's engines and onto the dirt, catching her breath. The hose was about the right length but didn't look much better than the one that came off Kimi's own skimmer. Felix came over and offered a hand to help her up to her feet. He held a metal coil in his other hand.

"Nothing else?" Alix said.

"I scanned the yard. We may find luck toward the back; there's a line of bikes and trailers. They at least have similar generators."

When Alix and Felix came into the back of the yard, two stirrols lifted their long necks and let out hard snuffs through their snouts. They stood tied to a wagon that floated behind them, against the back wall of the yard. A canvas covering was folded back toward the rear of the wagon and a woman's voice trailed out of it, cursing to herself. Clangs of metal followed, as if she dropped something heavy.

Alix moved toward the rear of the wagon as Felix put a calming hand on one of the stirrols. Before she could stick her head into the open flap, Alix heard the familiar click and whining charge of a plasbolt behind her.

"What the hell are you doing?" a voice said. It was sharp but young, perhaps confident only in the way someone would be from inexperience.

Alix held up her hands as she turned. "Easy. Just seeing what's going on."

The woman holding a rifle was no woman at all, but a teenage girl. She wore old boots and grey coveralls, but she'd rolled the top down to her waist. A patchy red shirt with frayed edges covered her umber skin. Her dark hair was wrapped in what probably once was a white cloth. Alix relaxed a little and smiled.

"Jo, can you give me a hand—" The woman inside the wagon cut herself off when she leaned out of the rear flap and saw Alix. "Who the hell are you?"

Alix didn't know which way to turn, but Felix coming toward the back of the wagon caused the young girl to sweep her rifle toward him. Her narrowed eyes looked shaken; the sentient was almost three times her size.

"Don't take another step, mister," she ordered.

The woman in the wagon jumped down, her boots hitting with a puff of dirt. She wiped her hands together and quickly went to the young girl's side. "Okay, what's going on here?"

"Saw this one snooping," Jo said, motioning the barrel of her rifle at Alix.

"Look, I wasn't snooping. It sounded like you needed help. And if you don't put that bolt down, this is going to turn south real quick," Alix said.

"For you," the woman shot back.

"No need for hostilities," Felix said, holding out his palms. "We are not here to take anything from you or hurt you."

"Well, why don't you move along, then?" Jo said.

Alix then recognized the woman who emerged from the wagon as the same one she'd seen in the street that morning. They both eyed one another, coming to the same realization at once.

"We're sorry," Alix said. "I'll leave you to your business. We're just looking for scrap parts over here if that's alright."

"Just stay out of our stuff," Jo demanded.

"Not a problem," Alix said.

She lowered her hands slowly and turned to Felix, but each pair hesitated to turn their backs on the other. Alix listened to Jo and the woman whispering to one another.

"Calm down, Jo. They didn't see anything," the woman said.

"What if she did, Sora? They might get us into trouble."

"With whom? They don't exactly look like the type to be in tight with Xypha or the marshal."

"You *know* who."

"It's fine. Don't worry about it. Let's just get this stuff tied down and go. I need your help."

Sora and Jo climbed into the wagon and Alix and Felix started picking through the scrap along the outer wall. Alix knew Felix heard the conversation too. Of course, he could *choose* not to eavesdrop on other people, and often did, but she could tell when his mind was somewhere else.

"They're up to something," Alix said with a smile.

"Yes, but I think it's only something that would endanger them, not anyone else. The parts they have in the wagon are nothing too unusual for a couple of valley farmers."

Alix smiled as she lay under a broken swiftbike. She wasn't surprised Felix had scanned the wagon and identified anything inside, but it seemed Sora and Jo hadn't much experience with sentients to know that Alix was the least of their worries.

"They don't have another induction coil, do they?"

Felix laughed. "No. Unfortunately they do not."

2

The Boss

Two men entered the Black Barrel saloon owned by Silas Purvida and dropped a body on one of the tables. They both took a moment to catch their breath from carrying the man wrapped in a bag from their skimmer. They stood in a fine establishment: a saloon, brothel, gambling hall, hotel all in one—and that was just above-ground. The main room sat empty this time of day, except for those who worked for Silas. Workers kept the tables polished and the floor clean. The saloon's bar reached down the length of the room on the left from the front door. A great mirror covered the wall behind rows and rows of glass bottles. The room had a high ceiling up to the second story, and a darkly-polished set of stairs went up to a balcony that ran perpendicular to the bar. Beneath the second story balcony, rooms for gambling and other business stayed separate from the food and drink of the main saloon. A gentle, sweet melody played from somewhere off in a far corner. The place wouldn't be packed until nightfall.

A tall, thin man with dark, deep-set eyes came out one of the back rooms. His hair was thin but styled well. He wore a dark vest over a light blue shirt, a gold chain dangling from the vest. Two Plasvelds hung at his hips. He shook his head disapprovingly as he looked at what the men had brought into the saloon.

"Who is this?" he said.

"Bandy. Got killed at some scrabhole in the desert," Dalton said through deep breaths. His rosy cheeks were even redder than usual, contrasting with his dark eyebrows and mustache.

The Thin Man took a moment to think, rolling a toothpick between his fingers. He opened the bag to see the heavy man inside, blood and spittle dried in his beard. His face was pale and cracked.

"What the hell are you doing, bringing him in the front door?"

"He's a heavy son of a bitch," the other man, Shaw, said.

"Alright, leave him here, and let's go up and have a chat."

The Thin Man led the other two up the set of stairs. The men behind him took off their hats and held them in their hands. Their expressions changed to that of reverence, fear that they might bear the brunt of a fury that needed a target, even if they weren't responsible for Bandy's demise. They passed doors on their right down the balcony. The door at the end boasted an ornate, colorful glass window. The Thin Man knocked gently with one knuckle and a deep voice permitted them to enter.

The office was all stained wood. A fireplace sat on one wall, unused. Sleek, gold lamps hovered around the room, all Xypha-made. A large desk commanded the center of the room, and behind it sat Silas Purvida, a barrel-chested man in a well-tailored suit of local textiles, grey and blue. His hair was slicked back, and he'd had a fresh shave, though his eyebrows had been neglected, his masculinity only bending so much. A cigar in a glass ash tray created a small trail of thin smoke up from the desk. He'd made himself rich at the expense of others in the valley. He owned much of the land around town simply by saying he did (and having the guns to back up his words).

The Thin Man pointed to a spot on the floor for the other two men to stand before he went to his usual spot in the corner. The Thin Man said nothing, leaned against the wall, and began rolling a cigarette. The large man at the desk set down a datapad and leaned back in his chair, which creaked beneath him. He picked up his cigar and took a drag as he studied the two men across from him.

"Dalton, Shaw. Well, let's hear it," he said.

"Sir, Bandy's dead," Dalton started. He waited, wincing for a reaction, but Silas gave him nothing, so he continued. "Seemed it was over a game of Solar. A few others were killed too."

If Silas Purvida had been anyone else, he would've slammed a fist on his desk, yelled obscenities, maybe even killed the man standing in front of him, but he wasn't just anyone. The Purvidas had been in the valley for generations. Silas's great grandfather was a farmer, laying claim to acres of unused land west of Verisport. He'd protected that land with his life. But it was Silas's father who tired of getting his hands dirty in the rich soil of Celestine. So, Simon Purvida split the family acreage into lots and welcomed a hundred families, whole villages of people who had the chance to leave Verisport and stretch their legs.

By the time Silas was a man, he'd inherited the largest segment of the valley, a great crescent shaped mass of prime farmland to Verisport's west that created a barrier between the city and the rest of the valley. Silas knew what he had on his hands, and he quickly tightened the noose. He had council members whose landholdings were outside of his own needing passage over his land to deliver their tenants' crops. Over the years he'd had several of them in his pockets, enough hired men to keep anyone from asking questions out loud.

"Who did it?" Silas said after his anger subsided.

"People who saw it happen said it was a woman and an artie."

Silas couldn't decide whether he was impressed by this woman or embarrassed one of his best captains had been killed by her. All he did outwardly was nod as he thought, keeping his rage inside.

"You have descriptions?"

"Yes sir. We had some people see them leaving the docks this morning. Seems they got a ship there," Dalton said.

"Xypha contract?"

"Not sure. Don't know which ship is theirs, but we'll find out."

"Bring them to me. Go find Wickford and put him to use."

Dalton and Shaw nodded and shuffled out of the room, gently closing the door behind them. Silas sat quietly for a moment, tapping his finger on his cigar. He shook his head and took a drag. He finally let his rage out, only just a hint. "I told Bandy I'd fucking kill him if he did this again."

"You want me to take care of this?" the Thin Man said.

"No, no, let them handle it for now. I want to know what ship they fly, or what business they have at the dock otherwise."

Deep below the fancy office and quiet saloon, Dalton and Shaw emerged from a stairwell fresh from their meeting with Silas. Before, they had been sheepish upstairs; now, they flexed their bravado. They passed all sorts of machinery that kept the lights on and the water running above them, but the chamber also acted as a garage, a hanger, and a chop yard for vehicles, ships, and a storage space for smuggled goods that passed under Xypha's nose. The piercing sounds of cutting metal, hissing steam, and roaring engines bounced off every wall.

Away from all the small craft being repaired, torn down, or built, there was one ship. It sat dark and alone, small lights running along the stone walls around it barely showing its whole shape. Tools and parts lay all around the landing gear, canvas sheets laid out with disassembled machinery neatly organized, one man at a workbench on the wall, cursing as sparks flew out around him.

"Wickford!" Dalton shouted. When he received no answer, he tried again, even louder, *"Wick!"*

The man at the workbench dropped his tools and turned around, a huge mask covering his face. He threw it back. "What?"

"Silas wants you to look into something for us."

"I'm busy," Wick said, nodding his head so the protective mask fell back over his face.

Dalton grabbed Wick by the shoulder and pulled him away from the bench, spinning him around. "Well, now you're busy with this. Boss has people you need to find and bring to him."

Wick took the mask off, which protected his eyes but didn't keep the rest of his face clean. He was covered in dirt, grease, dust, oil, and who knows what else. His eyes popped against the dark muck around them. He was smaller than the other two men, and he knew he'd already pushed his limit by dismissing them earlier, but he couldn't resist one more.

"You two seem pretty capable and like you've got some free time."

That earned him a punch to the jaw. Wick crumpled over, spitting on the floor to see if the blow drew any blood. He laughed when he saw it hadn't. Shaw dragged him to his feet again and pushed him against the wall.

"Descriptions are on your syncpad. Just find them and bring them back here," Dalton ordered.

"I'm the chauffeur now?"

"You're whatever Silas says you are."

Wick washed his face in a basin deep beneath the saloon. The light above the mirror in the washroom barely worked. He scrubbed at the muck with a wet rag, staring at himself in the faint blue light. He certainly didn't lament Bandy's death—the guy was a stirrol's ass. He also didn't pretend to think the job fell to him for any reason other than Silas anticipating trouble, and who cared if Wick was murdered trying to bring a couple of murderers in to face Silas's justice?

He slipped a red shirt over his head and picked up the belt hanging on the wall. The syncpad on his right arm showed some images of the two targets: a thin but muscular woman and the biggest sentient Wick had ever seen. He flipped through more images of the two captured from the dock's security cameras. Silas had his hand in everything; half the guys working security at the docks were his people. The marshal pretended otherwise. Wick put on a fake smile in the mirror one last time before walking out to a waiting skimmer.

He found the pair at Kimi's, a local hotel run by a fat man who had an even bigger mouth, but not the kind that aimed to manipulate anyone. He was about as self-aware as rock. When Wick asked about the woman and the sentient, Kimi simply pointed him to the back of the hotel. He walked around back and found the sentient sitting cross legged on the ground, machine parts in his giant hands. Wick leaned against the corner of the building until the sentient noticed him, which wasn't long. Soon after, the woman rolled out from under the skimmer on a creeper and sat up. Her eyes darted over to crates and things stacked against the wall between her and Wick. There lay her plasbolts. Wick chuckled quietly and put on that fake smile.

"You ain't going to need those."

"May we help you?" Alix said.

"Sure can. My boss would like to have a word with you."

The sentient remained seated, completely unconcerned, perhaps because he knew he could tear Wick in half in a second. The woman remained standoffish. She stood up and wiped her hands on her pants.

"Yeah? And who is that?"

"Silas Purvida."

That had an effect. It was always easy to name drop Silas and get results. Usually, people shut their mouths, or they dropped open. Nearly everyone in the valley knew who Silas was, and what he was known for; a path crossing with him usually meant bad news for whichever party wasn't Silas.

"I don't got business with him," Alix said.

"You *think* you don't, but I assure you that you do," Wick said. "You killed a captain of his."

"I've killed a lot of people, pal," Alix boasted.

"Maybe true, but this one happened a few nights ago, over a game of Solar? Ring any bells?"

Alix rolled her eyes. She rubbed her forehead and looked at Felix, who knowingly smiled back. "Alright—what does he want?"

"Beats me. That's why you got to come with me to talk to him."

"We're a little busy at the moment."

"I'm sure you are, but Silas doesn't like to wait. It's in your best interest to come along, now."

"He doesn't like to wait, and I don't like being called like a dog."

"The dog may not like being called, but it comes when called all the same."

Alix glared at Wick. Felix stood up and set down the parts he held in his hand. "We'll be right with you."

"I got a skimmer out front," Wick said as he jerked his thumb over his shoulder.

When Wick went round the corner, Alix stepped close to Felix, spoiling for a fight. "What'd you agree to that for? We don't have money to pay that guy off. Even worse, we walk in there and get shot."

"If he wanted us dead, this guy would've shown up shooting," Felix said. "Maybe we can get some work out of it."

"I'm already trying to work off one debt!"

"I'd rather not get into a fight with the valley's biggest snake."

Alix huffed and crossed her arms. Felix was right and she knew it, but she hated it. *Just my luck*, she thought. *Killing some moron at a card table who just happened to work for Silas Purvida.* It seemed that even when she began to fix one thing, yet another thing broke. Alix picked up her belt off the stack of crates and buckled it around her waist.

"Fine. When this goes sideways—and it *will* go sideways—I'll be prepared."

Alix and Felix came around to the front of the inn and saw Wick leaning against a skimmer. He smiled confidently, pleased with himself. Alix wasn't having any of it and pushed past him, putting her shoulder into him, then jumping over the side of the skimmer and into the beaten down passenger seat. The suspenders keeping the skimmer off the ground whined louder as Felix climbed in and the propulsion system had to account for the weight. Wick held onto the dash shield and stepped into the pilot's seat, then dropped himself down.

"Wipe that grin off your face," Alix said.

"Gee, I wonder why Bandy wanted to kill you," Wick replied.

He increased the thrust and the skimmer slid sideways across the street and pushed forward. Alix noted the maneuver, skillful and experienced. He piloted the craft well, but she wasn't about to let Wick know she thought he may be a serviceable pilot. *Any moron can pilot a skimmer*, she thought.

Wick decelerated at a large compound at the end of a street on the outskirts of town. Alix looked the place up and down, but Felix stared at the wooden doors, which stood open—not as an invitation, but as a show of strength and confidence that no one entered without Silas's leave. Alix started to enter, but Felix held fast on the boardwalk outside, a subtle tremor passing through his body's sensors. Alix looked back, knowing something was amiss.

"What is it?" She put a hand on her belt, keeping it a ready distance from her Plasvelds.

"There's a barrier on the door," Felix said.

"What is the hold up?" Wick had already walked in, not even thinking about whatever safety measures were on the doors to keep sentients out.

"Seems your boss has an issue with sentients," Alix glared at Wick.

"Wick, who are these two?" Dalton's voice cut in. He approached the door and held out a hand, still standing inside. "No arties in here."

Alix bristled at the slur and prepared to choke the man to death. Felix stepped closer, forcing the man's eyes upward. Alix caught one of the other men in the saloon moving toward them slowly, trying to seem smooth. She reached down, but Wick caught her wrist, moving almost as fast as she had. *Almost.*

"Do you want to die here?" he whispered to her. He looked at the others. "Relax. They're the pair Silas was looking for. Remember, the ones you told me to go find?"

Alix looked around the room at all the eyes on them. She knew a place like this could be full of bolts, and any of these drunks and gamblers dispersed around the room could be more than patrons. She also knew Silas's reputation. She relaxed her hand, and Wick let it go. Felix, however, still stood like a mountain filling the doorway, waiting for one of the men around them to speak again. Dalton looked away, unable to keep up his tough façade in the face of such a powerful being.

Dalton looked at each of them in turn. He casually put a cigarette between his lips. The man obviously took his job seriously, and he looked at Wick with disdain. Alix began to understand the hierarchy here, with Wick at the bottom, someone the others didn't like. Dalton was clearly a leader, but only a leader of the expendable vermin like Wick, which gave him an inflated sense of importance. He moved only his eyes from Wick to Alix, and then he stepped out of their way. With a quick movement by his waist, he put his right hand over on his left wrist, under his shirt. Felix looked down at Alix and nodded, knowing the barrier had dropped.

Wick smiled smugly as if he'd accomplished something. He walked by Dalton up the stairs, Alix and Felix behind him. Alix committed the leader's face to memory: gaunt with a thinning mustache, dark green eyes, and a red handkerchief around his neck. She looked him up and down as she passed, sneering. He followed them up the stairs.

Silas swiveled his chair around from a previous conversation when they entered. He held a cigar cutter in one hand and a fat Celestinian cigar in the other. Alix immediately noticed the Thin Man standing in the far corner, smoking a cigarette. He was tall, not quite as tall as Felix, but still a lean, towering presence. Though he stood tall and lean, Alix had seen plenty like him on Corto and fought plenty like him too. His muscles were strong as steel cables, even though they didn't particularly stand out.

"Wick, what's the meaning of this?" Silas sounded like a disapproving parent.

"These are the two you were looking for. They killed Bandy," Wick said, taking his hat off and revealing his balding head.

"One of which is an *artificial*," Silas said, sitting back in his chair, and rolling the cigar in his fingers.

"Excuse me?" Alix cut in, stepping toward the desk. She noticed a slight twitch out of the Thin Man in the corner, catching that he was left-handed.

"Now, darlin'," Silas said calmly, "I apologize if I gave offense."

"You asked us here," Felix said.

"If he ain't welcome here, then we'll be on our way," Alix added, preparing to turn and leave. She waited, though, and Silas looked at her through narrowed eyes. He smiled and put his cigar cutter on the desk as Alix crossed her arms.

"I did. And you came," Silas said.

Alix resisted the urge to spit in his face. "So why are we here?"

"Seems you killed a captain of mine, Bandy. I'm not going to pretend he didn't deserve it, as most of the men who work for me are loathsome sons of bitches, that's no secret. But I do care when I lose an investment."

"*That* man was an investment?" Alix said. "You should be glad I cut your losses."

Silas laughed. "Perhaps. Regardless, I had him preparing for a job that now I have no point man for. I can't afford to delay this job any further, and most of my captains are better elsewhere."

"You want to hire us?" Felix said.

"Something like that. How about you two take Bandy's place on this job, and we'll call it square."

"I don't work for free," Alix said.

"Seems to me you don't work at all lately. That ship you got in the docks ain't going anywhere and hasn't for well on half a circuit. Now, I wonder why that may be?"

Alix clenched her teeth. If it wasn't for Felix's calming touch, she probably would've just started shooting. Silas obviously had men inside at the docks and probably received a full background check on her and Felix, at least as far as their shipping activities went. It would be obvious they stopped abruptly when Xypha arrived. Maybe Silas hadn't figured it out, maybe he had, but seeing that she was unwilling to work with Xypha would've been enough for him to assume she had some kind of past trouble with the corporation.

Regardless, though, she knew the options were to either accept Silas's offer or shoot their way out of here. The latter option only created more problems. Besides, she could find a more opportune moment to kill everyone in this room who now stared at her, waiting for her reply.

Felix spoke first. "What's the job?"

"There's a train coming across the valley from White Sands. I've got some cargo that needs protecting."

"Protection from what? That's a Xypha train," Alix said.

"I'm extra careful," Silas said. "Anyway, you do this for me, and I'll consider your debt paid. Then, maybe, I'll have more work for you."

Alix glared at Silas, then looked over at the Thin Man, who stared back unfazed. She felt a pulse from her syncpad, a signal from Felix, one long pulse telling her he thought they should agree. She turned her eyes to his, and her face reflected how much she hated the idea. *What better ideas do you have, Alix—fixing an inn-keeper's skimmer?*

"Alright, fine," she said, looking back at Silas.

"Wonderful. Wick will pick you up from wherever you're staying tomorrow morning," Silas said. "Now, I've got other business to attend to, so please, show yourselves out."

Back downstairs in the main hall, Alix shoved past Wick, nearly knocking him over as she and Felix headed for the door. These vermin not only insulted Felix numerous times, but now she and Felix were working for them. She felt dirty just being inside this place, and her hands shook from the adrenaline. She wanted to shower off the disgust. Felix caught up with her and affectionately put his arm over her shoulders.

"This is bullshit," Alix said.

"I know," Felix replied. "Long game. We get out from under this debt, and then we can get another job. None of those bolts inside were worth their salt."

"Except that the thin fellow in the corner," Alix said.

"Well, one of him, two of us."

They passed through the front door, and Felix felt the low vibration move through his body again. This time, he studied the doorframe, his glassy eyes darting across the walls in rapid movements, able to sense the barrier placed there. It was a security system that detected sentients, driving home how unwelcome he was in the building. But now, he committed the design of the barrier to memory.

"The barrier on the entry is certainly Xypha tech," he said. "Dangerous to come back. There are probably more safety systems inside, but if so, they were inactive while we were there."

"That Dalton guy, he had a syncpad connected to the barrier," Alix recalled.

"Shouldn't be a problem."

After they walked a while back toward Kimi's inn, Alix sighed and hugged Felix's arm down by his side. "He's in business with Xypha. This is cutting it a little close."

Silas leaned back in his chair, fingers interlaced as he spoke to a man on a vizscreen. The Xypha officer wore the cleanest slipsuit anyone on Celestine had ever seen, and his dark hair was flat and arranged so perfectly in place. His face was as pale as milk, typical of Xypha officials, who hardly ever spent time under natural light and gravity.

"I got people for the train handled," Silas said. "One of them is an artie. I believe one of yours."

"They were all once one of ours," the officer said. "Is it going to be a problem? Any more schedule interruptions are unacceptable."

"We'll get it taken care of, Otto," Silas assured him.

"I do not wish to devote more resources to security when I was already assured there would be no risks across the valley," Otto said.

"It's a big valley, Otto."

"Funny—from up here, it looks rather insignificant."

The barb cut a little too close. Silas didn't like someone getting the better of him, and even less, showing that they had. His silence lasted a mere moment, but for him, it felt like an eternity, long enough to let Otto's inflated sense of self grow a little larger. Silas leaned forward and chuckled to himself, trying to keep his cool, but Otto spoke again before Silas could deliver his comeback.

"Report back when you have things under control."

The viscreen went dark. Silas sat motionless, now staring at his own reflection in the blank screen. He clenched his fists and then folded his hands together, turning to stare at the Thin Man in the corner, minding his own business, an unlit cigarette in his fingers.

"One of these days, I'm going to strangle that baby faced scrab myself."

"Don't you usually pay me for that?" the Thin Man joked in a monotone that normally frightened lesser men.

"Dig up what you can about the pilot and her artie friend. There's a reason they aren't paying the Xypha contract fee."

"It's an artie. Seems self-explanatory why they would want distance."

"I may pay you to kill, but do I also pay you to be a wise ass?"

The Thin Man smiled a toothy grin, looking down at his cigarette. He put it between his lips and looked up at Silas, who waited on an answer.

"No sir."

"Good. Now get to fucking work."

3

The Valley

Alix awoke just before dawn. She looked around the room at Kimi's inn, the pale moonlight casting a purple hue over the furniture, which cast dark shadows. She felt the hum of Felix's body, sitting up against the headboard, the roving electrical currents moving through him. She snuggled into him, pulling the blanket up and bunching it to her chest. Even in the comfort of the bed and Felix's cool, soft exterior, she felt uneasy.

She felt cornered, a feeling she had been all too familiar with, and fought like hell to keep it away. This was the closest she'd come to Xypha in years since she and Felix had to leave Corto. The job with Silas felt like a trap—not one he had set, but one she had walked right into and would never escape. It was like slipsand, pulling her in, and the harder she struggled, the deeper she went. Everything was going wrong; everything was taking her back, taking her down.

The sun would be rising soon, and if Alix was going to make a drastic decision, she was running out of time to do it. She dropped her head back on Felix's chest and sighed. She gently lifted the blanket and slipped out of bed. Their room had one window, which looked across the street to the west. Verisport slept quietly, only the wind making itself known, whistling between buildings, ruffling flags on rooftops and fronts of buildings. Beyond that, lay the valley: wide, rolling plains of chis grass, burrey trees, orchards, crops, farmsteads, and even more empty space. Compared to Corto, it was heaven, but Alix could only think of what it might become; what it *was* becoming, as Xypha slowly spread on this planet like it had done on so many others.

She needed a plan—to protect herself, to protect Felix.

Felix didn't so much sleep as he powered down and ran on the minimal systems required to keep himself aware. It was a mode he'd rarely achieved until he met Alix. Of course, instinct and habit kept the necessary safety measures running: proximity scans, heartbeat monitors, omnidirectional auditory sensors, the subtle changes in the air and the vibrations of the ground that only he could detect—plus, his memory bank, which he'd long ago used as a method of dreaming.

His cerebral unicore could not *dream* as humans did, but following the Awakening, sentients processed and replayed memories through distortions and in random selections to mimic the phenomena. Of course, there had been the debate about whether it was voluntary or if they had indeed achieved something akin to "natural" dreams. To Felix, it was such an effortless process it felt natural and any time he powered down, the sequence began...

Smoke hung heavy in the thick, hot air inside the fight room. The flickering old lighting focused on the ring, nothing more than a—

Spectators filled old bleachers and any space to stand in between. They screamed and spit, drank and stumbled all over the place as the fight carried on into its third round. Lamps moved about the room as well—

Like everything on Corto, the room was dirty, disgusting, and loud. Felix had no space to sit, so he stood between two sets of bleachers.

The fighters moved about the ring, one of them a sleek young woman, who just so happened to be beating the daylights out of a much larger man. Felix knew she could have won much earlier, but there was a flair in her that kept the fight going —

Alix looked up at him, her eyes wide. Spiros looked at Felix cautiously.

"Can I help you, big fella?" Spiros said.

"Nice fight," Felix said to Alix.

"Thanks. You interested?" Alix said, sizing him up.

Felix could not hold back his smile. She stared back at him, breathing heavily, her sweat, blood, and water-soaked tank top clinging to her small breasts.

"Buy you a drink?" Felix said—

Alix finished a fourth drink and smiled, trying to keep from laughing. Felix knew he was one of the biggest beings she'd ever seen. But she kept up her bravado.

"Is that right?" Felix said.

"Haven't you heard? I'm the best around." She held out her arms wide, motioning to the entire planet, it seemed.

"I've seen you many times," Felix admitted.

Alix laughed, and Felix looked at her. He knew it was an awkward thing to say, but he couldn't think of anything else. A sentient who could rip a man in half, afraid to talk to a—

The jungle made it difficult to walk. Ahead of him, three other members of his team moved as best they could, clad in dark suits, weapons on their backs. Felix carried nothing but a shining blade, half the length of his arm, which he used to cut through the—

Slowly, Felix's eyes flickered and let in the light of the room. They lit up themselves, dark blue, glassy orbs within metal sockets beneath the smooth silvery membrane. He saw Alix leaned against the window, her face turned down to the street. The rest of his systems slowly came up, and it took him a moment to compartmentalize the flood of information, the pure data that poured into him, like a crowded room full of voices. In three seconds, he silenced them, pushing them aside and focusing on Alix's breathing, which the current in his body matched without a second's thought. Her heart beat softly, imperceptible to anyone else, but he knew it intimately.

"You're awake," he said.

"For a little while," Alix replied. "Just waiting, you know?"

"You alright?"

"I've got a bad feeling."

"About this job?" Felix pulled on his trousers and eyed his old brown hat on a chair.

"About everything." Alix turned away from the window. "We're taking one step forward, and it seems three steps back."

"I think we'll pull out of it soon."

"Why?"

"Because we always do," Felix smiled.

His blue eyes were bright in the dim room. The sun began creeping upwards in the west, the light only just reaching inside. Alix came over and kissed him, holding his cheeks with her hands.

"We can always just kill them, I guess," she said. She walked to the chair where Felix's hat sat and tossed it to him like a disc. She sat in the chair and pulled her boots on. Her goggles sat on the vanity behind her, along with her hormone vials.

"Is that your plan?" Felix chuckled as he put on a shirt, the hat sitting beside him on the bed.

"It's no secret to anyone paying attention that Silas is working with Xypha. Whatever their relationship looks like, this is putting us a little close to the fire."

"It's true. I can't see how we get out of this thing without some risks, but I think we can play our cards right, and we'll just fall into the same crowd as everyone else out here: people who want to be left alone."

"What if he digs?"

Felix put on his hat, making sure it was angled just right. "Like you said, we'll just kill them."

Their laughter filled the room.

Outside Kimi's, Wick leaned against the same skimmer as the day before, waiting for Alix and Felix. He wore a dark hat, black boots, a dirty pair of red trousers, and a black shirt. He'd tied a black handkerchief around his neck. A puff of smoke blew out from under his hat brim as he lit a cigarette, before he looked up to see Alix and Felix step out of the hotel.

"Driver, take us to Silas," Alix said. She walked around to the passenger chair and dropped her rucksack behind it.

"Very funny," Wick replied.

He looked up nervously at Felix, who stood close to him, invading his space to reinforce how small Wick was in comparison. It worked, and Wick moved out of the way as Felix climbed into the back of the skimmer. Wick noticed that Felix carried no plasbolts on his waist.

"You uh, don't have any bolts on you?"

"I don't carry," Felix said as he situated himself on the bench seat in the back.

"Don't you think you'll need them?"

"That's what she's for."

Wick looked over at Alix who checked both Plasvelds, spinning them on the trigger finger of each hand, letting them fall smoothly into the holsters on her hips. She gave a sarcastic sneer to Wick and hopped into the skimmer.

"Wonderful." Wick sounded unimpressed.

Instead of returning to the front of Silas's compound, Wick brought the skimmer to the rear, where a large stone wall reached out from the back of the building from one corner to another. A gate opened, and they entered a yard with ready vehicles. Alix noticed a stable in one corner, with five stirrols lined up, saddled and ready to go.

"We're going out on stirrol?" she said to Wick.

"Can't you ride?"

"Of course I can."

Dalton and Shaw moved around the stirrols, packing saddlebags as Alix, Felix, and Wick approached. Alix groaned seeing those two again, and the prospect of a long ride into the valley with them sounded as pleasant as getting trampled by a brizcoe.

"You're late," Dalton chastised Wick as soon as he got within earshot.

"Good to see you too, buddy." Wick slapped him on the shoulder as he went by. He ran his hand reassuringly along the back and long neck of the stirrol he'd be riding.

The first colonists who came to the planet long ago domesticated these beasts native to Celestine. They were well-evolved to survive in the chis grass oceans of the planet, their slender necks and tall legs looking over the panicles, as well as able to pick fruits and leaves off burrey and twifruit trees. They were swift and graceful, and surprisingly sturdy for slender creatures. Felix got acquainted with one, petting its neck and tall ears. It nuzzled its nose into his other arm.

"Can it ride?" Shaw asked.

"Excuse me?" Alix snapped.

"Your artie. Can it ride?"

Alix stepped toward Shaw and knocked him right in the eye. The man stumbled back, tripped over a bag on the ground, and fell in the dirt. Dalton pulled his plasbolt, but Alix paid no attention to him. She stood over Shaw, grabbing his shirt collar. Felix called out to her, but she blocked out all noise. A singular focus took control, and she hit the man again, bloodying his nose. If Dalton wanted to kill her, he would have. Even though he held his plasbolt in his hand from instinct, he withheld his fire.

Felix rushed over to Alix and touched her back. She felt that and the current he sent into her, letting her know it was him. Her right fist trembled, knuckles bloody, her eyes ablaze with a fury that none of the men had seen from her until now. She didn't bring her fist down again, but let Shaw fall back into the dirt, which was now darkened and speckled with blood. Alix unclenched her teeth, but her fist remained locked in.

"You say that again and I will kill you," she hissed.

"Get control!" Dalton shouted as he holstered his weapon.

Felix held up a large, commanding hand to Dalton, assuring him he had things under control. His other hand lay on Alix's left shoulder, and he soothed her with a soft, buzzing whisper.

"Alix, it's okay."

She spit on Shaw as he tried to prop himself up on his elbows, his eyes and mind still completely in a fog, nearly unconscious.

"Look at me. Look at me, babe," Felix said, getting down on one knee to meet her eye level. She finally turned to him, her eyes red. "I love you. It's okay."

"Sorry," she stammered.

"Don't be."

"Are you insane?" Shaw said, his voice muffled and nasal as he stuffed a handkerchief in his bleeding nostrils.

Felix glared at Shaw, his eyes rolling and spinning, the deep blue color in them changing to a menacing red. Shaw quaked and crawled backwards in the dirt like weakened prey. Alix, her face hidden by Felix's large figure, smirked, and Felix looked back at her and winked as he changed his eyes back to blue. The color change meant nothing in a practical sense, but it did the trick.

"From now on, just shut your mouth," Dalton roared at Shaw. "Go clean yourself up so we can get going! I swear, it's like dealing with children around here."

The five riders on stirrolback followed the glassy surface of the Lipine River that cut across the valley. Alix let her hair out in the cool breeze, her goggles bouncing against her neck. Felix rode beside her with his sleeves rolled up, the sunlight playing across his bare arms, much like the reflections on the water. His hat was pulled low to keep it from flying off in the wind. They looked at the back of Wick riding ahead of them as Dalton and Shaw led the way. On their right, they rode along the wide sea of chis, occasional rolls in the land with burrey trees at their feet. The river wound along on their left.

Alix wondered what they were heading into. She expected a trip to White Sands where they'd catch the train back, protecting whatever cargo Silas was bringing in. But the trip to White Sands by stirrol would've taken a week. They must be meeting the train somewhere in the valley, but she knew there were no stops less than three-days' ride from Verisport, and nothing was loaded onto the train at Burreville except crops from the valley farmers. Protecting food seemed unlikely. Regardless of the reason for their being here, Felix made sure they synced their comms on a new private frequency, just in case. Neither of them trusted the three men who rode with them, not one bit.

When the hills rolled a little smaller into pure flatland, the Lipine curved northward, and so they did as well. The rhythmic gait of her stirrol would've lulled Alix to sleep if she wasn't careful. They stopped just after midday beneath a copse of burrey trees to shield them from the sun. Dalton and Shaw sat beneath the trees together. Shaw's nose remained red from the beating Alix had given him, and a white piece of tape stuck out brightly over the bridge. Wick sat alone on a rock, just a stone's throw from the other two. Alix and Felix stayed with their stirrols, letting them drink from the river. The soft movement of the water's edge washed over Alix's boots.

"How's your hand?" Felix said.

"It's fine. Better than his face," Alix laughed. "You think we're heading to Burreville?"

"The only logical place to intercept the train," Felix agreed. "But I see little need in doing so, unless there's illicit cargo being loaded there."

"Doesn't make a whole lot of sense."

"Maybe we're taking over for security on the second half of the trip."

"Possibly."

"Still, that's a two-day ride from here, and the train would pass through before we could get there." Felix could easily calculate the distance in his head. He had almost the whole planet mapped out in there.

"Why do I feel like we're being ridden out into the valley to be killed?" Alix patted her stirrol's head, water dripping from its lips.

"They could've just killed us in town. Who would care?"

"Ouch," Alix said playfully, acknowledging that neither she nor Felix were exactly important people. "That Dalton fellow could've killed me in the yard when I went after the other."

"Maybe he was afraid of jumping the bolt, so to speak."

"Or maybe he was afraid of *you*. Think you can tap into their syncpads?"

"Easily, but what encryption they have may alert them."

"Alright, well, let's just play along until tonight. Then we'll see what we're dealing with."

After a short rest, Alix ate a bit of brizcoe jerky as she climbed back into the saddle, and the group rode onward. They took to the chis grass in the afternoon, bearing northwest. The land sloped upward away from the river to the north, where Alix could see a wide orchard of twifruit trees, creating a dense, dark green and purple canopy.

It stretched westward along with them for several kilometers until ending and she saw wisps of smoke rising into the distance, likely the farmstead village that worked the orchard. The group turned due west after the orchard, and the sun began setting behind them. Cooler air came rushing into the valley from the west, blowing in her eyes, making them water. Leaving the stirrol to gallop on its own, Alix dropped the reins and lifted her goggles over her eyes to shield from the wind. Pollen and dust came with it as well, but she had no defense against that. Her goggles began their work of intensifying the infrared light to offset the setting sun, giving her a picture of the land ahead, clear as day. She watched Wick lift the handkerchief around his neck to cover his mouth and nose from the dust in the air.

Night fell on them quickly, and the air only grew colder. The larger moon rose bright in the northern sky. Clouds dimmed the stars overhead, but other than the moons, no other light could be seen out in the valley. The five riders seemed well and truly on their own.

Dalton lifted a hand and slowed his stirrol, cutting across a hill to his left, down the other side into a hollow. They could hear the river just a little further to the southwest. Burrey trees grew thickly in the hollow, giving them shelter from the wind and any rain that might fall overnight. They all dismounted, and Dalton, Shaw, and Wick tied their stirrols to tree trunks or solid branches. Alix and Felix simply removed the saddles and other tack, letting the animals roam freely.

"You lose those stirrols, and you'll have an even greater debt to pay," Dalton warned.

"Treat them well enough, and they won't go anywhere," Alix said. "You see, we've already bonded with ours. Mine seemed to be glad she wasn't carrying some cruel blowhard anymore. Didn't catch the name she was saying, though."

Wick laughed as he removed the saddle from his stirrol, though Dalton and Shaw grew furious. "Shut it, Wickford. We're eating here tonight. Why don't you get fire going and do your job?"

"Speaking of, what's our job?" Felix asked.

"When it's time to let you know, I'll let you know," Dalton said.

"Well, what else are we going to talk about over dinner?" Alix chimed in.

"I don't care what you talk about." Dalton's impatience intensified.

"Except what our jobs are on this adventure? Then you seem to care what we talk about."

"Your job is to do what you're told, when you're told!" Dalton huffed and stomped away, and Shaw followed along like a dog sticking close to its owner.

Alix shrugged and sat down on the soft grass.

"He's really a worse guy when you get to know him," Wick said, beginning to unpack his gear.

"No love lost between you two, I see," Felix said.

Wick set out a quick range, a metal coffee pot, pans, and a small chillbox. He started picking up sticks and branches from the nearby area. Felix helped by breaking hefty branches with ease into smaller lengths. They began stacking the wood for a fire.

"Well, like I said, I've gotten to know him."

After everyone finished their meal, Dalton and Shaw settled in for sleep. Wick kept the fire burning and didn't seem in need of rest. He stared off into the middle distance, the firelight dancing across his face, the night dark all around him. Alix and Felix wandered through the trees in the hollow, back toward the river. The bank was made up of small stones and sand, and the hollow opened just before it, with a single burrey tree on one side, shielding the entrance. The land sloped gently downward to the south, leaving a clear view for many kilometers. Alix leaned against the tree as Felix sat on the ground.

"You want to get any sleep?" he said.

"I'm okay. I'd rather not sleep with those three around anyway."

"Remember that time in White Sands—" Felix started.

"No, no, do *not* bring that up," Alix laughed, throwing a handful of grass at him.

"The look on the marshal's face when you came spilling out of that barrel." Felix's laugh was like distant thunder.

"Shut up," Alix pleaded, incapable of holding in her laughter. "I believe that was *your* idea to begin with."

She leaned her head over to his shoulder. He put his arm around her. The moons reflected on the surface of the river. "You know you can sleep. I will keep an eye out."

"Thank you." Her voice dipped lower as she relaxed and faded to sleep already.

The sound of ships' engines roaring in the distance mingled with the gusts of wind that howled over the open prairie. A small grey mass above, far overhead, moved slowly away from the surface. Lights blinked on its hull, and a trail of vapor swirled and spread out behind as it passed out of the grip of this world, and eventually, out of her sight. Alix lay on her back, staring skyward, watching the ships leave the Xypha port that stood almost a hundred meters away.

She shivered in the growing cold. Her clothes were threadbare and torn, stained from mud and blood. Her face carried weeks' worth of dirt, and her dark hair was a tangled mess. She looked like a wild animal, waiting in the cover of the grass to pounce. She was not a cunning hunter, but a weak and desperate cur. Pangs of hunger were overwhelming, and only sheer force of will allowed her to move from her hiding spot as night fell.

She waited in the grass for days after many more days and nights spent walking until she was broken and barefoot. Then at last, a great hulking freighter stood on the landing nearest to her hiding place. Between them, an old fence lined the perimeter, within which she had already found a break she could squeeze through. Beyond the fence, there were the fuel tanks: four standing tall in a row. She saw machines and hovering robots loading things onto the freighter throughout the day. Flat hovercraft moved autonomously, laden with massive containers, following one another in a line and up into the ship's enormous cargo hold.

But now, as night drew near, the ship was fully loaded and preparing to depart. A few men and women milled about the ship, but they were focused on the hull and the large hoses that ran from it. She at last decided to make a run for it, crouching so she could remain hidden in the grass, though it was almost as tall as her. She carried just a small handmade backpack with meager things she owned. In her waistband was a knife, small enough to fit in her young hands, made from a broken piece of metal and sharpened on stones for days. She breathed heavily as she ran, stumbling along the way, feeling weak.

At the edge of the grass and the fence line, Alix knelt, waiting and looking around. She made sure the coast was clear before squeezing herself through the torn fence and then running across a black expanse to the fuel tanks. She looked around each one before darting from one to the next. The freighter's cargo hold remained open as she stood with her shoulder against the fourth tank, her heart beating fast and heavy. She took a step forward but froze and then jumped back as two men worked around the stern of the ship, speaking together, pointing up to the hull, stopping and staring at it, then moving on again.

Alix made a break for it, sprinting as fast as her weary little legs could take her. She reached the massive cargo ramp, jumped onto it, and ran up into the towering cavern of the ship's hold. Containers were stacked three or four high, and to her they looked like skyscrapers. She gawked at them before realizing she stood out in the open, and she ducked into the small walkways that were open to her between some stacks of the crates. She sat with her back to one, catching her breath.

The ship rumbled, and she started at the abrupt sound of alarms and the hiss and grinding of the large ramp as it slowly closed. Alix shivered from the cold metal floor and the fear that overtook her. There was no going back now; she was bound for somewhere else, leaving this *world* behind. She didn't care where the freighter might take her. She pulled her legs in and gripped her knees.

The hold echoed with the sound of the massive engines roaring, and the ship vibrated beneath her. She jerked her head up abruptly, hearing oncoming footsteps. Panicking, she stood and looked around the corner of the container but saw no one down the narrow space between two long rows of stacked crates. Then, she realized the footsteps we coming up behind her, and she spun around to see a man. He stopped and looked up from a datapad in his hand in utter confusion. She stared at him, trembling, afraid.

"Who the hell are you?" he asked. "How did you get in here?"

She didn't say anything as her eyes welled with tears. He shook his head and came closer, typing on his datapad.

"You're not supposed to be in here," he said. "Let's go."

He reached for her with one hand, and she drew back. Frustrated, the man rolled his eyes and put the datapad in a small pouch at his hip. He came for her again, and her despair took hold, anger releasing as he gripped her thin arm in his hand. She screamed, the cry dying among the crates and the growing roar of the engines. She reached for the knife she'd made as he lifted her off the ground. She reached out and thrust the knife into his chest. He let her go, and she fell. He stumbled back and pulled the knife out, blood spilling down his shirt and onto the metal floor.

"You crazy son of a bitch," he gasped as he tried to walk away.

She looked at the knife then at him, leaning with one hand on a container and the other clutching his wound. He turned to leave, and she sprang up, grabbed the knife and ran at him, crying and screaming. She jumped up at him and stabbed him again as they both fell. He struggled only briefly, then slowly faded, his arms falling and lying beside him, his eyes dimming and closing. His skin looked pale, and he grew cold. She recoiled and dropped the knife. As she felt the strange sensation of the shift in gravity, the ship taking off, she stared at the dead body next to her. She wept uncontrollably.

"Alix," Felix said, his voice shook her from sleep.

Alix startled, sitting upright with a weak cry. She looked around and saw the river, the grass waving in the wind, Felix holding her in his arms. Her face was soaked with sweat, awash in terror as she looked at him.

"It's okay," he said. "You were having a nightmare."

She took a deep, ragged breath and shook out her hands. "I'm fine."

But truthfully, she wasn't. She could only picture that face all those years ago. She'd spent the rest of her life running, fighting. Now, it was all for nothing. Her rage grew. The past week raced through her mind —the *Shadow* locked in the shipyard, the money lost, the debts piling higher. Everything began to unravel. Her hands trembled, and she felt like her heart would explode. Her legs became weak, and she felt an intense tingling rising and spread through her body. She clutched her chest. Felix wrapped his arms tightly around her.

"It's okay. You're safe, you're here, Alix. I've got you. Deep breaths. Slow your heart."

She began to feel a rhythm in Felix's body wrapped around her, slow and steady. Alix struggled to match her breathing to the tempo. Her breaths came slowly, long inhales and exhales, shaking at first, then smooth. The frantic beating heart in her chest slowed, and the burning and shaking left her. Felix's eyes studied her, and she knew he was checking her vitals, feeling the sensations and signals from her body, just as she could feel his. She put a hand on his face and smiled, her cheeks flushed.

"Thank you," she said, and then gently kissed him.

4

The Train

When Xypha first arrived on Celestine a year ago, the first project the corporation's representatives began was a magnetically levitated train that connected the two principal settlements of the Isidis Valley: White Sands and Verisport. The company showed its power and influence by completing the project in nine months, all with materials brought on its own forward station now orbiting the planet.

The people of White Sands marveled at Xypha's resources, strength, and prosperity. Those in Verisport were more cautious, less eager to accept the new presence without suspicion. After all, White Sands was much more populated with the upper classes. Those who sought to distance themselves from the less desirable history of Verisport and its people found their own sanctuary on the other side of the valley where the river slipped into a vast, blue sea. Alix hated the place, except when it offered up naïve, rich buffoons to take advantage of.

After another day's ride and night's sleep, Dalton stopped the group at the bottom of a hill overlooking the train line. Its track was a singular strip of sleek omniite, brightly reflecting the sun. Measuring about five meters wide, the track housed electromagnetic currents that kept the train suspended a short distance above the ground. On either side of the track, concrete was poured, preventing the chis grass from taking back what had been stolen from it. To finish things off, a large fence lined the concrete pads, buzzing with electricity to keep the local wildlife and people from interfering.

"Looks good, Dalton, but I don't believe the train is supposed to stop here," Alix said, kneeling in the grass.

Atop the hill, they waited, but only Dalton and Shaw knew why. The chis grass waved around them. Dalton had cut away the blades to give them a clearer view. Their stirrols milled around behind them, unconcerned with anything.

"Alright, here's the story," Dalton finally began. "The train is due in an hour to pass by here. But, instead of going by, it's going to stop, just for us."

"Why?" Felix said.

"Because we're getting on it. There's an access gate here, and I've got the code for it, so we won't get killed by that fence."

"Alright, so the train stops, we get on, then what?" Alix wondered.

"When we get on, I'll let you know," Dalton said impatiently.

"What about the stirrols?" Wick asked.

"Who cares?" Shaw butt in.

"That's why we didn't take a skimmer," Alix noted.

"Congratulations, you've put it together," Dalton said. "Now, get down there and set them loose. Whatever gear you want to keep, bring it. Otherwise, it's staying behind."

"Are there passengers on the train?"

"Why does that matter?"

"Won't it be suspicious that the train just…stops in the middle of nowhere?"

"I'm sure Silas and—" He caught himself. "I'm sure everything has been thought of before now. Just do what you're told."

"You're a fine leader." She rolled her eyes.

Felix, Wick, and Alix headed down the hill to unburden the stirrols, leaving Dalton and Shaw alone at the hill. Alix hadn't quite begun to trust Wick, but she was more confident in his animosity for Silas's other men than she was in his trustworthiness. At least if push came to shove, Wick didn't seem like the kind to stick his neck out to save Dalton or Shaw. She could probably count on his self-preservation instinct, and Alix knew she and Felix could best the other two without much effort.

"So, who else was Dalton talking about?" Alix asked Wick.

"What do you mean?"

"Up there, he said Silas, and he was *going* to say someone else, but he didn't, like he wasn't *supposed* to."

"Beats me."

"Silas has a partnership with some in Xypha, that much seems clear," Felix said.

"Is it?" Wick seemed like he didn't care at all if it were true or not.

"Nobody is stopping that train but Xypha."

"You familiar with them, eh?"

"We've had our run-ins with them in the past," Alix added.

She dropped the saddle off her stirrol and gave it one last affectionate rub on the nose. It stamped its front hoof and pushed against her chest with its nose before turning and wandering aimlessly. The others joined it, sticking together but remaining near, just eating the golden panicles off the chis around them.

Alix was growing tired of being left in the dark. She stuck a finger in Wick's chest. "Look, I know you don't really march along with those two, so if there's something you know that you're not telling us, spill it, quickly."

"I know just as much as you do now," he protested. "Nobody really tells me anything either."

Alix mocked the orders given to Wick, "Go pick up these people; cook dinner for us out in the valley. Is that what you do in Silas's crew?"

"Pretty much. I'm about as worth as much as a stirrol to him."

"Then you don't have much reason to stick around."

"Well…" Wick's shoulders sagged, and he looked down at his boots.

"What? You mean to tell me if bolts start flying, you're going to protect his interest?"

"You don't understand."

Wick took a deep breath and gathered himself. Alix recognized that tough exterior, how the face tightened, and that façade to deceive those around you and yourself. Wick's face was stern and serious, but she knew better.

"Try me," she said.

"If you two want to talk amongst yourselves, figure out some grand plan to turn this thing in your favor go ahead, but leave me out of it." He stormed off, heading back up the hill, muttering to himself.

Felix watched Wick walk up the hill, "Something keeps him here, but it isn't loyalty."

"Fear," Alix said.

"Precisely."

"Well, if we have to, I'll give him something else to be afraid of."

The time dragged on, and Alix lay in the grass on her back, hands behind her head. Felix sat beside her cross-legged, in a meditative state. He extended his sensors with as much strength as he could, and he would detect the oncoming train before anyone else heard or saw it. The wind rustled the chis, creating a rhythmic hissing in the air, but Felix's audio receptors detected a distinct sound of a ship's engines.

His eyes brightened. "There's a ship approaching."

Alix sat up quickly and watched Felix, who stared into the distance, listening, searching, scanning. Dalton and Shaw looked over their shoulders in momentary confusion.

"Xypha class D-4," Felix said.

"That's a drop ship," Alix added.

Dalton checked his syncpad for the time. "Right on schedule."

"I thought we were waiting on the train?" Alix said. She didn't like the idea of getting on the train, even if it was to protect some cargo in a freight car, but Xypha drop ships came with Xypha personnel.

"We are. It should be in momentarily, so get ready," Dalton said.

"Here it comes," Felix added on cue.

The train glinted on the horizon. It already slowed its pace, far below the max speed of over four hundred kilometers an hour. From the rounded nose, the cab angled back and met the cylindrical shape of the cars behind it. The whole thing shined with white paint over the omniite frame. Gliding over the rail, it made no sound except for rushing wind. Slowly, it came to a stop right where Dalton said it would. The eight cars behind the cab contained no windows, so no passengers were on board.

Above them, the Xypha ship circled then made its vertical descent to the ground. The ship was rectangular, the stern angled sharply up from the deck where a ramp dropped down to load cargo. The ship's engines blew the chis below in wild swirling patterns. The landing gear stamped down the grass. The ramp lowered behind and another, smaller hatch opened near the cockpit, folding out from the side of the hull and forming into metal stairs from the cockpit to the ground. In all, six men emerged from the vessel, all wearing pristine white Xypha slipsuits.

"What are those men doing?" Wick asked.

"They're a repair team, engineers. Something must be wrong with the train," Alix said.

"Congratulations for identifying them. Now, go kill them," Dalton said.

Alix turned her head swiftly, staring at Dalton in disbelief. "You want us to *what*?"

"We're here to kill those men. So, do as you're told," Dalton repeated.

He had already drawn his plasbolts, snapping the cylinders in place, which began to spin and charge. Shaw covered his face with a dark handkerchief, his own weapon in his other hand. Alix tried to understand the mission, but her confusion began to fade away as she thought of heading down the hill and killing the men who now entered the protective fence and crossed the concrete pad to the train. The corner of her mouth turned up, and she shrugged.

"Don't mind if I do." She drew a Plasveld in each hand.

"Alix, wait!" Felix said.

He could not reach her, and she darted down the hill. Dalton and Shaw followed behind her, leaving Felix and Wick. Felix begrudgingly followed, mostly because he needed to have Alix's back. Wick thought for a moment about hanging back, or even making a run for it, saddling up a stirrol and leaving. But he delayed long enough to not actually have to fire his plasbolt, which he drew and trotted down the hill.

Four of the Xypha engineers stood on the near side of the train, their backs to Alix and the others. They focused on the open panel near the bottom of the driver's cabin and never saw or heard anyone coming. Alix had no idea whether Dalton and Shaw could shoot worth a damn, but she knew she could drop all four men without an issue.

She ran through the next few minutes in her mind. As soon as the shots would leave her Plasvelds, the other men would know to get the hell out of there. They saw six get out of the drop ship, which meant two were unaccounted for beyond the four in front of her. She scanned the train with her goggles, shifting through wavelengths and looking through the train to find the other two men. They were further back on the driver's cabin. They probably wouldn't even hesitate to run when they heard the shots, leaving behind the toolbox they brought with them. But there would be a moment of confusion, and they would have to drop the datapads, which were connected to the train. One of them might trip over the toolbox on the ground between them. Either way, the train hovered off the ground, but moving below it would be suicide. The engineers in front of her would have to go around the front, and so would she.

"Felix, you read?" she said into their private comms channel connected to her goggles.

"Yes, just behind you," he answered.

"Go over the top. I've got these four."

"Two on the other side, armed with plasbolts, not drawn. The four ahead are running diagnostic checks. They *think* there's something wrong with the train."

"There isn't?" Alix didn't understand.

"I do not detect any error."

"One step at a time," she said, but plasfire cut her off.

Dalton and Shaw had opened fire.

"Fucking idiots," she said under her breath.

They, of course, missed. Plasma rounds buried into the train around the four men. Some clipped through the fence, burning and melting the metal weave. Alix quickened her pace, and the engineers panicked. A lucky shot from Shaw hit one of the engineers, but only in the leg. *At least he slowed that one down*, Alix thought.

Her own shots did not miss. With the Plasveld in her right hand, she fired twice.

Zmmph zmmph.

One engineer who ran toward the nose of the train fell and tumbled forward—dead.

Her left moved and found its target crouching, the man's hands up by his ears.

Zmmph.

He crumpled to the concrete—dead.

She turned both Plasvelds to her right.

Zmmph zmmph zmmph.

The third engineer died as blood stained the white train and concrete.

Dalton and Shaw stood by the gate in the fence, fumbling with the code. As soon as they got it open, Alix shoved them out of the way, quickly heading for the front of the train.

Felix didn't need the open gate. He easily leapt over the fence, one foot hitting the concrete, a crack beneath him. He bounded up and over the train in another leap. Dalton, Shaw, and Alix only heard the screams and shouting of the men on the other side of the train—then, they were silenced.

Alix now walked, letting the last engineer crawl on his belly, dragging blood across the concrete pad. Her boots let him know who approached behind him until she stopped beside his body, and he slowly rolled onto his back. She looked down on him, her lips pursed, her eyes hidden behind the goggles. He held his one good arm up, the other stained with blood and the wound singed black. The man was not much older than Alix. Blood splattered his pale face, wet with tears and sweat. He could hardly muster a coherent word. She looked him up and down, from his gray boots up to the neural implant protruding from his skin over his left ear, a feature of all those in Xypha employ.

She remembered. Each shot she fired drew out the nightmares.

The dry, oppressive heat. Wind biting her skin.

Zmmph.

People in tattered clothes. Starving. Flesh clinging to frail bones.

Zmmph zmmph.

The men in bright white slipsuits.

Zmmph zmmph zmmph zmmph.

Alix's mind raced and her hands shook. Her heart pounded in her chest. The bright blue flashes in her goggles concealed the man at her feet as each plasma round hit him point-blank. His body flailed and burned then lay still, receiving the fifth, the sixth, the seventh, rounds with lifeless, dull thuds, accomplishing nothing but spraying more blood across the ground, burning new nightmares into Alix's brain to overwrite the old ones.

"Alix. Alix!" Felix cried.

She shook back to reality and wheeled around on her heels, pointing her steaming Plasvelds at him and everyone else, the cylinders spinning white hot. The others stared at her in horror, but Felix looked with love and compassion. She lowered her shaking hands, then dropped to her knees, her body suddenly giving out on her. Felix rushed to her side to catch her.

"Are you alright?" He gently pulled the goggles back from her eyes to see her weeping.

"I'm…fine," she stammered.

The Plasvelds dropped to the concrete, and she threw her arms around Felix's neck. He wrapped his around her.

"What the hell is the matter?" Dalton called out.

In a single motion, Felix stepped toward and yanked Dalton off the ground by the neck. Dalton felt weightless in Felix's powerful arm as he kicked and screamed, helpless. Felix's eyes spun and narrowed, he sneered, and silently squeezed until no air could escape Dalton's lungs. He threw the man to the ground and Dalton bounced off the concrete. Dalton gasped and put his hands to his throat, panicking. Felix turned and reached a hand to Alix, who put her small hand in his and stood. Dalton couldn't speak, could barely breathe. All he could do was answer with fear and violence.

He drew his plasbolt, and the charged whining preceded one shot racing between him and Felix.

Zmmph.

The round hit Felix, passed straight through him. The giant sentient barely registered the burning plasma round that sliced through his shoulder, in one side and out the other. Alix ducked as the hot round went right by her head. Felix turned to face Dalton.

The man on the ground looked up, eyes wide, and he dropped his plasbolt. Felix bent over him, and with one hand, pressed him into the ground. Dalton screamed in pain, as if a building now lay on top of his chest. Shaw stood motionless, struck by fear.

"Listen, if you try to hurt one of us again, I will kill you. Do you understand?" Felix's voice shook Dalton.

Dalton couldn't speak, but he nodded.

"If you even speak to one of us with any disrespect, I *will* kill you."

Felix lifted his hand, and Dalton gasped for air. Dalton curled up and clutched his arms to his throat and chest. Felix picked him up and steadied him on his feet. Alix holstered her Plasvelds and wiped her eyes. Wick strolled up, trying to find words to say, but the tension in the air kept his mouth shut.

Shaw finally tapped the syncpad on his arm and reminded Dalton of a time window that they had kept between them. Dalton nodded. Unable to utter a word, he simply waved Shaw along, and the other man took over from there.

"Alright, time to board," Shaw said. "Train has to move in less than two minutes."

"Lead the way," Felix said.

Shaw closed the panels the Xypha engineers had opened, and with a code supplied to him from Silas, he opened the door to the first car. A pressurized lock popped and hissed, and the door slid open. Each of them climbed inside a dimly lit car with heavy crates stacked in an orderly fashion. There were no seats of any kind, so the five of them had to sit on the floor or lean on the walls. Once the door closed, the blue running lights dimmed, making it nearly too dark to see.

Felix and Alix sat with their backs against the front of the car, a stack of large crates on either side of them, looking down an open space between stacks. Felix's eyes shone bright; his skin reflected the blue lights like water on a clear night. Alix brought her knees up to her chest and held them tight.

"What happened back there?" Felix whispered.

"Just a bad memory," she said, resting her chin on her arms.

"The Cradle?"

She closed her eyes and sighed. Felix did not pry further. He simply put his arm around her as the train shifted and built speed.

Alix could not keep the memories at bay. The cold train car, its dark ambient light, the metal floor beneath her, the metal at her back; it was all so familiar. She was back in the cargo hold of that freighter. The sounds of the engines echoed in the massive space. She felt the cold creeping into her bones as the ship entered space. The shifts in gravity made her stomach turn. Sitting against the large metal crate, she lurched and vomited. The ship's autogravity saved her from lifting off the floor.

The dead body of the Xypha officer grew cold as the blood on the floor thickened. She crawled to his feet and unfastened the man's boots. She kicked off the ragged shoes she'd worn for years and slipped the boots on, noticing the warm, supple lining. Hesitating for a moment, she felt through the man's empty pockets. The implant over his ear caught her attention, and she recoiled, but then reached to the man's arm and tried to remove the syncpad there. The sleeve took some effort to pull from the man's arm, and Alix poked at the soft screen but understood little about its function.

Alix stuffed the device into her bag and stumbled to her feet, trying to steady herself in unfamiliar gravity. She left the dead man behind and began exploring her new surroundings.

Her new world.

The train slowed some hours later as they neared Verisport. The train glided through a gateway into an expansive yard that had been constructed alongside the port compound. A singular omniite structure housed a warehouse and the operating offices for the line. Only three officers manned the station in rotating shifts. Night fell outside while Alix and the others rode in the windowless freight car. She wondered how they would leave without drawing attention.

"So, we killed six Xypha personnel, and now we're just going to pop out of this car like we're supposed to be in it?"

"Yes," Dalton said, his voice still low and weak.

"The officer on shift will not bother us," Shaw added.

"Great," Alix said sarcastically.

The train stopped. The sounds and vibrations faded. The pressurized lock snapped before the door slid open. Outside, strong lamps lit the yard in round pockets. The five passengers in the train casually stepped out of the freight car. One of the lamps bobbed away, as if someone moved it to shroud their departure from sight.

"Well, it was nice knowin' ya," Alix waved casually as she and Felix started off on their own.

"Wait. Silas would like to see you again," Shaw objected.

"Sorry pal, he said we're even."

"He says it's about your ship."

Alix stopped. She turned around and narrowed her eyes as Felix grumbled.

"What about my ship?" Alix said.

The whole way to Silas's place, Alix argued with herself. Had it really been that easy to convince her to come along? She sat in the back of a skimmer with Felix and Shaw as Wick piloted the craft and Dalton sat beside him. A cool fog hung in the streets and corners. A storm rolled its way out of town just as they were coming in, and every surface glistened with raindrops. *Silas is about to make an offer*, she thought. *Working for him to pay off her debt at the docks?* Alix considered it for a moment, but only one. She knew better than to trust a man like Silas. He wouldn't stop at paying off her debts at the port; he would squeeze until he didn't need her anymore. *So why am I about to talk to him again?*

She would do anything to get the *Shadow* back in the air. The idea gnawed away at her ability to reason. Alix was not overly cautious, but it seemed now, she was on a slope, gaining speed, unable to turn from the path.

Inside Silas's office, he tossed a small box on the desk, the crits inside clinking against one another. Alix wanted to snatch the box up but waited to hear the man's offer. Felix reached down and picked up the box between his thumb and forefinger.

"That's two thousand crits," Silas said, his back to them, reordering some papers and items on a bookshelf.

"I thought you said we were even?" Alix crossed her arms.

"Well, Dalton told me you two performed exceptionally well. Bandy was a good weapon to have, but not the best. Maybe I felt your work warranted a little extra."

"Or maybe you're trying to buy us."

Silas turned, a big grin on his face. He hadn't slept much, that was obvious in his eyes, and Alix noticed he subconsciously played with something in his vest pocket with his left hand. He ran his other hand over his mustache before he reached out, motioning to the parlor set up in the other half of the room. He walked that way, knowing Alix and Felix would follow him. He spoke as he walked.

"I know about your debt to the dock master. He and I are well acquainted. Your ship—the *Shadow*, is it? Seems you refused to pay the Xypha contracting fee when all shipping into and out of Verisport and White Sands moved to their control."

A woven carpet covered the floor, handmade from the best fibers in the valley, dyed with blues and greens. The red cushions on the furniture complemented it, and lamps hovered over small end tables between chairs and a couch. A large liquor cabinet and wet bar stood on the far wall. Paintings and art pieces hung on the other walls. A large window looked out, but not in, on the bar below.

"Why would I agree to be someone's errand girl?"

Silas retrieved three glasses and then hesitated. He looked over his shoulder knowingly, leaving one glass on the bar, upside down, as he poured an aged chisik into the other two. He turned and brought the glasses over, setting one on the glass table between the chairs and the couch. He sat down and took a sip.

"Apologies to your friend. I don't have anything he would like," he said, motioning his glass up at Felix.

Alix sat on one end of the couch as Felix stood behind it. He would've loved nothing more than to hurl the man through the window, sending him crashing down through glass and wood below, but he smiled.

"Do you have something to offer or not?" Alix said as she drank the chisik in one gulp. It was, indeed, extremely good, warm going down, but not sharp and unpleasant.

"I pay off your debt to the dock master, and then you come work for me, free of Xypha's reach," Silas said, taking another measured sip.

"Again, why would I agree to be someone's errand girl?"

"Steady work, steady pay—isn't that the goal?"

"And on the side, we'll be sent on assignments without knowing the details, murdering Xypha officers, is that it?"

Silas smirked and looked down into his glass.

"I find the fewer people who know something, the better. Some men do as they're told, and others do the telling. Which man are you?"

He looked up from his glass, his brow furrowed. Alix sneered back at him. The man had no protection. She thought of drawing a Plasveld and putting a hole through his eye or slitting his throat.

"It'd be a shame if we stained this nice rug," she said behind clenched teeth.

He acted as if he hadn't said it on purpose. "Ah, sorry, I apologize. Just an expression, you know? Dalton told me you had a temper."

He finished his drink and picked Alix's glass up off the table to go for a refill.

"What else did he tell you?"

"That you're a killer, and a killer is what I need."

"Where's the one who sat in the corner of your office the other day? Seems you got enough of them."

The bottle clinked on the glasses as the liquid flowed. With one glass in each hand, he turned. "I guess you'd say an errand boy on an errand."

"Just because I know how to kill doesn't mean I kill for hire." Alix took the glass, not passing up another quality drink.

"Everyone's got a price."

Silas took a sip. Alix hesitated, the glass poised in front of her lips.

Silas leaned forward and tapped the glass table between them, which lit up and turned into a touch display, projected from underneath. A three-dimensional map formed on the surface in pale blue light.

"You ever been to Keizur's End?" Silas said.

"A few times," Alix set her glass down on the table in the middle of the map projection.

"How's about you go back? Would ten thousand do the trick?"

Alix's jaw almost fell open, but she kept her Solar face. She looked over her shoulder at Felix, his blue eyes gazing down at her. The question hung in the air like a whiff of smoke. The sound rang in her ears. *Ten thousand.*

"What's the job?" She grinned, and then threw back her drink.

5

The Mechanic

One year ago…

Sora sat in the saddle atop a stirrol. She had stopped the mount on a hillock that looked over the valley to the west. A purple glow tinged the dark sky overhead, some trick of the magnetic field and atmosphere she didn't understand. A cool breeze sent the chis grass below her swaying, moving in undulations like a great ocean.

She rode out at night to enjoy the view, the cold air, the stars overhead. There were *billions* of lights in the sky. She could never count them all, and some moved as she caught a glimpse of a ship entering or leaving the atmosphere. Celestine was so remote, at the frontier edge of colonized space, that only a handful of pilots came and went, but she'd never met any of them. Verisport, the nearest city on the planet, stood so far to the east behind her its light could not pollute the sky. Her village may as well be the most remote point in the universe.

With a sigh, Sora adjusted herself in the saddle. The stirrol's long neck easily reached down and chewed the short grasses at its feet. She rubbed her hand reassuringly on its coarse hair. A flicker in the night sky caught her eye, a small light that grew in magnificence, and she waited for the moment it punctured the atmosphere and dimmed after reentry. But the light did not—it only grew until it reached a bright point and remained. It slowed in the sky, and some strange feeling came over her. She'd never seen something enter the space around Celestine like this.

Sora pulled a small vizscope from her saddlebag. She held up the eyepiece to her right eye and found the strange light in the sky. The craft entered focus: a silver, shimmering circular space station. She tried to guess its size and wondered who could be in such a vessel. Unknown to her, the waystation belonged to the Xypha sovereign corporation.

Present day...

Sora yawned in the driver's box of the wagon. Jo's head rested on Sora's shoulder as she slept. Instead of camping the night before, they decided to drive on. Jo made it a few hours before falling asleep with a blanket wrapped around her. Sora leaned her head to rest on her sister, a warm smile and memory moving her. She remembered Jo as a little girl, sleeping in her lap after their parents died. Sora herself was still a child then, barely sixteen years old, but Jo was even smaller, even more helpless. Despite having the village to help raise her, Sora instantly changed that day. No force in the universe would come between her and her sister.

She would do *anything* to protect her, to provide for her.

But the girl on her shoulder was growing, pushing for more, reaching for her place in the world. Sora had no doubts Jo would find it, take hold of it, and never let go, but the risks of the past year began to pile up, and Sora worried more than usual. Had she made the right decisions?

Should I have protected Jo more? Protected her from herself? she wondered.

It was a silly thought. Sora knew now, that although she was tough, Jo was made of sterner stuff.

The stirrols bobbed their heads as they galloped through the chis. The land began to slope upward as they neared home. The sun would be coming up soon, and as the stirrols crested a hill, Sora caught sight of the first slivers of light in the west. The chis gleamed with dew, the long stalks waving in a gentle breeze. The dark night sky began to crack into pink, purple, orange and red. High clouds drifted, the rising sun painting them in many shades. Sora smiled as she saw a thin column of smoke over an elevated plain ahead. The first fires of the day signaled breakfast, a hot bath—home.

Sora gently lifted her shoulder to give Jo a little nudge. Her sister groaned and pulled the blanket tighter to her neck. She spoke in barely a whisper.

"Stop…" She dragged it out to convey her annoyance.

"We're home; wake up."

The stirrols and wagon suspended behind them broke through the edge of the chis, entering a field of short grasses, cut deliberately to neatly define the edge of the chis grass sea around the village. A dirt lane ran up the hill, leading into the village at the flat top. The farmstead was built primarily of wood, but not without artisanship. The buildings stood around a square with a large stone cistern in the center. Some of the buildings were houses, built for multiple families, no more than two stories tall. Their exteriors were dark and polished with verandas along the front and some wrapping around corners to the sides of the homes. The light green roofs sloped gently.

Natural lawns of ryegrass covered the ground up to the square. Footpaths had been carved by generations of travel between and around the homes. Directly beyond the square stood a long, wooden building: a central meeting house with a great stone chimney, smoke rising from the fire inside, kindled anew for the morning.

Sora turned the stirrols off the lane onto another dirt path and led them around the rear of the houses toward another set of buildings set away from the others. A barn commanded the area, a structure much taller than anything else in the farmstead. Stables, pens, and pastures all contained within wooden fencing spread around the barn. Livestock waited patiently for their breakfast, congregating near the smaller barns, knowing from where the food would come. The people here raised stirrols, ibi, binox, and many chickens clucked all around freely.

Jo yawned dramatically, stretching her arms and legs. Sora jumped off the wagon and began disconnecting the stirrols from their harness. Jo ambled over to open the stalls, the blanket still wrapped around her shoulders. Once unharnessed, the stirrols calmly walked into the stalls as they had done hundreds of times. Sora shut off the wagon's suspension system, and it slowly lowered onto the ground.

"Sora! Sora!" a young child's voice came toward them.

A child with tangled reddish hair and a soft, rounded face sprinted into the stable, trailed by two other children. All three children were no more than twelve, dressed in hand me down shirts and trousers.

"Ein, what are you doing here this early?" Sora said.

"We…we were out with the ibi yesterday." Ein was both out of breath and trying to talk as quickly as possible.

"Take a deep breath," Sora chuckled.

"There is, uh, a ship out by the rail, and well, there were dead guys all around it."

"What?" Sora looked over at Jo with a horrified expression.

Sora got down to the child's eye level. "Ein, what were you doing down by the rail? I told you to keep clear of it."

Ein shook their head. "No, I know, um, the ibi like to the graze at the short grass, you know?"

"Right. Did you touch anything? The ship?"

"No!" Ein shouted in their defense.

"Did you tell Ben or Sim about it?"

Ein shook their head emphatically.

Sora figured that would be the answer, given that Ein and the others were not supposed to be anywhere near the Xypha rail line, but Ein knew Sora and Jo went there frequently, without the knowledge of any of the elders. It took a lot of bribing to get Ein to agree to keep their mouth shut about it, but they became a little fly, always nearby, always interested in whatever Sora and Jo were up to.

"Jo and I will take care of it. You don't have to worry about anything, okay? Just go get your chores done." She playfully ruffled the child's hair, much to their dismay.

The children ran off as Sora rubbed her hands down her face, releasing a weary, heavy sigh. The bath and breakfast would have to wait. Jo tossed the blanket onto the driver's box of the wagon. She no longer looked sleepy and pouting. Sora knew the look of singular focus in Jo's face, and when Jo reached into the wagon for her plasrifle, Sora tried to calm her.

"Jo, we're not going to get into anything."

"You don't know that."

"We're just going to go have a look."

"Well, if someone else starts trouble, then I'll be prepared, just like at Jesse's."

Sora rolled her eyes and relented. She remembered the woman in the scrapyard: her cool confidence, strong arms, and a knowing smile.

"There won't be any trouble."

"A bunch of dead guys around a ship by the rail? That's already trouble, sis."

They gave the two stirrols that had pulled the wagon a break, saddled up two more, and headed out. The rail line wasn't far from the village, and the land the farmstead once looked over had been cut in half when Xypha built it. They lost considerable crops and grazing land, leaving their primary crop, the twifruit orchard, under the villagers' care. The morning had not yet penetrated the canopy of the twifruit trees. Sora and Jo rode through the dewy grass and mist beneath the boughs and dark, purple leaves. The orchard rolled from one hill to another, and soon, their bright pink fruits would pop among the dark leaves like stars in the night.

Once the orchard came to an end, the short grass continued for a few meters before the chis staked its natural claim. The space between the orchard and the chis was like an alley between two lines of buildings. Sora turned her stirrol right and followed the line of chis, then reached a small cutout, just large enough for one person to walk through uninhibited. She and Jo carved the path, small enough to not be noticed unless you were looking for it. They dismounted and left the stirrols behind, then disappeared into the chis, the panicles high over their heads.

After a short walk, Sora knelt at the edge of a small cliff. Two old burrey trees stood on its edge, their roots exposed and reaching downward, tearing rocks from the ground as they grew, the stone tumbling down below. They had a clear view into the lower depression, where the rail line cut across the valley. Sora crouched down by the trees, one hand on the trunk. She removed a viscope from her bag and looked at the white ship, its rear ramp wide open, steps reaching down from the cockpit to the ground. Then, she panned over to the line and saw the dead bodies swollen in the morning light. Black jawix flocked to them, picking at the flesh and bones, squawking at one another, competing for the next bite with beating wings.

They had come here many times in the past few weeks to study the gate on the north side of the fence. It was the nearest access point to the rail line—for maintenance, they guessed. The scene down below proved them right.

Maybe there's something in that ship to open the gate, Sora wondered. "Xypha men," she said aloud, handing the viscope to Jo. "Nobody in the valley is stupid enough to do this."

"They're all *inside* the fence line," Jo pointed out.

"Two on the near side, so maybe they were surrounded."

"How, you'd have to get *through* the line?"

"Well, we've been trying to get through it," Sora reminded her sister.

"Maybe others have figured it out before us."

"Why has nobody been out to clean things up?"

"I want to go down there," Sora said.

Jo dropped the viscope from her eye. "Are you serious? What happened to 'we're just going to have a look'?" She mocked Sora with a deep, authoritative voice.

"Shut up." Sora pushed Jo almost off balance. She drew a plasbolt out of her bag and slung the bag across her body. "You stay here; cover me."

"No way. I'm coming with you!"

"You keep a look out, and besides, I trust your shot from here."

Jo would've protested more, but the compliment did its job. She smirked and brimmed with confidence. She put the viscope on the ground and picked up her rifle, making sure the rounds were charged. Then, she affixed the viscope to the rifle so she could get a better sight on the scene below.

Sora smiled at her. "Be right back."

"Hurry—and be careful," Jo whispered, as if there was someone who could hear them.

Sora ran down the hill. Jo watched Sora through the scope on her rifle until Sora disappeared in more chis at the bottom of the hill. Then all she saw of her sister was the agitated grass as she moved through it. Jo scanned the horizon, taking her role very seriously.

The Xypha dropship sat eerily silent, the grass all pressed down around it from its landing. Sora waited for a moment at the edge of the chis; when she was confident nobody was around, she headed for the rear ramp. She kept her plasbolt in hand, just in case. There would be a treasure trove of things she could pick off the ship, and given enough time, an infinite amount of information to learn, but she didn't have time and didn't want to stick around anyway. The scene gave her the shivers as she glanced over at the dead bodies closest to the ship: two men lying face down on the concrete pad beside the rail. They were the only two not covered in blood and burns from plasfire.

Sora craned her neck to look around and into the rear compartment of the ship as best she could. It was dark inside, save for soft yellow lights along the bulkhead and the ceiling that she assumed were always on. She stepped on the ramp with one foot, then another, fighting the urge to run away.

Her boots clicked on the metal ramp as she entered the ship.

Jo lost sight of her at that moment. She continued scanning the horizon.

The rear compartment was not much more than a small cargo space. There were no seats, but many lockers and compartments on the inside of the hull. She could tell that a workbench would emerge from a space between sets of lockers if she powered up the ship. Afraid to tamper with any electronics just yet, she ran her fingers over the sleek surfaces. A hatch stood slightly open toward the nose. Sora put her shoulder to the bulkhead beside it, then gently pulled the hatch open so she could look inside. There were two soft seats on the left, and she looked to the right to see two more. Nothing else.

This is obviously where workers sat while in transit, with easy access to the workspace and cargo. But there was no hatch to the cockpit from here. She turned around and worked up the courage to open the lockers. Expecting an alarm to blare as she opened the first rectilinear locker, she winced as she lifted the latch and popped open the door. Nothing happened, and she dropped her shoulders as the tension wore away.

Tools and hardware were attached to the inside of the container, as was the case in every compartment except one with strange food rations. A plastic box sat against the hull, and she fumbled with the latches until she freed it from its stowed position. She threw out any useless storage items and began tossing in spanners, batteries, wires, circuit boards, irons, spinclips, and much more. When it was too heavy to pick up, she tossed out some things and tested its weight again. *No problem.* She put the lid back on and latched it.

With a push from her boot, the crate slid down the metal ramp to the grass below.

Jo started at the sudden sight of the orange crate sliding out of the ship. Then Sora emerged and waved back to Jo, knowing her sister was watching.

Sora headed around to the cockpit stairs and climbed up. The cockpit was made for two. The windshield automatically tinted as the sun shone onto it, and all the screens stared blankly at Sora as she sat in the cushy seat. The mass of buttons and switches seemed overwhelming. Sora had tinkered with nearly every machine on this planet, but nothing like this. She reached for the dash but froze. Turning on anything would surely be a terrible idea. Instead, she searched around the seats and under the dash. Between the chairs sat a small lockbox. She tapped the little pad of an electronic lock near the handle, and a red light flashed. Sora brought the box with her and hurried out of the cockpit.

Back at the rear of the ship, she set the lockbox on the crate, studying them both. She groaned and waved both arms up at Jo.

Jo slung her rifle over her shoulder. She hurried down the hill toward her sister. Once they got within earshot of each other, Jo yelled first. "What's all that?"

"Tools, supplies, other tech that might be useful."

"The smaller box? It's locked." Jo picked up the lockbox and studied the lock pad.

"I want to know what's in it."

"Could be dangerous."

"Well, good thing I have you to protect me. Now, let's get this stuff back home."

They lugged the crate a few meters back toward the hill, but soon realized it would be a pain to carry it up the slope. Jo ran to get the stirrols and came back, riding one and leading the other. Sora lifted the orange crate onto her stirrol, holding it in the saddle. They didn't have any of the proper panniers or crossbuck to pack the stirrol, but Jo could make do. As Sora held the crate steady, Jo tied it security to the saddle. They tested the balance and figured it was good enough for the short ride home.

"Alright, let's go," Sora said, putting her foot into the stirrup of Jo's stirrol.

"Excuse me? You're in the back," Jo protested, handing the reins of Sora's mount to her sister.

Jo defiantly shooed Sora to get out of the way as she climbed into the saddle. Sora gave her sister a sideways look.

If Sora and Jo rode in from the orchard, they had a path to the barn without being seen by anyone else in the village. They'd only been gone for a couple of hours, but that was plenty of time for everyone to wake up and get busy with their daily routines. Luckily, they had the whole barn to themselves. Coming from the opposite direction as they had earlier in the morning, the two rode in quietly. Sora jumped down and ran to slide open a door at the back of the barn so Jo could lead in the animals.

Inside, straw covered the ground level, except for a washing bay with a stone floor and a drain. Six stalls ran the length of the barn, north to south. The tack room sat beside the north end of the washing bay, and on the south end was an open area with a door in the wall, leading into their shop. Above and on either side, bales of hay were stacked and packed tightly from the summer's growing. Many smells blended: the sweet, fresh hay, oils, leather, and grain mixes, plus the powerful stench of ammonia.

Sora kept the crate from falling onto the ground as Jo untied it. For the moment they stashed it in the tack room while they finished removing the stirrols' tack, sending them into their stalls. Jo gave them a twifruit each as a treat. Then, they carried the crate together through the door leading into the machine shop. The west side of the building was dedicated to their primary work in the village. Sora was the best mechanic between Verisport and White Sands. Jo was getting there.

Jo flicked on the lights.

The giant room was cluttered and greasy. A shaker sat in the center, its guts all over the floor in a state of disassembly. Tools, creepers, barrels, buckets, hoses, toolboxes, pans, nuts, bolts, springs, and panels —metal everywhere. Great metal arms reached down from rails on the ceiling, chains dangling with them. Overlooking the shop, Sora and Jo's apartment sat dark behind dusty windows.

They set the crate down beside their workbench that ran the width of the room beneath the apartment windows. Metal shelves covered the wall leading up to the windows, and each was packed to the breaking point with an absolute mess of stuff. Sora picked up the lockbox and studied it further. It was a dull black and smooth to the touch, but it felt like a material she'd never seen before.

"Let's scan it. Maybe we can see what's inside," she wondered aloud.

Jo already sat on a stool at the workbench, powering up their computer system. They had four screens in a rectangle set on the wall in the center, surrounded by crowded shelves.

"Alright, she's ready," Jo said.

Sora shook a dusty blanket off a large table and tossed it aside. The glassy surface of the table slowly lit up. She gently placed the box onto the surface and looked at Jo. A light beneath the box flashed and moved around, as if taking the preliminary measurements of the box. Then, a boom arm lifted itself out of the left side of the table, sat upright, and moved over the box automatically, lowering itself to just the right height. The arm passed over the box a few times, lights emitting from the underside. Sora's face glowed green from the table's light as she rested her elbows on the edge, chin on her hands.

The arm finished its work and Jo stood on the opposite side of the table from her sister. They watched as a reconstructed image of the box appeared next to it made only of light. It slowly rotated to show all sides to them.

Jo held up her hands in confusion. "It's just a box?"

"The scanner can't read into it," Sora said.

"Is that possible?"

"Well, I didn't *think* it was possible."

"Okay, so, how do we open it? *Should* we open it?"

Maybe she has a point, Sora thought, but she wasn't satisfied. Curiosity pushed her further. She picked up the box again and carried it to the workbench. From a shelf above it, she pulled a small plaspen. Then, she retrieved a protective mask that sat on a barrel near the half-finished shaker.

Jo watched her sister move with a purpose. As soon as Sora grabbed the plaspen, Jo protested. "Whoa, you have no idea what'll happen if you cut it open!"

"No, I don't," Sora said, putting the mask on then flipping it down over her face, hiding her smile behind the metal plate and thick glass window.

Jo backed away and sat down, bracing herself for the worst. Sora pulled on a pair of heavy gloves and activated the pen. She held it just as if she was going to write on the box. With her left hand, she turned the box around and over, then set it up on one side, with the lock down on the table. Sora couldn't make out if the box had hinges, so she picked a spot near the center line and started cutting.

Jo shielded her eyes as the pen lit up and sparked, a bright white light concealing Sora's progress. In a few moments, the pen shut off, and the light died down.

Sora dropped the pen on a cooling pad beside her. She flipped the mask up and cracked a smile. She'd cut right through whatever this box was made of, the cut straight and precise, the edges burned red, cooling in moments. She set the box down and turned it to look at the lock. She'd still have to cut through *that* if she was going to get the whole thing open.

"Did it work?" Jo said.

"Yeah, I cut through the back, but the lock still has a hold on it. I'll have to cut through it too."

"Well, you've gone this far," Jo said, a hint of disapproval in her voice.

Sora nodded her head so the mask would fall back over her face. She picked up the pen again, and this time left the box sitting flat. She moved back a touch on the stool to look at the front lock, then activated the pen. This time, she cut right below the lock pad, starting from the right side, straight across. Through the dark eye shield and the bright light of the plaspen, she could see the lock pad, rapidly flashing red. She didn't stop, but pushed on, across to the end of the handle, about where she assumed a locking mechanism might be.

She deactivated the pen and set it down. She knocked the mask back and waited for the cut to cool. The lock pad no longer flashed. With her gloved hands, she gently gripped the box on either side, then slowly lifted. Jo stood behind, hands on Sora's shoulders, barely peeking over them.

The box came apart in two. Inside, a thick layer of foam material cushioned its contents, lying neatly in cut out places. Sora discarded the top half of the box, tossing it onto the floor. She pulled her gloves off by the fingers and pulled the mask off next, shaking her hair out as the strap snagged a bit.

Jo and Sora leaned over the box, deciphering its contents.

In one spot cut into the foam sat another, smaller box. Next to it, in a perpendicular space in the foam, was a plaspen, but one much sleeker and better than Sora's. That much they recognized. Then, on the other side of the pen, was another small box with a red cross on it, within a red circle.

"Is this a first aid kit?" Jo asked.

"Seems like it," Sora agreed.

She lifted the first aid box and saw it snapped open easily. Inside were the usual small first aid items: a roll of bandages, tubes of antiseptic, needles, pills, and gloves. They were all packed so tightly, almost impossibly compact. They set it aside and lifted the plaspen from its place. It looked familiar to them, and so they studied it very little.

But the other box, black and sleek, posed questions. Sora lifted it out of the foam, and it seemed to have no further locks or security, so she unlatched it and opened it. A small, rectangular, metal object lay inside. It couldn't have been more than four centimeters in length, and it had a shiny, almost reflective surface. One long side curved down at one end, wider than the other, like the letter C cut in half horizontally.

Jo and Sora felt a sense of fear and confusion. Neither wanted to reach out and touch the object. They just stared at it.

"What the hell is it?" Jo asked.

"How should I know?"

Sora delicately felt the object with her fingers, then softly picked it up out of the foam cushion. The cushion around it was much finer and softer than the foam in the larger box. The metal object felt almost imperceptibly light. She let it rest in her palm and turned it over so they could look at the other side. Both were surprised to see it covered in a thin, translucent membrane that looked like it could be peeled off.

They didn't peel it back.

"Could it be, like a medical device?" Jo guessed, but only based on the other contents of the box.

Sora nodded, thinking. Jo could've been right; the quality of the plaspen did look surgical. Maybe this was an emergency medical kit in case of a crash.

"That's the best guess I have," Sora admitted. "Maybe we can scan *this* thing," she said, moving her palm up.

She spun on the stool and gently placed the device on the table surface. The table and arm repeated its process, light moving all over the small object, the arm going back into its place flush with the table edge.

A projection of the object materialized over the table, but larger than its literal size so they could study it better. Sora chewed on the inside of her lip as she stared at the projection of the thing, searching her knowledge and experience for any clue what the device could be. She'd worked on nearly every kind of machine on this planet, but this looked alien to her. At least it presented a project, one that she would hyper-focus on until she figured out its purpose.

6

The Marshal

The marshal's office boasted a good view of Verisport. He could see the bright, colorful awnings and flags of the market from his vantage point, many levels up in the tower at the center of the port. He could almost smell the twilight pastries and his mouth watered. The town had expanded quite a bit in his time, but it still paled in comparison to true cities on other planets like Thuli or Hass. Smoke drifted up from the shacks and tents on the outer edges, obscured by taller buildings and the morning haze.

Marshal Rayburn could draw his line straight from those who first came to Celestine, something not many remaining on the planet could boast. He'd never been anywhere else, too focused on turning Verisport and the valley into something that could be respected. This was his home, plain and simple.

The marshal sat at his heavy wooden desk, his fingers interlaced, staring out the window when Cole, his top deputy, entered. The young man in his mid-twenties was still eager and excitable—a little too excitable at times. He'd grown up on stories of duels, stirrol chases, remote mining towns with deadly games of Solar. Working for the marshal was a dream to the kid, and while it wasn't that in reality, the kid still tried to see it that way. He exhausted Rayburn at times.

"Morning, marshal," Cole said, sitting down in one of the two chairs facing the desk.

He handed Rayburn a cup of coffee, steaming hot.

Rayburn kept staring out the window. A datapad in front of him had received the report straight from Otto just before dawn. *Did that man ever sleep?* Rayburn wondered. He sighed, rubbing a hand over his gray stubble. Taking Cole out into the valley felt unavoidable now, especially since he'd done him the favor of bringing coffee.

"Cole, we've got to head out into the valley," Rayburn said finally.

He tapped the datapad and slid his fingers around, their large knuckles and hard callouses a stark contrast to the sleek tech. The windows dimmed and a map of the valley projected onto them. Verisport, Burreville, and White Sands were clearly marked, the Lipine River running through it all. A red dot appeared east of Burreville, pulsed, and then, with a tap on his datapad, the marshal drew up a photograph taken by a Xypha satellite.

The clarity was remarkable.

Cole wiped a drop of coffee from his chin after he nearly spilled it down his shirt. He coughed and choked as the image of the dead bodies startled him. Six Xypha engineers lay dead around the rail line. The train was gone, but by the position of the men it was clear it had been there when they died—when they were murdered.

"Otto sent this to me. Appears these fellas were murdered two days ago," Rayburn said.

"Two days? What took them so long?" Cole said.

"I don't know, but you and I have to go take a look."

"Otto pretty upset?" Cole winced.

Rayburn finished a sip of coffee, "Always. He's concerned about safety crossing the valley. I'm not stupid—"

"I never said you were," Cole interjected anxiously.

"That's not what I meant. I know a test when I see one."

"A test?"

"It's no secret Otto and I aren't on good terms. These fellas are killed, and it's my job to clean it up and figure out who done it. If I can't, then Otto's got a good excuse to get me removed."

Rayburn sighed as he tapped the datapad again, sliding his finger to remove the map projection and photographs from the windows. He stood with a groan, his chair and leg creaking. Rayburn was short and stocky, scars on his face. He walked to the window with an uneven gate, thanks to the old prosthetic just below his knee. Cole looked up at him with childlike awe and disbelief that anybody could possibly disapprove of Rayburn's conduct or service.

"Do you really think it would come to that?" Cole said.

Rayburn stared across the city, catching a lump growing in his throat.

He cleared it and turned around. "We do our jobs well, then it won't. Now bring the skimmer around to the west gate, the long bed one. We're going to have to bring those bodies back."

"Yes sir!" Cole set his coffee cup down on the desk, jumped to his feet, and saluted.

The marshal rolled his tired eyes, barely lifted his hand to return the salute, more like waving Cole out of the office. The young man left quickly to fulfill his duty. Rayburn walked over to the desk, picked up Cole's cup, and set it on a coaster.

Cole piloted the skimmer across the valley while Rayburn leaned against the door, elbow out the window. The cabin from the windshield to the back was all glass, letting the sunlight in. Rayburn kept his gray hat on to shield his eyes. As the chis parted around them, his thoughts dwelled on the fight he'd had with Otto when the Xypha officer first arrived. They'd wanted Verisport to be their primary port, but Rayburn knew the city wasn't happy with the idea. He fought tooth and nail to convince the council to keep Xypha out. It forced them to do business in White Sands, constructing their own port there. But that meant Verisport would fall to second, slowly waste away as Xypha sucked traffic from it until nobody had to fly in or out of the city.

Did I make a mistake? Should I have done something different?

In the past year, the winds shifted, and the council began to see it a different way. They slowly turned on him, one by one, regretting the decisions they had made. If Rayburn didn't command such respect, he figured the council would've given in months ago. The lack of business at Verisport, thanks to the Xypha contract system, made it only a matter of time.

Cole slowed the skimmer and turned it around before landing, the back cargo space facing the scene, making it easier to load the bodies. Rayburn climbed out of the cabin and immediately noticed a large area of the ryegrass tamped down by force. He snuffled and roamed around the area while Cole climbed into the skimmer's cargo space. He pulled a handheld scanling off the inside wall and booted up.

Rayburn walked up to the fence, and he heard the faint buzz of electricity. He eyed the concrete on either side of the sleek metal rail. Two Xypha men in white slipsuits lay on this side of the rail, face down on the concrete. No blood pooled around them, but two jawix stood on the bodies, alert. The marshal sucked his teeth and punched in the gate code that Otto had given him.

Behind him, Cole surveyed the area with the scanling, waving it all around, the beeping wearing on the marshal's nerves. Rayburn looked down at a spot in the concrete, cracked and depressed. He put his boot over it, eyeing the size difference. Cole walked up beside him, the scanling emitting an undulating tone in Cole's left hand.

"Turn that thing off," Rayburn growled.

Cole followed the order. He looked down at the cracked concrete in front of them. "What happened here? Almost looks like a footprint."

"It is a footprint," Rayburn said quietly.

"Ain't nobody got a foot that big, much less one that can make a dent in concrete."

"You're right—no *human being* has a foot that large or that powerful."

Rayburn walked toward the two bodies nearest to them. Cole stooped over the broken concrete, wanting to turn on the scanling to detect any clues from the "footprint" but hesitating, and deciding against it. He returned to the marshal's side as Rayburn stood over the bodies, hands on his hips.

"No blood," Rayburn said. "Killed from some kind of blunt trauma, maybe."

"That's unusual. Those fellas over there were shot down by plasbolts."

"Mm." Rayburn chewed on his lip and walked to the rail, his boot clinking on the omniite.

The south side was a bloodbath. Two men lay near one another, efficiently shot down—only two shots. The other two were a different story. *That meant at least three attackers.* One was a good shot, one shot with an unsteady hand, and the third didn't shoot at all.

"This one is gonna be tough to get in the skimmer," Cole said, his voice broke as he tried to cover his mouth and nose.

Rayburn walked over to the last body, dried blood everywhere around it, splattered up to a few meters away. The man lay on his back, face locked in terror. His chest was almost entirely missing. But the jawix didn't pick it clean without help. The chest cavity was empty but burned and blackened by plasfire. *This one sent a message,* Rayburn thought.

He ran his finger over his bottom lip as he examined the scene, running through the possible scenarios in his head. There was no doubting that many in the valley were unhappy with Xypha's presence here. Many of the valley farmers had expressed their anger when the rail cut straight through the valley, cutting them off from free passage north and south. But the idea of farmers attacking Xypha engineers out in the open like this seemed unlikely. The train *was* here when the shooting started. It would've been stationary so the engineers could work on it, whatever malfunction befell it, but it was here. *Someone knew these engineers would be here.*

Rayburn stared into the dead, horrified face of the man at his feet. He put his finger out like a plasbolt and pointed it down at the man. *Someone stood here and shot this man repeatedly.* He turned and looked toward the south gate: locked. *And they were given the code, knew how to crack the code, or came in from above.*

The possibility gnawed at him. He clenched his teeth. He didn't want to go there, but signs began pointing that way. The ambush itself may not have been personal to start, but whoever killed *this* engineer made it personal. Across the whole of Celestine, there was only one person Rayburn knew who had a personal vendetta against Xypha who also ran with a very large sentient.

"Cole, get the board and get these fellas loaded up. When you finish, we're heading back into town," he shouted.

"You giving me a hand?" Cole said, looking up from his scanling.

"Nope." Rayburn walked back to the skimmer.

The whole trip back to Verisport, Rayburn reflected on his primary suspects: Alix and Felix. He hadn't spoken to them in months, and the last time they had, it wasn't pretty. He still felt weighed down by the guilt of what he said. His pride stood between them, then and now, but it wasn't always that way, and he remembered the time they first met.

Decades ago...

Rayburn spilled a drip of coffee on his shirt. He cursed and wiped his chin as he looked down at the dark stain on the white shirt beneath a dark blue vest. He pulled a handkerchief out of his pocket and rubbed at the stain, but no luck. He groaned when the bell on his door chirped.

"Yeah, who is it?"

"It's Ed," the voice called from behind the door.

"Alright, get in here."

One of the marshal's deputies entered and removed his hat. The marshal was impatient, annoyed at himself, and Ed immediately regretted bothering him.

"We got an issue downstairs," he said.

"Keep going."

"Well, a ship landed in port earlier, and while unloading cargo, workers found a little boy, no more than 12 years old, stowed away in a container."

The marshal stopped rubbing the stain and looked up at Ed, confusion on his face. "A boy? They trafficking or something?"

"No, no, the pilot had no idea."

"And you believe them?"

"Well, yeah, or…I did, I guess."

The marshal rolled his eyes at Ed's lack of confidence. He stuffed the handkerchief back in his pocket and stood, retrieving his hat from a hook on the wall behind him. A long sigh left his mouth as he fixed the hat on his head and left the room, Ed following behind.

"Let's see what we're dealing with," the marshal said.

Outside, dock workers crowded around a docking bay door. They laughed and cracked jokes, as if they had bets on how a game would turn out. Ed used his best authoritative voice to break up the crowd and get them to quiet down. The marshal shot disapproving looks at the lot of them.

The docking bay held a dark freighter. Cargo containers were already stacked behind it, autoloaders sitting still, since the workers stopped what they were doing when they found the stowaway. The pilot, a short, keyed up man, ran up to Rayburn and Ed and launched into a panicked defense.

"Marshal, I swear I had no idea this boy was in there. I just picked up the crates on Corto like usual. Everything checked out, and there was nothing unusual about the cargo," the pilot stuttered.

The marshal put his hands on his hips, looking into the cargo bay. "Nothing unusual? Except the kid in the crate?"

"I didn't know!" the pilot insisted.

"Nobody got the kid out yet?"

"We couldn't. He's got a knife and damn near stabbed me when I found him."

"You didn't strike him, did you?"

"No sir!"

"Alright, I'll see what we can do."

The marshal's boots clicked on the metal surface of the ship's cargo hold. He moved slowly, keeping a sharp eye out. The hold was almost empty, but there were still a few crates a small kid with a knife could hide behind. He didn't want to approach things with his plasbolt out, but he kept his hands near his waist.

"Hey kid," he said in a gentle voice. "My name's Rayburn. I'm here to help you."

The marshal heard no reply. He found the open container, one of the first that had been loaded into the hold. The lid lay on the floor beside it, and inside were blankets, a rucksack, scattered food and crumbs. The marshal raised the back of his hand to cover his nose.

Suddenly, a young scream echoed. The marshal wheeled around as a knife grazed his arm. He stepped aside as a small child stumbled from missing his attempt to stab the marshal in the back. Instead of drawing his plasbolt, the marshal snatched the kid's arm. He squeezed tight, twisted the kid's wrist, and the knife fell to the floor.

"Easy!" the marshal said. "I'm not going to hurt you."

The kid was violent, wild, like a cornered animal. The marshal kicked the knife away and held the boy in both hands. His face was dirty and bruised, his eyes wide and frightened but determined to fight. The marshal breathed slowly.

"Hey it's okay, I'm not going to hurt you. Just calm down, alright?"

The boy continued to writhe and kick until the marshal let go.

Suddenly free, the boy froze, unsure what to do. The marshal knelt to eye level with the boy. He smiled and held out his hand. It earned a cautious and still angry stare. His little chest heaved, but he began to calm down.

"Do you have a name?" the marshal said.

The boy didn't answer.

"Would you like some food?"

The boy hesitated, then nodded.

"No strings attached. Well, except you can't try to stab me again," the marshal winked.

The boy tried not to smile but failed.

Today...

Back in the office, Rayburn flopped into his chair. He couldn't stop thinking about Alix. They had grown apart over the years, but the final wedge between them seemed almost inevitable after the Xypha prospectors showed up: one small ship and two men. Alix was adamant, but Rayburn had a duty, a responsibility to the people of Verisport and the valley. He couldn't make the decision only based on her feelings. He received the prospectors kindly. Alix left for Corto. The distance between them only widened, even when she returned. But still, a shadow crept over them ever since.

The marshal turned his nose up as he typed the commands to call Otto. He waited, and waited no doubt Otto making him sweat it out. Then, the man appeared on the vizscreen on Rayburn's desk.

"What is it, marshal?" Otto snipped.

"You know what it's about, Otto," Rayburn began with an exasperated sigh. "I have some questions about the incident on your rail line."

"Ah, yes, so you went out there?"

"Of course. How likely is it that someone possessed the gate codes?"

"Impossible." Otto shook his head. He looked at Rayburn like a fool for even asking the question. "Our men are instructed to keep them closed, to prevent intrusion, even while on-site."

"Well, what about the ship?"

"What ship?"

"The dropship that was there. It was gone when I went out there."

Otto pursed his lips. "Right, well, we had to retrieve it as soon as possible. It was recalled through remote piloting."

"But you'd leave six dead men for the jawix?" Rayburn waved his hand in disgust.

"That ship costs more than a hundred men," Otto said in a matter-of-fact tone.

Rayburn bristled at the vacant expression of the man on the screen. He couldn't comprehend the attitude on display, the disregard for his own people. "What were they out there to fix?"

Otto waited a moment before answering, his eyes looked elsewhere, as if checking another screen. "System malfunction with the accelerator. The train began to lose speed, so the driver issued the stop command and requested inspection."

"How often does that happen?"

Otto shrugged. "Rarely, but it does happen."

"You have mentioned to me before that there have been hits on the fence. It is possible this was escalation. Perhaps whoever was tampering with the fence found a way through. Perhaps they hacked your gate codes."

"I seriously doubt that," Otto said.

Rayburn almost said it—that one of his suspects was a sentient. Otto would have been surprised by that, and maybe it would've shut him up, but Rayburn didn't trust Otto and didn't want the man to have any information that might cause him to interfere.

"Well, this was obviously someone opposed to your being here. Honestly, I am not surprised, but I have some suspects, and I will talk to some more people down here."

"I trust you will take swift action. Security across the valley is our top concern, and it seems that is becoming less reliable."

"Good talking with you, Otto, as always," Rayburn said sarcastically.

He shut the call down, and Otto disappeared from the vizscreen.

That son of a bitch.

To make matters worse, Cole walked in. The kid's face was way too enthusiastic and smiling for Rayburn at this moment. Cole held up a datapad triumphantly and sat down. "Want to see the scanling report?"

"Not particularly," Rayburn groaned. "But let's have it."

"Alright," Cole said, throwing the projection up on the windows as the lights dimmed.

All sorts of numbers and readings came up on the windows, substances found and analyzed at the scene, chemicals, residual footprints, everything. But the one thing Cole was so excited to show the marshal was the south gate.

"See this, on the lockpad? Normally, we can't get any kind of data from these things, Xypha tech and all, but I found a fingerprint on the gate itself. We barely have a useful database, but *this* one was a positive match. Some guy named Dalton, didn't have a last name."

An image of the man appeared on the window with his record of arrest. He had a long, thin nose, a scar on his bottom lip, rosy cheeks, and a black mustache. His eyes were sunk back beneath big bushy eyebrows.

"One of Purvida's men," Rayburn said.

Cole's enthusiasm faded in an instant. "That so?"

"Either way, good work, Cole," Rayburn admitted genuinely. The young man brimmed with confidence and gratitude. "Looks like we've got to pay Silas a visit, now."

Rayburn stood and lifted his hat off the desk, setting it on his head, covering the grey hair. Cole stood up quickly. "Why don't you stay here?"

"Are you sure?" Cole swallowed. "Mr. Purvida has a *reputation.*"

"Trust me, kid, nobody knows that better than me."

The marshal knew how to handle Silas, and he didn't want to have Cole's anxious energy around while they were sitting in a snake pit. When he walked in the open door of Silas's saloon, Rayburn was surprised to find Silas behind the bar. The barrel-chested man looked relaxed, and several of his goons sat around, playing cards or cleaning something. A Thin Man leaned against the bar in his shirtsleeves, a Plasveld shining in clear view on his left hip. The marshal pushed his hat back on his head.

"Hello, Silas."

"Rayburn. To what do I owe the pleasure?" Silas smiled, wide and knowing. "Perhaps you'd like a drink?" He moved behind the bar with skill, for Silas wasn't always the man in charge. He picked up a bottle and poured the marshal a fine drink of local chisik.

Marshal Rayburn looked around at each man in the room, studying them through narrow eyes, looking for Dalton. No such luck. He eyed the Thin Man with disdain—Silas's man, who did his killing and buried the bodies.

"Looking for a man of yours," the marshal said, ignoring the drink. "Name's Dalton."

"Ah, what has he supposedly done?" Silas drank his own glass of chisik.

"Do you know his whereabouts?" Rayburn grew impatient.

"Yes, I do," Silas said, looking down as he poured another glass. "But you and I both know that without some kind of evidence or written order of the council, I can't just turn over an innocent man to you."

The marshal put his hands on his hips, one Plasveld on his right side. He noticed the Thin Man shift his eyes there, ready. "I got his prints on the Xypha rail fenceline. If he's around, I would appreciate the chance to ask him some questions."

"Now why would Dalton be out in the valley messing with Xypha's fence?" Silas wondered aloud, as if he knew the answer to his own question.

"Look, Silas, I know you and Otto have arrangements."

"Last I checked, that wasn't illegal," Silas said correctly.

"Well, what about the murder of six Xypha engineers? I believe that's against valley law."

"And you think Dalton did this crime?" Silas looked at him with a furrowed brow, scoffing at the possibility.

"There's data that puts him at the scene," the marshal said. "And I would like to know his whereabouts day before yesterday."

"And you've got no other suspects?" Silas said it into his glass, right before polishing off the chisik and staring daggers at Rayburn.

He knows about Alix and Felix, so they were there with his man. How could she be so stupid to get mixed up with someone like Silas?

"Investigation is ongoing, and it won't go much further if I don't get a chance to talk to those who may have been there," the marshal said.

"You know Otto and I have arrangements, and you know one of them is security. Sure, Dalton was there, but not day before yesterday. I had him on another errand."

"Where?" the marshal snapped, not giving Silas a chance to think of a lie.

But the man took the chance anyway. Silas poured himself another drink, a sly smirk on his face. *He always enjoyed the competition between them*, the marshal thought.

"I believe it was at Bruce's chop shop," Silas said finally. "Had him making some deliveries and pick-ups. I know Otto is perturbed by this incident. His confidence in local justice is, let's just say, shaken."

The marshal stared as Silas comfortably threw back his drink and let out a satisfied sigh as he held up the glass and looked straight into Rayburn's eyes. There was nothing else to be learned, so Rayburn sucked his teeth and reached for the bottle of chisik. He picked it up and read the label aloud.

"Seventy-five years old, Black Barrel." He was impressed.

"My father's distillery," Silas noted with pride.

Marshal Rayburn took a drink directly from the bottle, and Silas barely managed to hide his anger. The marshal licked his lips, nodding. With the bottle in-hand, he tipped his hat with the other hand and left the saloon.

As Silas watched the marshal leave, his temper flared. The Thin Man picked up the glass poured for the marshal and drank it. He, too, kept his eyes on the marshal as the old man walked out the door.

"Get out to Keizur's End," Silas said to him. "Take whoever you need with you."

"And Dalton?" the Thin Man said.

"He's tragically killed in the fight," Silas replied.

"Yes, sir," the Thin Man pushed off the bar and tipped his wide hat to his boss.

The marshal decided to walk back to his office. He needed the time to think and enjoy the crisp air of the changing season. Summer was gone, and harvests would soon be coming into Verisport. That meant a lot of traffic coming in from the valley, and now, much of that would be coming in on Xypha's rail line.

He walked along the wooden boardwalks beneath the awnings and balconies on the front of many businesses and houses. Out by Silas's compound, many families lived in tenements stacked on top of one another. Children ran around in the afternoon sun, kicking a ball, chasing chickens or each other. Their laughter was a stark contrast to the dark business that went on around them.

Rayburn had been the marshal for over forty years, Silas his adversary for almost as long. Both came from old families, original settlers on Celestine, but their chosen routes to power could not have been more different. Silas's father was indeed a legitimate man, owning significant swathes of land to the west of town, growing, expanding his holdings and businesses. One was the Black Barrel chisik distillery, which still operated under Silas's eye in Verisport. But Silas used his money to bleed his land's tenants dry, to keep them down, and poor. He became a gambler, a smuggler, running illicit drugs from Corto, cornering the market on salvage, and running a successful saloon, casino, and brothel. He even owned a casino in White Sands, to the dismay of the "fine" people out there.

Rayburn made his family proud when he entered in the previous marshal's services at seventeen. When it was time for that marshal to retire, he chose Rayburn as his successor. Only 30 years old, Rayburn suddenly became the council's arm of the law, back when it actually meant something. Now, the council was weak, afraid, bought. He tried to hold on to whatever semblance of justice that he could, which meant low-hanging fruit. His deputies kept the streets clean, and the duels and random murders over Solar tables shifted out of town. People loved him for it, but the cancer in Verisport still festered. The council had no will to hold Silas accountable, and Rayburn didn't have the plasbolts to start a war.

As much as he hated to admit it, Silas served a function in the outskirts of town. While the marshal could push the deadly and dangerous criminals from Verisport's center, eventually, he ran out of momentum. But Silas had an iron fist, and that Thin Man, to rid the outskirts of any remaining vermin.

But Xypha was an escalation the marshal had neither the energy nor strength to meet. Alix told him all about Xypha, how they would get in, spread, and destroy. At the time the prospectors showed up, he was foolish enough to think he could keep things under control. He told her she was overreacting. *I won't let that happen*, he said. *You have to trust me. I will keep them in line.*

What a fool, he thought.

Rayburn walked through the market and found his favorite restaurant tucked into the corner of the buildings around the square. The woman at the door greeted him warmly as he tipped his hat, but a smile eluded him. She looked at him with pity as she directed him to a table outside. Shaded by an awning, he removed his hat and set it on the nice, white tablecloth. A man swept through without a word and brought him a glass of water.

He set the bottle of Black Barrel on the table next to his hat and drank the ice-cold water. All around him, people moved. His table was situated at the edge of the restaurant's outside seating, leaving him close to the foot traffic passing by. Conversations came and went with the people, and the shouting, bartering, and haggling in the square made a symphony. It was not a deftly composed piece, but natural and free flowing. He loved to listen, to close his eyes and take in the sounds. He didn't know how much longer he would be able to do that, so he cherished every chance he got.

But then, he found it difficult to focus on the music. The gnawing thought kept breaking in, interrupting his reverie. He sighed and rubbed his hands on his face. He would have to make a call and accuse Alix of murder.

7

The Shootout

To the southwest of the Isidis Valley, Celestine's lush green chis grass seas dissipated into dry and semiarid land, cracked and marked like a crumpled piece of paper someone attempted to lay flat again. A range of mountains reached around for thousands of kilometers, running northwest from the equator. Beneath swirling white clouds with purple edges, the green landscape faded into various hues of orange, yellow, and brown. It was a land not worth much to anyone except folks who wanted to be left alone.

Amid this barren, dusty land, at the bottom of a steep ravine lay a ramshackle town called Keizur's End. The gorge had once been carved by a river, long-since dried out, and the stream bed became the main road splitting the town in half. Buildings lined the rock walls on either side, some built into the stone itself. Unlike Verisport, there was no omniite here, each structure built only of wood and stone. The town was old, dating back to some of the original settlers on Celestine. They went where they thought valuable minerals could be found, but instead they broke open the rock and dirt without luck, only to find they'd turn to dust themselves.

Keizur's End experienced periods of abandonment. When miners left the region empty-handed, someone else moved in and built houses and storerooms on top of older buildings. They tore buildings apart to make new ones. Some stripped wood and took it elsewhere, leaving only frames knocked over by winter winds. For decades, it housed only those fleeing another life, fleeing from or cast out by authority.

They gambled, drank, stole, killed, and died, but it was at least a place to lie low where nobody asked you any questions, except what might be in your pockets.

Alix threw back yet another glass of chisik, the large glass bottle less than half full. She, Felix, and Wick sat together in a noisy saloon with dim yellow lighting from aging lamps. Wick reached for the bottle, but Alix snatched it first and poured another glass while staring at him. After downing the glass, she looked out the window and sighed. Wick waited a moment, watched Alix, then slowly slid the bottle across the table to pour himself a glass.

"So, who are we looking for here?" he said, scanning the busy room.

Alix still stared out the window.

"Oh, him? Yeah, sure, I will definitely notice him, no problem. I'll keep an eye out," Wick said as if Alix hadn't ignored him.

He waved down one of the servers who wore a tight dress that had been repaired one too many times by hand. She had bright blond hair and wore too much makeup, aiming to catch the attention of the desperate men coming through. She winked as she came up to the table.

"Can we get another?" Wick held up the near-empty bottle.

"Why don't you order dinner?" Alix said, still staring out the window.

"You hungry?"

"Nah."

"Great company you are."

The server returned with another bottle, and Wick ordered a big dinner while Alix tapped her fingers on the table. Felix reached over and touched her shoulder. She stopped tapping and instead reached up and gently gripped Felix's fingers with her right hand, the left under the table.

"So, how did you two meet?" Wick said.

"On Corto," Felix replied with a smile.

"No shit?" Wick finished one bottle.

Alix snatched the other bottle and poured a glass before Wick could get started on it.

"Yes, I flew in and out of Corto a lot," she said.

"What were you doing on Corto?" Wick pointed his glass at Felix.

"Working," Felix said.

"Doing what?"

"What it takes to survive." Felix was unamused. His memory of that time was dark and cold before he walked into Spiros's place to watch the fights and found Alix.

"Aren't we all?"

"Is that why you work for Silas?" Alix cut in.

Wick groaned. "Is that why *you* work for Silas?" He took a drink. "Why are you here, anyway? What did he offer you?"

"Ten thousand," Alix said.

Wick missed the glass while pouring. "You're kidding me."

"No." Alix took his glass from him and finished it.

"That's killing money."

"Yes, it is." She filled his glass and slid it across the table.

He wilted under her eyes, which burned a hole through him. "So, who are we here to kill?"

"You're not here to kill anybody."

Wick's hand shook as he held his glass up to his lips, just a slight tremble that he was sure they noticed. He laughed to himself as he took a drink. He began piecing it together. "So, why'd we come all the way out here?"

"Because nobody gives a shit what happens in Keizur's End," Alix said.

Wick filled his glass nearly to the brim. He drank it in two gulps. "Everybody's got a price," he said, cocking his head and clicking his tongue.

"What was yours?" The chair under Felix creaked as he leaned back.

Wick looked at the sentient, his large arms, hat set back on his head. Wick expected him to look cold, like the job didn't matter, that Wick didn't matter, but there was sympathy in his artificial eyes.

"A debt I should've known I could never repay."

"So why would he want to kill you?" Felix wondered.

"You mean he didn't tell you?"

"I didn't ask." Alix raised an eyebrow.

"Smart." Wick drank directly from the bottle, his despair reaching an apex.

Alix shook her head and looked away. She bounced her leg under the table, since Felix had politely indicated she should stop tapping her fingers. *Why does this feel so wrong?* she wondered. She didn't know a thing about Wick, and he seemed a harmless fellow, at least to her. Her face twisted as she debated in her mind. *It's not the killing. Something else is wrong, here,* she said to herself.

Wick reached into his vest. He pulled out a small disc and laid it on the table. He rolled his left sleeve back and tapped the syncpad, bringing up the projection of a ship from the disc.

Alix felt a lump in her throat. The freighter was not much different from the *Shadow*. The ship appeared to be about the same length, similar overall capacity, although it had different angles than the *Shadow*, more curves on the bottom of the hull. There were two large engines on either side at the stern. When Alix decided to speak, she had to clear her throat.

"What's she called?"

"*Procella*," Wick answered. "Storm, tempest, or some such thing."

Alix lifted her left hand, the Plasveld she already held under the table now revealed. Wick swallowed and froze. Alix took a deep breath and stuck the Plasveld back in its holster. The server returned at last with a large plate, packed with meat, vegetables, and bread, all steaming. It was by no means a gourmet meal—just what they could fill a plate with and would fill a person's stomach. She set it down in front of Wick, who stared at it with a different feeling: not his last meal, but now the first since his stay of execution.

"It was almost ten years ago. I knew of Silas through my—well, I had trouble paying off the loan on my ship. Silas said I could work for him to pay it off."

Wick stabbed at the plate with a fork, eating like he wanted to kill the animal that was already dead in front of him. He chewed and spoke between every bite.

"Then, two years turned into five turned into I don't fucking know how many."

"You had the ship; couldn't you just leave?" Felix said.

"Yeah," Wick scoffed, "just leave! Why didn't I think of that?"

"Well, why didn't you?"

"None of your fucking business." He continued eating, tearing at the piece of bread like a predator.

"What if *we* could get your ship back?" Alix said.

"You don't get it." Wick let out a short laugh with food jammed into one cheek. "He doesn't lose."

"All winning streaks come to an end." Alix spoke from experience.

"Not Silas," Wick insisted. "He's always got a card up his sleeve."

Alix knitted her brow, her eyes darted around the room as the realization dawned on her. She spoke out loud a rhetorical question. "Why did we come all the way out to Keizur's End?"

She looked at Felix, eyes wide.

Felix snapped his head toward the door.

The wooden doors swung open as the Thin Man strutted through, his head down. He wore a duster down to his ankles, undoubtedly concealing plasbolts, while a wide grey hat concealed his face in shadow. A small spark lit under the brim of the hat. He looked up and around the room, strolling toward Alix's table. His boots knocked on the wood floor, loud in Alix's ears. The saloon fell silent except for his footsteps.

"Captain." He tipped his hat to Alix.

"Turn and walk away before something happens to you," Alix said.

The Thin Man took a long drag on the cigarette. "I'm sorry, captain, but things aren't going to go the way you think."

"An errand boy on an errand," Alix repeated Silas's words from back in his office. "I'll let you live, and you can go back to Silas and tell him that this whole business is settled."

The Thin Man shook his head. A breathy laugh escaped his lips. He nodded at Wick with a sinister smile. "I'll let you finish your meal."

He tipped his hat again and calmly walked outside.

"There are ten men with him out there," Felix said.

"Whether we did the job or not, he was going to make sure none of us walked out of here," Alix said.

"He never loses," Wick reiterated, his voice distant, defeated.

Alix pulled her goggles down over her eyes. As the lenses lit up, her mind kicked into action. She wasn't going to die tonight. *Especially not in this shit hole,* she thought.

"Wick, you and me in here. Felix see if there's a back way out of here," she said.

"Out back? This place is built into a damn mountain," Wick said, waving an arm behind him.

"You with me or not?" Alix shouted.

"Alright, alright. I'm with ya."

Alix drew both Plasvelds and spun up the chambers. Felix moved quickly through the saloon toward the back of the building. Alix stood and looked around at the other patrons, who stared back at her, anticipating trouble, which happened often enough in Keizur's End. Women sat on men's laps, and the bartender stood frozen, his hand under the bar, gripping a weapon no one could see except Alix through her goggles.

"Anybody staying here has got something to lose," she shouted.

Some of the women jumped up and began to leave, despite the drunken protests of the men they entertained. Some of the men stood cautiously, unsure if they could leave the saloon or if walking through the door was a death sentence.

Then, the Thin Man's voice broke the silence.

"I know there are a lot of bolts in there. The woman, her artie friend, and the other fella with them—anyone who brings me a body, I'll give five thousand crits!"

Alix and Wick stared at one another. The eyes in the room turned mean, toward the two of them, calculating how things would go if someone began shooting. Through her goggles, Alix could see through every man in the room, wondering which would be stupid enough to step up. Everyone waited, eyes fixed on Alix and Wick. She saw some hands move beneath tables, trying to avoid detection. She fired a shot.

Zmmph.

The plasma round ripped through the silence and through a man to her left.

His plasbolt clattered to the floor from his dead hand.

Another moment of silence.

Three men jumped to their feet, kicking back their chairs as they drew their plasbolts in one motion, but Alix ripped them apart. Wick kicked their table to the floor, the bottles and glasses shattering across the floor, food flying with them. He ducked and ran. The bartender drew a long Cortis-12 from behind the bar.

Thoomp. Thoomp.

He killed two men who had drawn their plasbolts.

Alix ducked from the heavy rounds behind her, but they weren't meant for her. She dropped to the floor and rolled toward the bar. Wick popped up from behind it, already hiding there. He covered Alix's movements with his own plasfire as the room filled with blue trails of residual light, heat, and smoke. The air crackled hot. Almost ten men lay dead already. Wick stopped firing and dropped down behind the bar as Alix jumped and slid over the bar top, crashing into bottles and glasses. She fell to the wet floor.

"So, why did Felix leave?" Wick shouted.

"Don't ask questions!" Alix said.

She sat up and put her back to the room, drawing deep breaths. The plasfire intensified, glass shattered, and various liquors spilled and splashed all over them. Wick tucked his head between his knees to shield himself further. Alix looked to her right in time to see the bartender slammed to the wall and ripped apart by plasfire, his Cortis-12 falling out of his hands. Boots shuffled on the floor as men changed positions around the room, measuring their movements to not get caught in a sudden storm.

Alix moved position too, sitting across from Wick, facing the room. Her goggles showed her everything, looking through the bar and registering each man left alive in the saloon. "Four men left. They're moving to get around us on each side. Take the two on the right."

"I can't fucking see them!" Wick said.

"Just go on my signal."

Alix crawled away from him and stopped by the dead bartender. She stared through the bar for a moment, then looked over to Wick and nodded. She aimed precisely through the wood of the bar, her Plasveld tracking the men who crept slowly across the room.

Zmmph.

The wood in front of her burned as she fired a hole straight through it, taking down one of the men.

Out beyond the bar, the three remaining men looked at one another, at the dead man, and back at the bar. Their confusion caused them to freeze.

Zmmph.

Alix fired again with lethal accuracy, through the bar and the chest of another man.

Wick jumped up at the same moment as Alix let the second shot go. The last two men stood looking over to their right, shocked to see the second man fall dead, caught by what they believed were blind shots. They saw Wick too late, and he killed them both with repeated, excessive plasfire from both plasbolts.

"You got another pair of those goggles?" he said at last when the whistling rounds and the spinning chambers died down.

Alix jumped back over the bar top, ignoring the question. She leaned against the wall and spoke to Felix through their comms channel.

"Felix, any luck?"

"I've got nothing," Felix responded.

"Shit. We've taken care of the idiots inside, but the Thin Man and his goons are still outside."

"I'll be back there in a moment."

"What the hell is he going to do? He doesn't even have a plasbolt!" Wick said, shouting but trying to keep his voice down.

"Will you shut up?" Alix turned back to him, "Follow our lead and you'll live."

Her goggles adjusted and Alix saw the men outside, their hands glowing from charged plasbolts. One of the men, however, stood without bolts in-hand: the Thin Man. *Could I get a shot off at him from here*? She shook her head; she should wait for Felix so there wasn't plasfire coming through when he returned to the main room.

"Not bad, captain!" the Thin Man said. "How many more men you going to take with you?"

Alix rolled her eyes, wishing every man in the town would shut their mouths.

"How many more you got?" she shouted, her voice carrying through the cool night out into the lane. She turned back to Wick. "This is gonna get messy."

Felix returned from the back rooms, crouching as he came through a doorway, shaking his head. "No exits." He knelt beside Alix on one knee.

"There's a Cortis-12 behind the bar." Wick motioned with a plasbolt toward the bar, imploring Felix to pick up a weapon.

"No," Felix said emphatically.

"What's the building to our left?" Alix nodded that way.

Felix scanned through the walls, "Looks like a general shop."

"Wick, you got a light?"

"Aye, captain," he said, sort of sarcastically. Reaching into his pocket, he tossed her a box of matches.

Alix looked at him, and her goggle lenses spun and became clear so Wick could see her eyes behind them. "Look, you stick with us, we get out of here. We get out of here, then we get our ships back."

Wick nodded. He looked at her earnestly, his eyes wide and watering. He steeled himself, a confident smile breaking across his face. As much as Alix didn't want to admit it before, they were in the same boat now. They were both trapped: Silas had taken something fundamental. They both wanted the same thing. Alix could see it—he believed her, he believed *in* her. She nodded, and then the lenses once again darkened, opaque, a blue glow at the edges. Both plasbolts in hand, she looked back into the street. They had run out of time.

"We make an exit through the store. Wick, you cover us from in here. Then we catch them in a crossfire."

"Wait, how are you making an exit *through a fucking wall*?" Wick was dumbfounded. Although Alix's goggles had spun back to dark circles, he could still feel her staring daggers. He held up his hands and nodded.

Alix lit three matches at once and walked to the bar. She tossed them onto the liquor-soaked bar top, the alcohol catching fire, moving along the pools and spills with a quick rush. Wick began to sweat, his palms slick as his nerves peaked. Alix walked coolly from the bar and tossed the matches back at Wick. He absent-mindedly tried to catch them, even though his hands were full. He fumbled, and the matchbox bounced onto the floor.

The fire grew as it reached the end of the bar, curving around it toward the wall, before it hit the liquor shelves. The fire burst into larger flames, and soon, the saloon would go up in a blaze.

Felix studied the opposite wall and picked his spot. Alix held up both Plasvelds, charging the cylinders and waiting for Felix. He slammed a heavy shoulder into the wooden wall, and he almost lost his balance as the wood cracked. Wick took a deep, deep breath and held it in, watching Felix crash into the wall. He realized the plan and kind of felt like Alix was a genius.

Flames spread on the wall, to the floor, licking out toward tables and chairs. Glass popped and shattered. The men outside waited. Wick held his plasbolts at the ready. Another smash into the wall with his shoulder was all it took for Felix to break through. He ripped at the boards, tossing them on the floor. There was only a small cavity between the buildings. Felix let a punch go, and his fist broke through the outer wall of the store. He pulled his hand back and kicked at the boards. If he could fit through the hole, Alix would fit easily. Climbing through, he ripped a few boards out of place, and Alix followed him into the dark shop next door.

Wick took the hint. He leveled his plasbolts and began firing out the saloon windows. With the fire on his right, Wick couldn't see much out there, but he knew his plasfire would send the men scrambling for cover. *They stood out there in the open like idiots anyway.*

The men standing on either side of the Thin Man opened fire on the saloon, but they ducked and ran as they did so. Wick dropped flat on his stomach as plasfire cut the air above him. The saloon windows shattered, shards of glass vaporizing as the rounds passed through. When a gap in the plasfire presented an opportunity, Wick jumped up again, firing wildly. He crouched and dropped when necessary, his feet slipping in the blood and the liquor. His boots caught on a body, and Wick fell, tumbling and rolling over a dead man. He cursed the body and himself for being so clumsy as he flopped against the wall near the front door. With a quick click, he ejected the plasma cylinders from his plasbolts and pulled new ones from his belt.

Alix and Felix moved around the tables and shelves of goods in the shop. Luckily, all its lights were out, and Wick made enough of a commotion in the saloon to distract Silas's men from hearing Felix crash through the wall. Felix crushed the lock on the door with one hand and left it hanging open; they would need to move quickly. Alix leaned her left shoulder on the wall, looking down the wooden boardwalk in front of the buildings built into the cliff face. Luckily for them, crates and barrels created barriers around the shop. She wasn't sure if she could make the run across the street herself, but Felix could.

"You cross the street?"

"Sure." He nodded.

"If we don't make it out of here—" she began.

"Don't," Felix smiled. "We will." He pulled her in close and kissed her passionately. "But I love you."

He ran out the door like a rush of wind, sucking the air out behind him. Alix crouched and moved stealthily, hiding behind the crates and barrels. The men in the street didn't notice Felix at all. He disappeared into the darkness. Alix took a deep breath, hoping Wick was still alive. *What a weird thought. Why should I care if he's living?* She shook her head and laughed to herself. Then, she turned and aimed her Plasvelds.

Silas's men were scattered in the street, standing in the open like fools. *They had little to fear. We were the ones who were trapped*, she thought. First, she scanned for the Thin Man, but none of the men looked like him, their builds all wrong. She began to worry.

Snap out of it.

She opened fire.

The street lit up with the blue lines and trailing steam. She hit one man and he fell into the dirt. So much noise came from the saloon, it took one of their comrades dying for the others to notice the crossfire. They all ducked and ran. Alix raised again to fire, tracking them as they moved. It took more shots this time to take down another.

Where's Wick? Is he dead in there? She ducked back down as some of Silas's men sent plasfire her way. None of them were particularly great shots: they just needed to overwhelm. She looked around the crates at her back toward the saloon. Flames brightly lit the place with dancing yellow and orange, glass strewn all over the boardwalk. Her goggles struggled to adjust to the changes in light, the intensity of the fire. She saw Wick moving, thankfully.

He burst through the door, screaming like a madman as his hat flew off his head. Flames burned on the back of his jacket. Diving off the boardwalk, Wick spread plasfire from both plasbolts, a whirlwind of chaotic energy, blue streaks burning through the air in many directions. His body hit the dirt, a stray shot kicking up a cloud of dust around him. He rolled and rolled, putting out the flames on his jacket, still screaming. Surprisingly, nobody shot at him. Alix couldn't stop laughing.

She jumped up and gave Wick some covering fire. With one Plasveld, she kept two men pinned down on her left, and with another, she put enough rounds through a barrel that the man behind it screamed, shook, and fell out into the street.

"Let's move!"

Wick stumbled to his feet, running as fast as he could, shooting all the way. She kept Silas's men pinned down, allowing Wick to get across the street and into a dark alley on the other side. One of Silas's men jumped up from a barricade hidden in shadow, and Alix saw him in the corner of her eye, the view in the goggles flashing on her right, detecting the threat. She tracked with her Plasveld in her right hand, shooting him dead in the chest.

That moment of distraction was all the Thin Man needed.

A round pierced Alix's thigh, searing through her flesh, burning the dirt behind her. She stumbled and cried out, searching for the source of the shot. The goggles' gentle pulse of light told her to look up, and the outline of a man in a window was shown to her. She clenched her teeth, pushed herself up and limped toward the opposite side of the street.

Fuck, that's it, she thought as she moved slowly, dragging herself through the dirt, Plasvelds in hand.

She was an easy target now.

Suddenly, someone grabbed her beneath the arms, but Alix kept shooting. She heard a groan and yell from the person pulling her expending all his strength to get her out of the street. They finally reached cover in an alley, and the person fell over behind her. She tilted her head back and saw Wick sit up, breathing heavily.

"You okay?" he said.

"No, I'm fucking shot," she barked in pain.

"You're welcome."

She discharged the plasma cylinders from her Plasvelds and

reloaded quickly. Her hands began to shake as she pushed the new charges into the chambers.

Fuck.

"Felix, you there? I've been hit, but it's not lethal," she said as if he stood right beside her. "Thin Man is in an upper floor window."

Silas's men outside regrouped, moving around the street to take up new positions. The fire in the saloon burst out of every window, and the town cared little for the shootout happening around it. Men rushed from other buildings now, screaming and pointing. People ran from the hotel and gambling rooms beside the saloon, and above it, men, women, and children cried out from their windows. With buildings stacked up the cliff face, intricate stairs zigzagged up the structures from one level to another. The rickety stairs filled with people trying to escape. Buckets began passing from one man to the next until they could rig a real fire hose.

"They have the ravine exit covered," Felix said at last. "I could take them out, at least a dozen."

"We might not make it there," Alix admitted, the pain still burning and pulsing in her left leg. *At least I'm not bleeding out*, she thought, thankful for the cauterization of the plasma.

"Alright, coming to you," Felix replied.

Alix tried to stay calm. Her heart pounded in her chest, and sweat ran down her face, beginning to creep in under her goggles, burning her eyes. She shook the cobwebs from her mind, trying to focus. Her goggles showed her the movements of Silas's men. What she had thought were ten, now seemed to multiply, and Felix said there were a dozen more at the mouth of the ravine.

"I don't know how we're going to get out of this," she said.

"Hey, don't give me that shit," Wick growled, picking her up and holding her steady as she almost collapsed on her wounded leg and hopped on the good one. "You said stick with you, and I'll live. Well, I'm sticking with you, for better or worse, because those sons of bitches sure aren't interested in anything but killing me."

Alix laughed through her tears. Wick's face was bloodied and covered in soot and dirt. At least it wasn't his blood on his face. He began to walk deeper into the alley, Alix hopping along with him, her arm over his shoulders, his around her.

Felix came up to them out of the darkness, startling Wick, who nearly let Alix fall to the ground. She let go of Wick and threw herself at Felix, knowing he would catch her and effortlessly hold her up. He looked down at the wound, and she awaited his assessment.

"Looks okay, not bleeding. Didn't hit the bone or an artery," he said.

"Ah, well, everything is great then," she said, dripping with sarcasm.

"Is there not another way out of this hellhole?" Wick looked back toward the street, seeing the shadows of men and women running, fighting the fire.

On the north side of the ravine, homes, shops, hotels, brothels, stables, and machine shops formed a patchwork of buildings on the ground. Above them, more homes, shops, brothels, places for gambling, and whatever else someone wanted to do ascended the rock face. As the ravine went along, it became narrower, almost down to the width of one person, then opened back up in some places, making it difficult to navigate.

Felix looked all around them, through the buildings, trying to process as much information as he could as quickly as possible. Then, he found it: a smuggler's tunnel into the rock. He looked up, following a shaft to the top: a lift.

"I've got it. Let's go."

He carried Alix in his arms so they could move quickly. Wick watched behind them, looking over his shoulder as they moved through the crisscrossing alleys between the buildings. Some were packed so heavily with junk, Felix had to barrel through, leaving a path for Wick to follow if he could manage to avoid tripping and stumbling over the debris.

Zmmph.

A plasbolt round whizzed by them before Wick turned and fired down the alley. He saw a shadow move and duck out of the way. He turned and ran again, bouncing off a wall to avoid scattered junk Felix had knocked over.

Zmmph zmmph.

Wick ducked and ran awkwardly, firing behind him without looking. *How much further?* he wondered. He could barely keep up with Felix, who seemed to whip past each corner out of sight just as Wick rounded the previous one.

"Wait up!" Wick shouted. *The place is a fucking maze.*

He rounded a corner and ran directly into Felix's back, like hitting a brick wall. Felix didn't budge, didn't even flinch from the impact, but Wick fell back on his rear, plasbolts flying out of his hands. Wick hollered and reached his hands up to his bleeding and probably broken nose.

"Son of a—"

"We're taking this tunnel," Felix said, unconcerned that Wick had just barreled into him. He reached out and helped Wick to his feet.

Wick scrambled to stuff a handkerchief into his nose. "Great."

Felix cleared debris and found a locked wooden gate over a natural tunnel in the rock. He ripped the gate off its hinges and tossed it into the alley behind them to create a barrier for anyone who might be following. It would at least slow them down for a few seconds.

Wick noticed Alix sitting on the ground, holding her left leg, nearly unconscious from the pain. Her goggles had been pushed up onto her head, and her eyes drooped. Felix picked her up again and turned to Wick.

"Let's go. The lift is about thirty meters back."

"Just warn me if you're going to stop," Wick stammered, holding his nose, handkerchief red with blood.

Where the hell are we going to go when we get to the top? Felix wondered. Alix needed medical attention, and while he was skilled enough to handle anything, he didn't have the materials needed to tend the wound. First, though, they needed to not get stuck in the small tunnel. Felix's shoulders rubbed against the walls as he walked bent over from the low ceiling, trying to keep from hitting Alix's legs on anything.

Finally, they reached an old lift, operated by an ancient hoist motor. He had no idea if it could hold his weight, but they had little choice. He set Alix on the floor of the lift, which was simply a square with no walls, metal poles on each corner, the frame over their heads holding the motor. Felix hit the button on the rock wall, and the motor whistled, whined, groaned, and shook as it began lifting them upward.

"This thing is a deathtrap," Wick said, looking up as the motor slowly wound the cable, each clang and jostle scaring him to death.

After the shaky, creaky ascent, the lift stopped. Felix smashed through the wood and metal doors and locks. They were in another cave, but one built into a plateau at the top of the ravine. There were crates everywhere, wooden barrels, stacks of cloth and heaps of bags. Everything looked like it had been left there for years, dust on every surface.

Felix gently set Alix on a pile of bags, which were filled with grain, at least making something soft enough for her. He checked her vitals, relieved she was stable.

"Don't suppose there's medical stuff in here?" Felix said to Wick. "Look around."

Wick nodded and got busy digging through everything in the cave.

"How are you feeling?" Felix asked, smiling and gently stroking Alix's red face.

"Wonderful," she said with a ragged breath. "Feels like there's a rod through my leg, but at least I'm not dead."

"I told you we'd make it out of there." He winked.

She laughed, but the pain assailed her, and she tried to stop. She reached for her leg, the laugh turning into a cough as tears ran down her face. But still, she laughed, and Felix with her. He kissed her, and she gripped the back of his neck, holding the kiss for as long as she could.

8

The Reprieve

Alix sat uncomfortably in the saddle. Despite the stirrol's gentle rhythm galloping over the desert back into the high plains of the valley, Alix's leg burned and ached with every hoof fall. The chaos in Keizur's End caused by the fire allowed Felix and Wick to retrieve the stirrols they tied up, and it seemed the Thin Man and his posse had left. At least Felix saw no sign of them, and if he said they were gone, they were gone.

Back in the smuggler's cave, the best Felix could do was wrap Alix's leg, which meant a ripped leg off her trousers mid-thigh. So, she not only rode with significant discomfort due to the wound, but the saddle also rubbed against the inside of her leg, which was less than pleasant. The night had come and gone, and another night approached now as they rode northwest from Keizur's End. Felix rode close beside her, within arm's length in case she keeled over. He commanded the stirrol skillfully, but not harshly. Wick led the way.

Despite Wick's reservations, he told them of a safe place where Alix could rest and they could mend her wound. He said the place was safe, but he also hesitated to even bring it up. Alix expressed skepticism that any place Wick went was safe, but what choice did she have? So they rode into the valley on the southern edge as the high plain dropped into the chis grass.

At last, Wick held up his arm and slowed his stirrol with a gentle "Whoa there." He turned the mount back and around as Felix and Alix caught up to him. The land sloped down ahead of them, and just a short distance away, they saw a house. Smoke trailed from its chimney. Fences created several pens around the house, and ibi wandered in a great white and grey blob, moving together like a cloud in the wind. A man on stirrolback rode along with the ibi, then around and back, guiding the herd into one of the pens.

"That's my brother, Wes," Wick said.

"Lovely place," Felix noted, taking in the green below the red and orange sky, which would soon shift to purple.

"Yeah, well, he isn't going to be pleased to see us."

"Why doesn't that surprise me?" Alix grimaced. "Look, if we don't get moving down this hill, I might fall off this stirrol."

"Alright, just let me do the talking." Wick spurred his stirrol forward.

Felix smiled at Alix, his hand on her shoulder. She forced a smile through a fog in her mind. With a click of her tongue at the stirrol, it raised its head and trotted forward. Felix went with her. Up ahead, the man, Wick's brother, had managed to get his flock into the pen and closed a wooden gate behind him. It wasn't until he turned around to lead his stirrol into a barn that he saw three riders coming down the hill.

As Alix got close, she saw the man wore handmade clothes, brown overalls and a dirty, faded blue shirt underneath. His hat looked like it had been trampled by every ibi on the farm, the brim bent back almost straight up in the front. A brown beard with grey patches covered his face. Just as Wick said, it was obvious he wasn't pleased to see them.

"Howdy, Wesley," Wick said as he rode up within earshot.

"Wickford, what are you doing here?"

"We need some shelter and first aid."

Alix raised her hand, her eyes drooping, her body bent over, almost lying on the stirrol's neck. "Been shot over here! Would love some chisik or whatever you got for pain."

Wes looked at her, seeing her leg dangling without a pant leg to cover most of it. He looked up at Felix, furrowed his brow, and then looked back at Wick.

"Anna is not going to be pleased," Wes said. "But we will give you some time to patch up that leg. I've got some things inside."

"I appreciate it," Wick said truthfully.

"Come on, you can let your stirrols into the barn."

Wes led his own stirrol by the reins while Wick and the others rode behind him. Felix kept his hand on Alix's arm, holding her up as her body swayed and her head nodded. She could barely keep her eyes open any longer.

Everything on the farm was made of burrey wood and stone. The house itself consisted of one large square building, with a few smaller rectangles built onto it, making it sprawl out but remain one level. The center of the house was all stone, plastered on the outside with clay, dried and painted. Some of the additions were wood, or wood and stone. A stone chimney rose from a large rectangle addition in the back.

The wooden barn stood taller than the house and about a hundred paces behind it. They rode by the pens full of ibi and stirrols. Chickens poked at the ground all around the house. Behind the house stood a large stone well. Alix couldn't see any sign of technology, and truly there was none.

Felix dismounted his stirrol and let Wick lead it along with his own into the barn. Felix gently helped Alix down from the saddle.

"Let me go warn my wife. Wait here," Wes said then walked away into the backdoor that led into the kitchen.

"Seems you two aren't on the best of terms," Felix said when Wick returned to get Alix's stirrol.

"Nah." Wick pulled the reins over the stirrol's head so he could lead it. "We haven't spoken in years."

Alix dropped her head on Felix's shoulder as he held her in his arms, legs draped over his left hand. He shook her when he saw her about to pass out.

"Stay awake."

"Ugh." Alix let her head fall back and looked up at the sky then returned it to Felix's shoulder.

Wes emerged from the house, impatience on his face. He looked at the three of them then drew in a deep breath. "You can stay one night, but you sleep in the barn. You're welcome in the house for supper and to fix that leg."

"Thank you for your generosity," Felix said in his most gentle, soft tone.

"Well, come on."

They went through the kitchen and turned left into a storage room. Felix laid Alix on a workbench Wes had cleared off. The smell of wood fire and smoked ibi filled the entire house. If Alix hadn't been almost unconscious, the smell would have filled her with joy. A bright light overhead was simply Wes holding a lantern up by his head before he lit two others in the room. Felix didn't need them, but it was a nice gesture.

Wes bent down and pulled a box off a shelf, setting it on the bench beside Alix's legs and flipping open the lid. The kit was the most advanced technological thing he owned, it seemed. Clean bandages, antiseptic, string, needles, syringes; Felix moved the contents around with his finger to see what he would be working with.

"Can you get some hot water?" he said to Wes.

"Sure thing." Wes left the room.

"Fuck the water; give me some chisik," Alix moaned.

Felix chuckled and put his hand on her forehead, "I'll see if they have some."

He met Wes at the storage room door, where Wes handed him a pail of steaming hot water, taken from a kettle already hot by the fire. He also had cloths over his shoulder, which Felix took and laid over the lip of the pail.

"Do you have something for the pain?" Felix said.

"Unfortunately not," Wes replied.

"Here." Wick showed his face around the corner, holding out a flask. "It's all I got left."

"It's something," Felix said, taking it. "Apologies for any noise and any…language."

Felix turned and closed the door behind him, at least it would minimize Alix's outbursts. He gave her the flask, which she emptied very quickly. She fell back on the tabletop as Felix unwrapped her leg.

"Alright, babe. Patch me up," she said.

Felix was as gentle as he could be, washing the wound with hot water and the cloths. Then he went to work stitching her up. He knew she would have some pain for a while, and the leg would be weakened, but at least it wasn't infected. She clenched her teeth between breathless outbursts. Felix clipped the string with a small pair of scissors and looked up at her with a smile.

"Alright, roll over."

"The back?" Alix exhaled.

"It went in and out," Felix confirmed.

Alix whined as she rolled over, putting her arms up and tucking her face into them. She almost kicked Felix when he started on the back, stitching up the hole, slowly (a little too slowly for Alix's liking) and carefully. It was over in a few minutes, but Alix would've sworn it had taken an hour.

"All done," Felix smiled.

"Glad that was good for you," Alix joked as she rolled over onto her back again.

"I'll wrap it up just in case," he said. "Don't suppose you have another pair of pants?"

"Why? I thought you liked my legs." She winked, feeling the chisik worm its way through her body, a warm and cozy feeling.

"I certainly do." He kissed her bare knee.

"Maybe Wesley's wife has something I can have."

Felix helped her off the table and held her up, one arm around her. He opened the door, and she limped out into the kitchen. A woman wearing an apron looked up at her, as if Alix had snakes coming out of her ears. Alix looked around and turned up one side of her mouth. Fresh bread, vegetables, and a large ibi leg were all steaming in metal pans. Alix looked at everything with big, wide eyes, dying to eat everything in sight.

"Sorry for the disturbance," she murmured. "I'm Alix."

"I hope you're okay," the woman replied. Then, she added, "I'm Anna."

Alix pointed toward the door and awkwardly hobbled out, joining the others at a large wooden table inside an even larger room. It had to be the largest room in the house, with the table set off to one side to create a hallway from the front door all the way to the kitchen in the back.

"Thanks for the chisik," she said to Wick as she slowly sat in one of the handmade chairs. She grimaced and sat up a little when her leg touched the chair, then settled for good.

"You owe me." Wick pointed at her.

"So, what's the story with you two?" Alix asked.

Wes and Wick looked at one another, wondering who would explain it first, or if either of them would at all.

"That bad, huh?" Alix said.

Anna came in carrying the large pan with a blackened ibi leg on it. She set it down and cleared her throat as Wes pulled his gaze away from Wick and apologized. He pushed back his chair and followed her into the kitchen. They both returned with the rest of the food and a stack of plates.

"This smells incredible, Anna," Alix said.

"Thank you." Anna sat across from her.

Out of the corner of her eye, Alix caught a young boy peeking around the corner to her right. She looked at him directly and smiled, waving with her fingers. Anna saw the boy too.

"I told you to stay in your room. I will bring dinner to you and your brother," she scolded him, but she didn't raise her voice.

The boy disappeared in a flash, and Anna took a deep breath.

Everyone dug in, passing plates and pans around the table. Alix and Wick ate furiously. Wes and Anna looked at the two of them awkwardly, but not as awkwardly as they looked at Felix, who sat there, seemingly staring into space.

"Uh, do you…need anything?" Wes said to Felix.

"What? No, of course not." He tried to smile and reassure the man.

"It looks to us like he's staring a hole in the wall, but he's actually quite content, shutting down a little to conserve energy and rest," Alix said with food in her mouth.

"Actually, I'm staring at you," Felix said, "and your horrible table manners."

Alix choked as she laughed, covered her mouth, then swallowed and drank a lot of water. Anna smirked and blushed as she ate.

"It's delicious, Anna," Wick said.

"Thank you." She looked up at him for just a moment.

"So, I hope you all aren't in some kind of serious trouble," Wes said. "Plasfire through the leg. Where were you all when shit hit the fan?"

"Keizur's End," Wick said. "We *were* in trouble, but now, I'm not so sure what we're in." He poked at his plate with his fork, keeping his eyes down.

"Trouble," Felix reiterated. "Silas won't stop looking for us."

"Silas?" Wes said in shock, dropping his fork. "Dammit, Wick!"

"Why do you think this is *my* fault?" Wick raised his arms in defense.

"Things usually are," Wes pointed out.

"It's not Wick's fault. Not exactly," Alix said. "We got involved with Silas too. And, well, I'm assuming you know him well enough to know that he double-crossed us. We were foolish to even think he'd hold up his end of our deal." She looked over at Felix.

"What deal was that?" Wes said.

"To kill your brother," Felix replied. "For ten thousand crits."

The table fell silent. Anna looked at Wesley wide-eyed, holding her fork in midair as Wesley raised his eyebrows. "And you didn't take it?" Wes laughed.

"Trust me, I was this close," Alix said, holding up her thumb and forefinger.

* * *

It wasn't the worst place Alix had ever slept, Wes had spread blankets over straw in the barn for her, Wick, and Felix. Anna thankfully loaned Alix a pair of trousers made of sturdy, dark blue fabric. A lantern sat on a wood crate in the middle of the stall. Alix stared at the flame dancing behind the glass. Felix filled a corner, sitting cross legged, already descending into his meditative dream.

"So, what happened between you and your brother?" Alix said to Wick without looking away from the lantern.

Wick sat in the doorway, staring out into the cold night. "You know, there was a time he was the one indebted to Silas," Wick said, his voice distant. He lit a cigarette.

"He doesn't seem like the type," Alix said.

"Once, he lived on a farm, on land owned by Silas. He wanted out."

"So you helped him?"

"We made a trade. Wes's land debt was paid, and I went to work."

Alix stared at Wick's back, but his voice and his drooping shoulders told her what she needed to know. Wick puffed smoke into the air.

"That doesn't sound like you."

"What? Doing the right thing?"

"Well, yeah."

They sat in silence for some time. Wick jammed the cigarette on the door frame and instead of flicking it into the barnyard, he put it into his shirt pocket. "Maybe it isn't," he said.

Alix laid back on the straw with her hands behind her head. Many years ago, she slept on a bed no better than this. Then, she lay on a beaten, discarded mat, barely what she would call "soft." Instead of looking up at the framing of the barn by lamplight, back then, she stared up into darkness, pipes crisscrossing the shaft between metal walls. She had a small, stolen hoverlamp, a little silver globe with a pale blue light. Anything she owned she stole from the refuse chambers below. The quiet hum and vibrations of machines all around her put her to sleep as the radiant heat from a central heating pipe kept her warm.

How long she spent in that hole, she had no idea. She felt a vibration in the syncpad on her arm. She didn't even bother looking at it, but simply swiped away the incoming call. She yawned and drifted off to sleep.

Wick lit another cigarette and scratched an itch on his forehead with his thumb. Maybe he sensed the frustration coming and began pacing outside the barn. Wesley walked around the corner and leaned against the barn. Wick gave him a sideways glance as he took a long drag.

"Well? You here to give me a lecture?" Wick said without looking at his brother.

"You can't be showing up here, Wick."

"Alix needed help. We had nowhere else to go."

"Since when do you care about anybody else but yourself?"

Wick looked up at the bright moon, blowing smoke into the wind. "I saved your life, didn't I?"

"You did *that* for yourself."

Wick hung his head.

He remembered almost twenty years ago. The two brothers stood around their mother and father's table, at each other's throats. A weight had fallen on them, a man at their door with an ultimatum. The image of their father shattered like glass; they struggled to make sense of the bigger picture. One of them had to go, and Wick *needed* to go.

In the moment outside the barn, Wick curled his upper lip. "We'll be gone at first light." He flicked his cigarette into the dirt, the ember slowly fading.

Felix woke Alix in the morning. She blinked rapidly, looking around and sitting up on her elbows. Her leg ached in the cold. She winced and rolled over, groaning at the fact that she was no longer asleep. Felix tapped her again, playfully tugging on the blanket.

"Go away," she complained.

"We've got the stirrols saddled. Anna brought you some coffee and breakfast," Felix said.

Alix rubbed the sleep from her eyes then stuck a hand up. "Help me up, dear."

Felix took her hand, and Alix climbed to her feet. Her leg remained stiff, but the sharp pain from the day before faded into a dull throb any time she moved. She ran her hand through her hair, shaking it out, still a tangled mess.

Wick cinched the girth on his stirrol's saddle. Alix greedily snatched the coffee and sausage from a metal plate sitting on a ryegrass bale by the door. She sat on the bale and looked up at Felix while chewing.

"Where are we going to go, now?"

"Back to Verisport, I guess," Felix said.

"Are you kidding?" Wick shouted. "Ain't no way we can get back there alive."

"You got a better idea?" Alix shouted at him with her mouth full.

"Well, I didn't tell you about this before, but the reason I guess Silas wanted you to kill me is because I've been stealing from him," Wick said.

"Great." Alix rolled her eyes, drinking coffee from a metal cup.

"I had a partner, a scrapper in town I funneled scrap to instead of it going to Silas's yard. Their name's Jesse. A little place on the east side of town."

"You just said we couldn't go back to town," Alix reminded him.

"Right, I wasn't suggesting that, at least not yet. I know a place we can lay low."

"Well, spit it out!" Alix was impatient, and the breakfast was nearly gone.

"I also know a girl who often was at Jesse's—her name is Sora. She's a mechanic from a farmstead in the valley, land owned by Silas."

"Why would they take us in?" Felix wondered.

Wick smiled wide. "Because we were planning a robbery together."

Alix couldn't believe they were following Wick's lead *again*. But at least his first idea had been pretty good. She got a good night's sleep, and it had been quite a while since she had food that good. Her leg still throbbed while riding. She tried not to think about the possibility of the wound never healing completely.

They rode north as fast as their stirrols would take them. As soon as they hit the chis, the stirrols were in their element, back home. Alix let her hands run through the golden panicles of the chis as it went by. She knocked seed pods into the air, and they puffed into white clouds catching the wind.

When her syncpad vibrated again, she looked at it this time. The marshal attempted to reach her. She hesitated, unsure whether she wanted to answer. The last words he said to her floated to the top of her memory: *I have to serve the people of this valley. I can't make decisions based on your personal vendetta.*

Her anger boiled over, and she swiped the screen to ignore the transmission. She hoped he knew how he had failed; she hoped he knew exactly what he'd done and how she had been right. *Of course I'm right*, she thought. *He has no idea who he's dealing with, and the valley is already suffering*. And that brought up a key problem in Wick's plan to reach this farmstead: the rail line split the valley in two.

They galloped nonstop until they reached the rail line in a familiar spot. Wick halted at the top of the hill where they had launched the attack just a few days ago. He sent a transmission to someone through his syncpad, and Felix detected the return signal even before Wick received it. With powerful binocular vision, he saw two women atop a hill across the rail line, low fields between them. They crouched beneath burrey trees, and one of the women held a plasrifle to her shoulder while the other looked through a vizscope.

"Your friends?" Felix said.

"Huh?" Wick looked at him then back to his syncpad to catch the return transmission from Sora. "Yes, that's them," he said, looking at Felix suspiciously. "You can see that far?"

"How do you get through the fence?" Alix said.

"Well, I have the passcode to the gates." Wick smiled proudly.

"You don't think they've been changed?" Felix said.

Wick stuttered, "I, uh, didn't think about that."

Felix smiled and patted Wick on the shoulder. "Don't worry, I can get us through." He kicked his stirrol forward down the hill.

Wick looked at Alix. "He's not carrying me as he jumps that fence."

Alix threw her head back and laughed as she spurred her stirrol to follow Felix. Wick groaned and followed along, annoyed.

Felix dismounted at the gate and simply touched the lockpad with two fingers. The pad changed from red to green in a few seconds, then Felix opened the gate and looked over his shoulder to Wick, who sat slack jawed. They led their stirrols through on foot, and Alix looked at the concrete around them. The dead bodies were gone, but blood still stained the white surface. She bristled as she passed where she'd killed the engineer in a blind rage. That rage melted when she looked up and through the north fence, to see the same woman she'd seen in Verisport, at the salvage yard.

Alix felt her heart beat a little faster, and she started to flush. Sora wore her hair braided and tied behind her head, wrapped in a red headband. She wore a grey, utilitarian jumpsuit, but the top half was rolled down to her waist, the arms tied loosely. Sora's beautiful brown skin contrasted the white tank top she wore.

"Wick, what the hell are you doing? Who are they?" Sora said in a disapproving tone.

"Relax, they're fine. They're with me," Wick said.

"I can see that," Jo said, her plasrifle at the waist, still holding her finger near the trigger. "But who *are* they?"

"I'm Alix; this is Felix."

"And you trust them?" Sora said, not acknowledging the introduction.

"I tend to trust someone who decided not to kill me." Wick led his stirrol through the north gate.

Sora pursed her lips and then glared at Alix. Jo's furrowed brow and itchy trigger finger raised the tension in the air as Felix closed the gate behind them. Alix slung the reins back over her stirrol's neck. She couldn't climb into the saddle on her own, so Felix gave her a leg up.

"What happened to you?" Sora said.

"Got shot in the leg." Alix shrugged.

"Keizur's End," Wick explained.

"So why are you all here?" Jo demanded.

"We need a place to lay low," Wick said.

Sora thought, and Jo sent a nonverbal signal to her sister, one Sora knew intimately. Jo did not approve, and she did not try to hide her disdain for Alix and Felix. They had no business here. Sora looked at Alix and the way her hands lay on the horn of the saddle, reins between her long fingers.

"Alright, come on," Sora said reluctantly.

"Lead the way." Alix smiled.

Jo rolled her eyes and slung her plasrifle over her shoulder as she tromped back toward the farmstead ahead of the others. Sora called out to her with plans of delivering some kind of reassurance, but her sister was already set, and there was no talking her down. Sora regretted her decision to welcome Alix and Felix as she watched Jo head back up the hill. In the end, Sora tilted her head to beckon Alix, Felix, and Wick to follow.

They approached the village through the twilight trees, heading straight for Sora and Jo's barn. Alix took stock of the land: the long, central meeting house, the family dwellings spread all around it, the barn towering over everything else. There was room enough for their stirrols, and the creatures were pleased to be free of their burdens. Alix envied them, brushing her stirrol's sweaty back with her hand. Sora watched Alix as she hung bridles on a line of pegs on the wall.

"Do you need immediate medical attention?" she said to Alix.

"No, no, Felix fixed me up already. Just hurts like hell." Alix blushed and quickly thought she should have dismissed Sora's concern; she would've looked tough.

"That your partner?"

Alix nodded with a smile.

"I'm Sora. My sister is Jo." Her own smile was not a warm and inviting one but one of forced politeness. She remained standoffish.

Alix found it intoxicating all the same.

"Pleased to meet you," Alix said, extending her hand. Sora hesitated but took Alix's hand with a gentle shake.

"Sorry to intrude on you like this. Wick was pretty adamant this place would be safe, but he did say you'd not be pleased to see us."

Sora watched as Alix picked up the saddle off the ground despite her injury and muscled it over onto a wooden stand by the stall. Alix leaned back on the saddle, her sleeves rolled up above her elbows, a dark, dingy vest over top of it. Sora realized she was so caught up in Alix's movements, she didn't even register what was said to her.

"Sorry." Embarrassment washed over her.

They both stood in an awkward silence. Alix smirked, knowing when someone was paying close attention to her body, but Sora's gaze did not trigger the bristling anger and defensiveness that usually came with such a thing.

"I remember you from Verisport," Alix finally broke the silence.

Thank the stars. Sora felt relieved she didn't have to be the one to start the conversation again.

"So do I. You were at Jesse's shop." Her tone turned harsh, disapproval on her tongue. "You were being nosey around our stuff." Sora crossed her arms, her eyes chastising Alix.

"I remember your sister pointing a plasrifle at me."

"What do you expect?"

"That's fair." Alix brushed her hair behind her ear, just beneath the strap of her goggles.

The stirrol beside them puffed air through its lips, shaking the hair on its neck as if telling them to knock it off. Sora walked over to an empty stall and opened the door, the stirrol following her inside, knowing the familiar routine. Alix leaned on the sill of the open window looking into the stall. The stirrol did a slow turn, and Sora made sure there was water available.

"So, Wick says you're planning a robbery," Alix said without a whiff of tact.

Sora threw up her hands as she walked out of the stall and latched the door. "He told you?" she said, then under her breath, "That fucking loudmouth."

Alix raised her eyebrows, knowing only after the fact that she should have been more discreet. "Sounds exciting! When are we going over the plan?" Alix followed Sora as she walked out to the side of the barn, toward the door leading into the shop.

"Never."

"Come on, we can help! Felix and I have pulled off *many* robberies." Alix laughed, remembering each one and how they may have been successful, but they weren't exactly executed to perfection.

Sora spun around just before the door inside and glared at Alix. Quickly, Alix turned her face from amusement at her own escapades, a great dumb grin, back into a no-nonsense scowl. Sora sensed Alix was imitating her expression, having fun with her, poking holes in the armor. *Dammit she is adorable*, Sora thought.

"You three will stay inside." Sora pointed her finger at Alix then switched to her thumb, pointing back at herself. "My sister and I will talk to the elders to see if you can even stay here."

"Okay, okay, I'm sorry!" Alix put her hands up and just barely squeezed by Sora, making sure she brushed her shoulder against her, just ever so slightly.

Sora bit her tongue, holding back a storm of words that surely would have put Alix in her place. Instead, she watched Alix walk through the door and into the shop.

Alix wandered around curiously, attracted to the shaker half-assembled in the middle of the room. She was actually impressed with the sophistication of the tools and equipment that Sora and her sister owned. Above her, the lights in the apartment windows shone through thin curtains. Alix knelt at the shaker, poking her head into the guts of the machine.

"Please don't touch anything. It's all in a very specific place," Sora said, walking by Alix toward the stairs up to the apartment.

"Sure looks that way," Alix shouted from within the shaker. "What's wrong with this thing?"

"Don't touch it!"

Sora's boots on the metal stairs echoed in the shop and she rushed into the apartment like a gust of air. Jo was already busy getting spare blankets together, still looking annoyed. Their beds sat in opposite corners of the room, Sora's beneath the windows, while Jo liked the comfort of sleeping in the corner with solid walls. A kitchenette lined one wall, and they had a small table and two chairs in the middle of everything, covered with used dishes and small pieces of the shaker Sora worked on reassembling any time she sat down to eat.

"I can't believe you said they could stay here!" Jo said, arms full of brown blankets.

"Look, I'm sorry. I can kick them out in the morning," Sora said as she anxiously picked up dirty clothes off the floor.

"Are you kidding me? You wouldn't kick that woman anywhere."

"What are you talking about?" Sora waved the handful of shirts that she just picked up off the floor.

"You *know* what I mean."

Sora sat on her bed as Jo headed down the stairs. Jo was right, and she *hated* when Jo was right. Sora tossed all her dirty clothes into a basket in the corner. A loud metal clanging rang out downstairs.

"Don't touch anything!" Jo shouted from far across the shop.

Sora smiled.

At the bottom of the stairs, Jo walked through a sliding metal door and down another set of stairs into a storage room below ground. It was the best that they could offer until speaking with Sim and the other village elders. A single light in the center of the ceiling lit the room, which normally was total chaos, but Wick and Felix had been stacking boxes and other junk onto metal shelves standing against the wall. Jo dropped the stack of blankets onto the floor. A couple of beaten-up cot mattresses were all they had, and only two of them. Felix wouldn't even be able to fit his entire body on both laid side-by-side. The glorified flat pillows would probably squish into a layer no thicker than the blankets once someone laid down.

"This is the best we can do." Jo was curt and immediately went back upstairs.

The sisters nearly ran into one another as Jo came up the stairs and Sora came down from the apartment. Sora put on a big, exaggerated smile, reminding Jo to not be such a jerk and as an apology for bringing these people into their space. Jo did not return the smile and stormed back upstairs to be alone. Sora felt guilty; she couldn't blame Jo for being annoyed.

Looking across the shop, Sora saw Alix's head just above the shaker. When she walked around the machine to see what Alix was doing, she found the woman sitting on the floor, holding a small cell converter in her hands, now streaked black from grease. Alix just finished reassembling the converter and turned it over in her hands to make sure all was right.

She looked up and happily held it up to Sora. "All fixed!"

"We told you not to touch anything." Sora took the converter anyway, and set it on a rolling shelf.

"Sorry, habit. It helps me clear my mind, you know?" Alix wiped her hands on a towel nearby and stood, finishing the wiping on her pants.

I do know what you mean, Sora thought. "Your friends are down in the storage room. Jo got some blankets, but that's the best we can do. I have to talk to Sim, and maybe we can get you some better accommodations."

"Hopefully, we aren't here very long," Alix said, but in her mind, she hoped that was a lie.

Sora didn't want to agree with her. She was a little disappointed to hear Alix say that, but outwardly, she didn't show it. "Well, I'll be right back. Just don't touch anything else please. Jo will kill you."

Alix smiled and held up her hands as she walked through the shop. She weaved in and out of the tables, toolboxes, and barrels, like a ship avoiding celestial objects. She leaned and turned dramatically around each obstacle to show Sora that she didn't lay a finger on anything else. Sora laughed at the joke, shook her head, and left.

The afternoon sun emerged from behind clouds with touches of violet. It was truly a beautiful day in the valley. People moved all through the village, going about their usual business. Children ran around playing, but Sora walked with a purpose. Behind the large meeting house, a community garden sat within a white picket fence. Several women tended to the vegetables, gourds, and some fruits, while others used the wooden tables nearby to repot flowers and trailing plants that lived in and around their homes. That's where Sora found Sim.

A woman in her seventies, Sim had been the village leader for most of Sora's life. She was chosen for her positive outlook, fairness, joy, and laughter. *Everyone* loved Sim, and the woman had been like a surrogate parent to Sora and Jo when their parents died. The other villagers alerted Sim to Sora's presence through their friendly greetings as Sora approached. Sim looked up from beneath a floppy straw hat that protected her skin from further blemishing. Beneath the hat, her gray hair was piled up into a bun. She smiled brightly when she saw Sora.

"Good afternoon, Sora!"

"Hey." Sora stopped on the other side of the picket fence. "Can I talk to you for a second?"

"Of course, dear."

"Um, privately?"

Sim put down her trowel on the table, a shadow passing over her face as she worried what Sora might tell her. "Is everything okay?"

"Sure. I think so. I mean, yes, no one is in any trouble."

"Well, that's a relief. Let's go inside. I could use a drink of water."

Sim's home was just beyond the garden, right across a dirt footpath from the meeting house. A simple veranda wrapped around the front and one corner. The windows sat open, blue curtains flapping in the breeze. Sora stood in the parlor as Sim poured water into two cups. Sim sat in a wooden chair on cushions she'd made herself.

"What's on your mind, Sora?"

"Well, I have some friends in the shop. They need a place to crash. Jo and I don't really have comfortable places for them. I was hoping there was room somewhere to put them?"

Sim nodded along as she listened, taking long drinks. "Friends?"

"From Veris. People I've worked with over there." Sora hated lying. She realized she couldn't vouch for any one of the people in her shop right now. Her skin tingled as she looked at Sim, who studied her.

"I don't see why not. I am sure we can find beds for them," she said. "How many?"

"Three, but one of them is, uh, a very large sentient."

Sim held her cup near her lips. "Oh?" She brought the cup down and held it in both hands on her lap. "Well, I can ask around. At minimum, they can stay in the meeting hall. We will rustle up some beds if we must."

She stood up and set her cup on a little bookshelf by the chair. Sora downed her cold, crisp water with relief. She hugged Sim tightly, wearing a big smile. "Thank you, Sim."

"No problem. Just make sure you can vouch for these friends," Sim said in her ear.

Sora held on for a moment longer, stuffing the feeling of anxiety down before she pulled away. She nodded, and Sora knew Sim knew she wasn't being completely honest about all this. Regardless, Sora took the win and the fact that Sim wasn't calling her out directly and left happily.

In the evening, everyone gathered in the large dining hall. A huge fire burned in the center within a stone firepit. A great metal hood hung several feet over the pit, and carrying the smoke up through the chimney. Long banquet tables stretched from one end of the hall to another. Families and friends sat together, the room full of conversation. Children ran up and down between the tables, laughing and playing, ignoring their dinners, or claiming to have already finished them.

Alix, Felix, Wick, Jo, and Sora sat at the far end of an otherwise empty table. Their dinner wasn't exactly as carefree and chatty as everyone else's, especially Jo, who had no interest in talking to anyone. Sora knew better than to try to force her sister into feeling any differently. *She would come around. Jo needed to be mad every now and then,* she thought.

Eyes around the room sent glances their way, and some lingered longer on Felix. He wasn't uncomfortable with the looks, as most were not hostile, but merely curious. Several small children hovered nearby, studying him. His smooth head shimmered under the lamp lights in the hall, and his own inner lights moved and glowed just beneath his silvery membrane. He smiled gently at anyone who met his eyes.

Alix ate furiously until her plate was as clean as it began. Wick sat like a satisfied ibi that just cleaned out its trough. Sora didn't feel too hungry and only nibbled, her mind in deep thought. Sim came up to them, and Sora's eyes widened when she noticed. Cleaned up and wearing a simple floor-length tunic, Sim greeted their guests.

"So good to meet you! I hope you enjoyed your meals," she said after Sora went around and introduced each of her "friends" in turn. When Sim reached Alix, she lingered in a delicate handshake and glanced down to Sora with a knowing smirk.

"My compliments to the cooks!" Wick said.

"I came to tell you that your friends here can stay in Merian and Cooper's new out building. They've been working on it for Cooper's mother, who is getting up there, and their boys are also getting older. They'll swap places, the boys taking Cooper's mother's house, and Cooper's mother being a little closer, where Cooper can care for her."

Sora nodded along, her eyebrows raised as high as they would go, waiting for Sim to finish. Suddenly, the woman realized she was rambling and giving away far more information than needed. She waved her hands dismissively, catching herself in a runaway thought.

"Sorry about that. Anyway, Sora can show you where they live, and you can take your things there. We've already set up cots inside, but I'm afraid there are no other furnishings yet."

"It will do just fine," Alix said.

"Good to meet you!" Sim waved and left.

"So, what do you do for fun around here?" Alix asked, her arms folded on the table.

The question caught Sora off-guard, and she mumbled and stuttered. "It's just Jo and I, we usually read and work in the shop, I guess. Take stirrol rides."

"How about tonight?"

Sora looked around the table. "What do you mean?"

"Do you want to take a ride tonight?" Alix bobbed her head with each word.

"Oh, you mean all of us?"

"Count me out," Jo said.

Felix smiled and shook his head "no thanks." He knew that Alix wanted to go alone with Sora, and Sora was too afraid and nervous to admit she wanted to go as well, just the two of them. Wick started to say it sounded like a lovely idea, but Felix kicked him under the table, and Wick coughed and changed his tune. Felix rubbed his hand on Alix's back.

"You two should still go if your leg is alright with another ride."

"It's fine," Alix dismissed his concern, although it was just for show.

"I would love to walk around the village," Felix added. "This place is very peaceful, very kind."

Sora was proud that Felix took an interest in her home and judged it so positively. She looked at Alix and then averted her gaze when their eyes met. Looking down at the table, her eyes drifted back up just a little to Alix's arms, one atop another, her long fingers tapping. Wick cleared his throat and spun around on the bench to stand up.

"I shall retire for a smoke," he spoke with what he believed to be a refined and gentlemanly accent.

Jo got up with her plate without saying a word, much to Sora's disappointment. Felix kissed Alix on the cheek and dismissed himself, eager to take that walk in the cool night.

Sora led her stirrol with a hand on the bridle, she on its left, Alix on the animal's right. They walked for some time across the village, westward, in silence, each waiting for the other to speak. At the edge of town, Sora tossed the reins over the stirrol's long neck and climbed into the saddle. Alix put a foot in the stirrup, grimacing at the pain in her other leg. Sora offered her hand, and Alix smiled as she took it and swung herself into the saddle behind Sora. With a whisper and click of her tongue, Sora commanded the stirrol forward, and it gracefully moved toward the chis grass around the village. The panicles were not yet opened and rubbed against Alix's feet and knees as the stirrol gently moved. They rode west, and Alix thought of the river away on their left, hidden only behind the hillocks that rolled along beside it. The leafy tips of burrey trees could be seen over the hills. Blue and purple shadows spread over the valley.

The stirrol shook its slender neck and head as the chis grass tickled its snout. Stirrols were adapted well for the valley, their necks able to see over the height of the grass, and their strong back legs could send them bounding through in great leaps to avoid predators. The people of the valley domesticated the stirrol, but many wild herds still roamed the land. Alix always liked their gentle nature, though she rarely had need for one of her own. Sora had been raised on them. She barely had to hold the reins in her hands to stay in control. Alix could tell Sora and this stirrol knew one another well. It even seemed like the stirrol knew exactly where they were heading. Alix held onto Sora's waist as they moved in the saddle. The stirrol disturbed a flock of shins that flapped their wings and flew up over the chis, and Alix's heart fluttered away with them.

"Does the stirrol have a name?" Alix said, her lips near to Sora's ear.

"Rey."

"I've never owned a stirrol. Never really needed one."

"Rey and I have been together for almost my whole life. I don't like to think that I *own* her. She and I are equals."

"Right, I didn't mean to—" Alix was embarrassed.

"It's okay. I wasn't accusing you," Sora laughed. "Rey and I come out here almost every night. I love the valley most at night."

"Why?"

"Because it's cool and quiet, and I love the dark shadows and purple fog. And you can see the stars."

"Have you ever been up there?"

"No."

"I gotta say, I'm having a hard time saying it's more beautiful than down here right now."

Alix felt Sora laugh. She pressed her cheek to Sora's back and felt the rhythm of the stirrol's gait move them. Alix closed her eyes and smelled Sora's hair and clothing: a cool breeze on a summer day, with the distant scent of flowers carried on the wind. Alix felt them climb a hill and then Sora halted Rey at the top. The hill was bald, with the chis only growing up around it, leaving it as a fair vantage point for kilometers all around them.

"Here we are," Sora said.

Alix leaned away from her so Sora could dismount. Alix jumped down gingerly, and Sora let Rey wander freely, though the stirrol didn't move much besides dropping its long neck and snout to the short grass to eat. They stood by one another, looking out across the valley toward the horizon.

"When I was young, I started coming here, counting the stars. It was after my pop told me that some people lived out there. I couldn't believe it."

They sat in the soft grass, barely a space between them, but the distance still felt like a whole kilometer to Sora. She wanted to lean toward Alix, press their shoulders together, but they sat like two magnets with the same pole, some invisible force keeping them apart.

"Where are your parents?" Alix said.

Sora hung her head. "They died when I was young. Jo barely knew them."

"I'm sorry." Alix regretted the question. The distance felt further now.

"So, what about yours?" Sora said in return, unable to think of something else to say.

Alix laughed awkwardly. "Well, I, uh, don't have any parents."

Sora's head snapped around giving Alix a puzzled stare. "What are you, a sentient?"

"No, no, definitely not." It was Alix's turn to avoid looking Sora in the eyes. She stared up at the stars, thinking she could see through time and space, back to that place, that horrible place. "It's called the Cradle. Xypha built it, and it's where I was *created*, I guess."

Sora couldn't manage a word. She was so filled with confusion, pity, horror, and a remote anger.

"See, the thing Xypha needs most of all, is workers, people who make it possible for an infinite expansion across planets. It's kind of difficult to depend on nature for that, so they...engineer us."

"Are...are you serious?" Sora instantly regretted her own question, but how else could she respond to such incomprehensible information?

"I definitely am," Alix gently laughed to ease the tension. "I don't even know how it works, but Felix told me they create labor supply through artificial growth and DNA manipulation. Also, rich people can *design* their ideal children this way."

"Were you a…labor person, or a rich child…person?" Sora stammered through the right words to say, then immediately kicked herself.

"I don't know." Alix shrugged. "But," Alix sighed heavily, "when I was created, it was not *this* body I was created in."

Sora watched Alix's face contort, twist itself in pain, fighting back tears, and a lifetime of hurt and fear. She put her hand on Alix's back to soothe her, to say, *it's okay*.

"I was created to be a man," Alix said. "But that was not me. Always, there was the feeling they had made a mistake. I would stare at myself in the mirror as a kid, and I didn't believe the reflection I saw."

"That must have been hard to process," Sora said.

"Yes, but…" Alix wiped a tear running down her face. "I escaped. I became me."

"I'm glad that *you* are here."

Alix's hands shook, and she continued crying silently. She glanced over at Sora and saw the sadness on her face.

"I'm sorry. I didn't mean to upset you," Sora said.

"It's okay. I wanted you to know."

Sora smiled and looked down at her legs crossed in the grass. Her heart went aloft, and her hands felt clammy as she swelled with a childlike anxiety. She felt confused and fought against the urges to kiss Alix.

"How'd you meet Felix?" Sora said.

"Now, that is a story worth telling." Alix laughed for real. "We met on Corto." Alix smiled, remembering that disgusting, dark, muddy fighting pit.

"I know that one; that's the nearest planet to us."

"Yeah, compared to Celestine, it sucks. Very dark and dirty."

"So, how did you meet?"

"I was a fighter, and Felix approached me after a fight, invited me to have a drink."

"A *fighter*?" Sora said.

"One of the best." Alix elbowed Sora, and Sora put a hand over her mouth to hide her laughter. "That's how I got the *Shadow*."

"That's your ship?"

"Yeah…" Her voice trailed away as she stared across the valley, now completely bathed in moonlight. She began the story, feeling warm and comforted again.

* * *

Many years ago...

Like everything on Corto, the room was dirty, disgusting, and loud. But Alix shut out all the noise, a smile on her bruised, dirt-smeared face. She danced around in the pit, which by this time of the night was becoming a mudhole. Ale, chisik, spit, blood, and worse ran into the ring from everywhere around them, the old walls rotting away from the bottom, barely holding up. Her fists were cracked open, though most of the blood on them was from her opponent, a man almost three times her size. She had forgotten his name. His left eye was swollen shut. Mud and blood caked his loose shirt, the original color long lost. Even the v-shaped stain of water poured down his bald head and sponged on his face to clean his cuts didn't reveal its original color; it simply stained it a horrid brownish pink.

He lumbered in clumsily and swung a heavy right. Alix ducked and backed away from his stumbling momentum, which carried him into the wall. A gleeful shout from the crowd came as he tried to steady himself. Out of the corner of her eye, she caught a glimpse of Spiros, standing with his arms crossed beneath a hoverlamp. He shot her a look and shook his head like a disappointed father. She winked in return.

The momentary lapse of focus nearly found her clocked by the man's left, but she could feel it coming, bending backward far enough to just avoid the haymaker. It was all he had left. She sensed the wall behind her, stepped aside as he came forward, then put a rapid set of jabs into his ribs, at least two broken. She drove her heel into the back of his knee, and he dropped into the muck, gasping for air. Alix moved around him, leapt, and delivered a final blow to his orbital bone. It fractured, and he fell face first with a heavy thud. The room filled with the deafening screams of winners and losers.

Alix stood in the ring, her chest heaving beneath a tight tank top stained with the man's blood. *Another one down,* she thought—about the tank top. Medics rushed in to wake the man and check on his wounds. Alix stepped past them and into her corner, removing tape from her wrists and hands. Several spectators filed by, giving her slaps on the shoulder and calls, whether thrilled that they had won again betting on Spiros's best fighter or furious that the giant of a man couldn't beat a five-foot-nine, 180-pound *woman.* Either way, she smiled through catching her breath, balling up the tape and tossing the balls into a metal waste can that usually held bloody towels and waste. She picked up a sort of clean towel from the bench outside the wall and wiped the sweat and dirt from her face as Spiros approached through the crowd of spectators.

"I told you not to play with them like that," he said.

"What?" Alix replied through the towel over her face. She dropped the towel and smiled. "People expect a show, right?"

Spiros tried to keep a stoic face. He turned his attention to his large, hairy arm and the syncpad on his wrist. He watched the accounts fluctuate as they paid out winners and absorbed the hard-earned credits of the losers. Alix awaited her twenty-percent cut.

Now that the crowd was almost gone, a huge sentient approached them. He wore a weathered black hat pushed back on his head revealing his deep blue eyes, a clean white shirt, sleeves rolled up to his elbows, and a black vest. Alix looked up at him, her eyes wide. Spiros looked at the sentient cautiously.

"Can I help you, big fella?" Spiros said.

"Nice fight," the sentient said to Alix.

"Thanks. You got next?" Alix flexed her bravado and sized him up.

The sentient held back a smile. Alix knew a sentient of his size could hardly move around in the mud pit with another fighter.

"No, just wanted to buy you a drink."

Alix thought about the offer and nodded. *Why not?*

"What's my cut, Spiros?"

"Twelve."

"Not bad. Drinks are on you, pal," she said as she hopped over the wall.

She started walking away, tossing a rucksack over her bare shoulder. She raised a hand to wave at Spiros behind her as she walked. "Give me a ping if you need to fill a space."

"I've always got space for you, darlin'!" Spiros called back as she and the sentient walked away, a hoverlamp following them silently.

In the smoky haze of a nearby saloon, Alix threw back drink after drink while the sentient kept buying. After she rapidly finished off the third, she raised an eyebrow. "What's your name?"

"Felix."

"Well, Felix, it was nice to meet you, but unfortunately, Spiros don't let sentients and humans fight. The odds don't ever make financial sense."

"I wasn't interested in a fight," Felix smiled.

"Good, 'cause you'd lose." Alix finished a fourth drink and looked at Felix sideways. This sentient was one of the biggest beings she'd ever seen, but she had to keep up her defenses. Besides, playing hard to get couldn't hurt.

"Is that right?"

"Haven't you heard? I'm the best around."

"I've seen you many times," Felix admitted.

Alix saw his eyes rapidly spin and look down at the bar. She hadn't spoken to many sentients since she'd been on Corto, and even fewer after she was *her*self. But in the moment, she could read Felix's embarrassment at admitting that he'd been watching her fights. Perhaps he'd just now worked up the courage to speak to her. Alix laughed at the thought—a sentient who could probably rip a man in half afraid to talk to a *girl*.

Now...

Back in the valley, Sora laughed boisterously as Alix relayed the story. Sora wasn't sure which parts, if any, were true and which parts she embellished, but Alix insisted on the truth of it. This woman, who was a bit smaller in build than Sora was the best bare-knuckle fighter on Corto? It beggared belief, but Sora didn't care even if Alix *was* lying. She felt even more attracted to Alix's confidence, the swagger that surrounded that wounded, crying girl from minutes before. It made sense to Sora that someone like that would hone her technique, become tough as nails. *Who else was going to protect that girl inside?*

"So, you two are, uh—" Sora awkwardly began.

"Partners? *In love?*" Alix leaned in and gave Sora a playful elbow. "Yes, we are. But we are not limited to each other."

"I see."

They shared a long, deep stare, their bodies drawn in, and it felt like they would collide.

Night in the village became a pleasant glow of fire and old hoverlamps. A pleasant aroma filled the town from the meeting house and individual cabins around it. The smell of baked twi-fruit, boiling broths, roasting bellroots, minlots, burrey seeds, and flame-grilled couley meats held back the oncoming chill of night. The moons rose into the sky over the village, the chis grass swayed in the wind and a purple haze hung over the twilight orchard. Felix couldn't believe the swirl of smells, sounds, and sights, seemingly lifting him on a pleasant wind, making him feel as weightless as zero gravity.

This place is like a dream. It's quiet and the people are kind. Could we have a life like this? he wondered. The thought of Alix on a piece of farm equipment made him laugh, but the thought of feeling the dirt, the bark of trees, the skin of a twi-fruit, made him smile and dream. *There is great reward in helping things grow.* The thought was a far cry from where he began all those centuries ago.

There was no possible future in which he and Alix could live in a place like this or have a life this quiet—not with Xypha around. There was no reason in hoping. He came back to reality. Alix would get the *Shadow* and get off-world as quickly as possible. The more he looked out over the twilight orchard and the bright moon, the purple fog in between, he knew a time would come when they couldn't look out over such expanses. Xypha would sniff them out. His code proximity and Alix's DNA would give them away. They'd be hunted.

Xypha would ravage this world, like so many others. The natural world would bend and break beneath the machine, the *need* for more, the insatiable pursuit of power and meaningless wealth. *What does Xypha want here?* Felix asked himself. *There must be more to it than fruits and grains.*

Late in the night, Alix tip toed into the bare cabin provided by Sim to her and Felix. Wick had been given one to himself. *Thankfully,* Alix thought. She pulled off her shirt and pants and climbed into the narrow cot next to Felix. She instantly felt his currents rise and his awareness travel back to the present. A possibility danced through her mind, an allure of home, safety, and beauty. She loved the life she and Felix built together, moving back and forth between Corto and Celestine. The *Shadow* had always been their home, a home they chose, one that went with them. *Could they make a new life, here? Could home be a wide, beautiful valley, instead of the cold, hard bulkhead of a ship?*

Alix stared at the wood beams and gables that held up the roof of the cabin. Everyone had been right, and Felix barely fit on the narrow bed, but as he lay on his side, he silently laid his large hand over Alix's bare stomach.

"Do you want to stay here?" he said.

"Would you stay?" Alix could see him leaning over her, his eyes dimmed, but still bright in the darkness.

"I would never leave you," Felix replied. "My home is wherever you are."

Alix gripped one of his large fingers in her hand. "I'm afraid."

"We have much to fear, but look at what we have here—to fight for."

Alix put her left hand behind her head as Felix laid his palm up and she rested her right hand within it.

"All my life, I've been running. Maybe it is time to stop."

9

The Deal

Rotation 23...

Otto sat in a white chair attached to the bulkhead of the Xypha waystation by a long, mechanical arm. His feet rest comfortably in individual footrests attached to the chair. With the control panel in front of him, also attached to the chair, he could move his seat over a wide nerve center in the ship. Everything around him was stark white or a pale gray. Men and women sat at their stations around the room, and below his feet lay the planet Celestine. Half of the nerve center floor was a massive, curved piece of glass. Otto suspended his chair over the window, looking at the display projected on it that only he could see, being the lead forward officer, and having the projection calibrated only for his neural implant.

He ran through the calculations again and again. Silas claimed to have the situation in Verisport under control. *Under control*, Otto scoffed. The council in Verisport had denied their landing in its much larger spaceport. The people in charge in White Sands were far more amenable to Xypha's presence if it meant enriching a small few. Silas was charged to deliver Verisport to him, open its spaceport for business. That was the deal, but Otto remained skeptical that the man could deliver.

They'd been over the planet for *weeks*. Otto was behind schedule, an unacceptable reality. So, he issued the order: drop ships would begin landing at White Sands immediately. They had a fleet of twelve ships, and more than seven hundred tons of cargo. Omniite, fabricators, engines, ground vehicles, food and water, tools, clothing, computers, fuel, furniture, weapons, and of course, a crew of six hundred and twenty-two. With only three drop ships able to use the port at a time, it would take days to offload everything. There was no longer time to wait.

"Drop-72, begin your departure," Otto ordered, speaking aloud to no one in his presence but knowing his voice carried through his neural implant and the station's communication systems to the drop ship's pilot.

"This is Drop-72. We are clear for departure."

Otto watched the rectangular ship emerge from beyond the window's field of view and nose down toward the planet. It entered the atmosphere at a gentle angle, then turned and descended sharply back toward the surface. He watched the complex systems within the station monitor the ship and crew's every possible signal, from an engine to a heartbeat.

"Drop-35, prepare for departure," Otto said.

"This is Drop-35. Engines are square, preparing for departure," came the pilot's voice in return.

The first ships carried necessary supplies to construct their own offices at the White Sands shipyard. Soon, it would be the only relevant office, but the locals didn't need to know that. In the meantime, Xypha promised omniite upgrades to the shipyard, hardware, and programming improvements, all under a symbiotic façade.

"Drop-35, begin your departure."

"This is Drop-35; cleared for departure."

A second drop ship glided through the space between the station and the planet. The ship's hull lit bright red, orange, and then the white heat of reentry. Otto checked the time on his control panel: two minutes, seventeen seconds behind schedule for the day. He rubbed his hand down his face and groaned. Impatiently, he called out to the final ship.

"Drop-19, you are cleared for departure."

Rotation 679...

Otto sat at the desk he'd brought with him on this expedition from

Thuli. Made of fine seronia wood, the white desk contrasted with the deep, red hue of the carpeting. The walls were smooth omni, coated white. Behind Otto, a window stretched from one end of the office to another, looking out at the curvature of Celestine below, the darkness of space everywhere else. Everything in the forward officer's stateroom reminded him of home—fine sofas, a wide bed, the finest art from Thuli's present nouveau movement, bottles of aged wine. Of course, no one else on the ship was allowed such luxuries.

Most of the ship's crew were now planetside, performing work in and around White Sands. They'd constructed the rail line by Rotation 478, a little behind schedule. The improvements to White Sands' pitiful shipyard were in progress, turning what was once just a three-pad facility into twice that size. Otto reviewed notes and reports on all projects underway, projections for the future. He drank a sip of red Moullivet as he stared at the glass screen above the desk.

Even whiter than the desk was his Xypha-standard slipsuit. Unlike when he worked in view of his inferiors, now, the collar was unclasped and loosened. Stubble began to return by this late hour, and he would need another shave to keep up acceptable appearances. But for now, he was alone and enjoyed the peace and quiet. He scratched at the edge of the sleek neural implant above his left ear. On the screen in front of him, a map of the planet focused on latitudes below the Isidis Valley. The high desert and rocky canyons created a difficult challenge before the planet's equator. With only his thoughts, he instructed the ship's computer to calculate and show the best course through the difficult terrain.

A transmission interrupted the view on the screen, much to Otto's annoyance. With a wave of his hand, Otto swept the map off the screen, then pulled the transmission alert down. With another motion of his hand, it filled the screen, connecting his private frequency to that of Silas Purvida. Otto twisted his face into displeasure and interlaced his fingers.

"What is it, Silas?"

"Did I catch you at a bad time?" Silas said.

Otto was not in the mood for any meaningless jousting. "Get on with it."

"Well, as you know, the marshal is looking into the killings of those four engineers of yours. I believe I've got him on the right trail that will jeopardize his position."

"You *believe*?" Otto was not impressed.

"The woman and artie I roped into the job? Turns out they're personal friends of the marshal. My man dug up some background on them. They're pilot and copilot of a light freighter that's grounded in Verisport. Didn't want to pay your contract fees."

"This is all very fascinating, Silas, but I fail to see why this call is warranted."

Silas shifted in his seat and cleared his throat. "You may need to meet with the council."

"They are welcome to call."

"In person," Silas clarified.

Otto curled his lip and turned up his nose. Going down to the planet surface did *not* appeal to him in any way. He'd been only once since arriving here. The air was not to his liking, the heat, the smells, the people. Everything about the place disgusted him.

"Why should I appear in person?"

"Showing up to the council to voice your displeasure would go a long way to spooking them into action."

Silas had a subtle smirk on his face, and his tone of voice hinted that he enjoyed that Otto had to come down from his *perch*. Otto was sure his physical presence was unnecessary, and that Silas only suggested it to make Otto uncomfortable. The man got under Otto's skin, like dirt under his fingernails. *That* thought almost made Otto gag.

"What is the likelihood this woman and artificial would be apprehended? I thought your people were going to take care of them, to ensure the marshal could never complete his duties?"

"Yes, well," Silas obviously searched for a way to cover his tracks, "my men are on their trail. They have not yet returned to Verisport, that much is clear."

"It takes one conversation with the marshal to jeopardize *our* deal."

"Which is why we need his feet to the fire, and why you need to come down here and hold them to it."

Otto rolled his eyes and let out a sigh so Silas could hear how upset he was. "I will be down tomorrow."

"Looking forward to—" Silas said with a wry smile.

Otto swiped away the call from his screen, cutting Silas off before his last word. He sat for a moment, thinking, tapping a finger on the white wood surface. Then, he swept his hand back in front of the screen and manipulated truncated folders until he brought up a beacon signal. He periodically checked the signal since he had his engineers killed. Every few hours, he sent a ping to the missing implant, stolen from the engineers' drop ship. The implant would power on long enough to receive and return the signal, a few seconds, and then return to its dormant state. It remained in a small farming village in the valley.

Whoever had possession of the implant clearly did not know what they had, and moreover, did not know how to connect to the implant. He stared across the room, tapping his finger on his bottom lip. If he revealed this information to the council, he could convince them that the murderers came from this village and stole tech from the drop ship. *Perhaps there is an opportunity there for more pressure on the marshal*, he wondered.

Rotation 680…

That Otto descended from the Xypha station to Verisport caused quite a stir among the council members, as intended. Three of the seven council members were there to greet Otto as he walked off the ship, straightening his pristine white shirt, gold buttons up the left side of his chest, collar tight around his neck. Four old men stood together, waiting on him. The marshal was one of them, while the other three were council members: Harold Volster, Clarence Nord, and "Dell" Plainview.

Two men followed Otto off the ship as his security. Otto looked bothered, annoyed; annoyed at the smell of fuel and oil, annoyed at the heat, annoyed that he was even *here* doing this legwork. The day was cool for any Celestinian, but Otto was used to the cold, filtered, recycled air of living in space. He'd lived on Thuli for years before finally reaching a point in his career that he was assigned a true job as a forward officer, but really, it was nothing more than being a gopher for other, older men in the rings around Thuli.

He'd dreamt of seeing the worlds Xypha had colonized, where Man had extended his reach to places far beyond. In reality, he sat in an office waiting. Xypha had, in many ways, exacerbated its reach. No new planet had been colonized in Otto's lifetime, despite the constant talk and planning of such an act. Then, he received a message, and that changed. Celestine was the target, and he was charged with paving the way. That mission proved more irritating than he could possibly have imagined.

As the dusty, thick air entered his lungs, Otto coughed. He put a pristine white handkerchief to his mouth and nose as he shook hands with the four men waiting outside his ship. They all voiced pleasantries, formalities, and Otto tuned them out entirely. The marshal's gaze lingered on him, and Otto registered the suspicion. The man knew Otto and Silas cornered him, but he had little power to prevent it. Still, Otto remained on his toes.

The air inside didn't offer much relief. The council chamber lay on the fourth level within the large complex around the flight tower. The council dais curved around one end of the room, two men and two women already seated in their respective places. The three who greeted Otto went to their seats, and Otto stood alone, hands behind his back, before the dais.

"Ladies and gentlemen," he began. "I am here to express my displeasure with the execution of justice in this land. The marshal has brought no news of those responsible for the murder of six Xypha engineers, a loss that we will not tolerate without fair compensation."

"Mr. Otto, I have been assured Marshal Rayburn is doing everything within his power to find the guilty parties," Madeline, one of the council members, spoke.

"With all due respect, councilwoman, as Xypha's representative in this system, I must reiterate the company's position that *any* hostilities towards our workers, our *property*, will be handled by local jurisdictions, up until local authorities have demonstrated an incompetence that prevents Xypha from obtaining justice and compensation for its losses. I deem that demonstration to be now, at present."

The council members exchanged confused glances. They understood that Otto's words were a clear threat, but the council had no strategy prepared for such a demand. Marshal Rayburn spoke up for them, as he often had to do.

"Council, if I may. I believe there is more to this than Otto wishes to tell." The council gave the marshal their attention, deferring to his authority. Even if the sun was setting on his legacy, they still respected it.

"At the scene, I picked up many signs that this attack was not just some revenge killing, but a calculated maneuver. Investigating such a thing takes time, and careful consideration."

Otto narrowed his eyes at the marshal, who stood off to his left. The marshal suspected Silas, and possibly even Otto, but of course, he had no proof of such a thing. Otto had the ammunition to undermine this accusation.

"Tell me, marshal, what suspects do you consider?"

The marshal shifted his weight, easing the pain in his amputated limb. The council eagerly awaited his response. "Right now, I have reason to believe Silas Purvida may have had a hand in this." He said it with such hesitation, it was clear he was not eager to make the claim and had nothing to back it up, other than his gut feeling and Silas's reputation.

The council's response was a mix of surprise, fear, and skepticism. Harold, who had to climb out of Silas's pocket to attend any council meetings, scoffed at the idea. The marshal waited for the councilman's admonishment, but Otto interrupted.

"I am skeptical of such a claim. In my internal review, I have evidence that points elsewhere."

"One second, Otto. What are you basing this accusation upon, marshal?" Harold Volster spoke up.

"What I know is that a man known to be in Silas's employ was at the scene. Silas claims he was out there *before* the crime was committed."

"Yes, Silas and I have arrangements for security. Needless to say, security offered by the marshal and his men does not have my confidence," Otto said.

"What evidence do you have, Otto?" Nelson pressed the issue, as he'd been coached to do.

"We have seen this sort of thing before," Otto began. "Many artificials remain hostile to our presence, even if their ties to Xypha's past are minimal. Satellite photos of the scene indicate an artificial took part in this."

"Council, I still believe the orchestrater of this crime should be held responsible, not just those who did the killing," the marshal tried to interject.

"Well, marshal, let's start with the ones who pulled the triggers," Nelson said impatiently. "If one of those folks wants to implicate someone else, then we will hear the case."

"I have a lead that may aid the marshal's efforts," Otto smiled. "Some equipment was also stolen from the engineers' drop ship. Now, I have triangulated the stolen equipment's location to a farmstead, less than a kilometer from the scene of the crime. I will gladly turn over this location to the marshal so that he may accelerate his investigation."

The marshal glared at Otto, knowing he had no choice but to accept the overture. The council seemed to think this was a great idea, their nods and murmurs pleased with cooperation between the two parties. The marshal forced the most pained, insincere smile Otto had ever seen.

"I will check it out," Rayburn said.

"Then if this matter is not concluded within the next three rotations, I shall return and seek even greater restitution." Otto bowed and walked out of the chamber, his two security officers opening the door for him.

"Otto!" the marshal's voice carried down the corridor.

Otto paused and turned on his boot heel. The security officers flanking him were on alert, the marshal red in the face. "Yes, marshal?"

"Why didn't you share that information with me when we spoke earlier?"

"It was not information I had at the time. It takes some time to perform an internal review and inventory of the drop ship."

"I would appreciate the location now."

"Certainly." Otto nodded and smiled. He withdrew a datapad the size of his palm from his pocket. With a few taps and swipes, he looked up and put the pad away. "All done."

The marshal looked down at the syncpad on his left arm and saw the pinned location in the valley.

"Now, if you will excuse me, I would really like to get back to my station."

Otto buckled himself into the jump seat while the pilots prepared to take off and brought up a connection to Silas. The man was in his saloon, not his office, as evidenced by the background of liquor bottles on shelves.

"We should be able to move forward in three rotations. I gave the marshal a lead to follow," Otto said.

"What lead?"

"Some of our tech was stolen from the drop ship, and it appears to be at a farmstead near the rail line. From what you've indicated, it's land you own."

"Send it to me," Silas requested.

Otto sent the same map ping to Silas that he'd given the marshal earlier. Silas, his projection above Otto's syncpad, looked down at the map just out of Otto's display.

"Yeah, I know it," Silas confirmed. "There's nobody there who would be a problem. Probably just someone scavenging."

"Whether the marshal finds our tech or not, I do plan to retrieve what is ours."

"Be my guest!" Silas clearly did not care at all about this farming village.

The drop ship began to shake. Otto unceremoniously killed the transmission before they began to break out of the atmosphere. Another reason Otto hated going to the surface: his stomach refused to adjust to the changes in G-forces as the ship escaped Celestine's atmosphere. He could see out of a window across from him, the entire field of vision black, a haze of light below them from the planet.

The drop ship approached the station, finding the open docking bay on the underside of the hull. Otto tried to steady himself and his stomach as the ship's gravity shifted and he fluctuated between slight weightlessness to the autogravity generated by the station's power core. Otto waited until the drop ship engines hummed down to silence before he unbuckled himself from the seat. It took a moment to readjust, but he smoothed his jacket before leaving the ship.

Silas leaned an elbow on the bar holding a glass of chisik. Not only did he just learn of the stolen Xypha technology, but Harold had also updated him on the council decisions from the meeting with Otto. Possibilities ran through Silas's head, thinking of the farming village, Harold's growing list of demands and false security. He downed the glass in his hand and clapped it back on the bar. The councilman was eager to improve his position, and although he did whatever Silas told him to do, it was clear Harold began to think of himself as more than an instrument. Harold was a fly who would need to be swatted the more of a nuisance he became.

But Silas dwelled on the farmstead, a village on land once owned by his father, one that lost land allotted to them when Xypha built its rail line. Of course, Silas split the parcels deliberately, creating opportunities to put more paying tenants on the open spaces. Generations of his family before him had once toiled that land themselves. Back then, the first ships landed in the grass around the small central cluster of tent buildings and framework for permanent structures. The settlers had nothing but the moons, the stars, and the great chis grass sea.

Silas had rejected his family's history, its toil and meagerness. He couldn't care less what Verisport had once been. He only cared about what it could be, and whether he would be seated at the head of the table. Xypha would bring people, wealth, and power to Celestine, and if he was not careful, that wealth and power would slip through his fingers.

He'd pressured the council through his various associates, but the marshal's legacy and his family's reputation still held greater sway. Silas felt as though he approached the twilight of the marshal's time, but it may take a stronger push. Otto expected to *own* the port in the end. It would take more than one hundred thousand crits to make that happen. Bribes could only take him so far. Fear would be an even greater motivator. Violence in the valley was one thing, but disruption and violence in Verisport itself would press the council into action. People would seek a stronger hand—his hand—to guide them.

10

The Splinter

Alix and Sora lay beneath the tree shaker, arms up, awkwardly twisting and reaching, wrenches in-hand. The wrench slipped off a bolt and out of Alix's hand, clattering against the metal and almost hitting her in the face. She growled and cursed while Sora laughed beside her. Jo cracked a smile at her workbench.

Sitting down the bench from Jo, Felix leaned over a small capacitor. His eyes scanned and sliced the capacitor into a three-dimensional render. He identified the problem, the quartz matrix had been knocked out of its housing. Jo and Sora had been trying to put it back into place without taking the capacitor apart entirely. Felix picked up a pair of scrits with his large fingers and reached inside the matrix, delicately moving, holding the crystal in place. With a small jolt from the scrit, the crystal spun, and the matrix energized around it. Felix sat back and handed the capacitor over to Jo.

"Piece of cake," he said.

Jo took the octagonal capacitor, turning it over in her hands. Her demeanor thawed—she liked that Felix was so quiet and calm. She felt comforted by his presence. As he smiled, lights in his face seemed to grow brighter around his cheeks.

"Thanks," Jo said.

"Happy to help."

"I'm sorry for how I've been acting," she admitted at last. She looked down at the capacitor in her hands, feeling guilty.

"It's okay. We are all pretty defensive. Alix and I keep our guards up a lot, too."

"She and my sister seem to like one another." Jo set the capacitor on the bench.

"Does that bother you?"

"No, well, I mean, it's just always been me and Sora. No one has ever come between us."

"I assure you that's not Alix's intention. You two have more in common than you think."

"Me and Alix?" Jo looked surprised.

Felix chuckled. "Oh yes. You both have a fire, and you keep it locked up tight. But often, that only means it puts more pressure on you, and when it finds release, it can be dangerous."

Jo looked at him sideways and sarcastically said, "You make that sound so positive."

"Like most things, it can be, or it could be harmful. Harnessing that fire and pointing it in the right direction is the real skill."

"So, who is Alix directing her fire at?"

Felix paused. "Anyone who threatens what she loves."

Suddenly, his mood shifted. He narrowed his eyes and looked around the shop and listened. Jo couldn't hear anything unusual except the sounds of Alix and Sora working beneath the shaker, but fear swept through her seeing someone like Felix change in an instant. She could see his walls go up: something had alarmed him.

"What's wrong?" she asked him.

Felix held up a hand. Jo went silent. But it wasn't a sound that Felix detected—it was a pulse he felt deep in his body. The pulse came in a familiar rhythm. He quickly spun through the archives of his memory, searching for pattern recognition. Another pulse. This one was close by, and it seemed to mirror the rhythm of the first, almost like a reply. Felix stood, and Jo stared wide-eyed at him, shaking with fear. He looked through the walls, the machinery, every surface, and finally, through the floor. That's where he found it.

With a grave look, he turned to Jo, looming over her. He tried to remain calm, but in this moment, he feared the worst. *Had they been drawn here on purpose?*

"What? What is it?" Jo asked, genuinely confused and afraid.

Felix whispered so as to not frighten her further. "There is Xypha tech here."

"What are you talking about?" Jo shook her head.

"Where is it?" Felix insisted.

Jo raised her voice. "I don't know what you're talking about!"

Alix and Sora slid out from under the shaker, sitting on their respective creepers. They looked at one another, thinking Jo's temper had boiled over. *It wasn't like she'd been a gracious host*, Sora thought. They both stood and saw Felix standing close to Jo, so close that she began to back away. Alix knew that look in Felix's eyes, the language of his body. She snapped her eyes over toward her Plasvelds in her belt hanging on a chair several paces away.

"There is Xypha tech here," Felix said in the exact same tone as before.

Jo looked at Sora, her arms up and out. Alix stepped away from Sora cautiously, toward her Plasvelds. Sora looked at her sympathetically yet defensively.

"Alix, what is he talking about?"

"Drop the act," Alix said, her anger rising. "If Felix says it's here, then it's here."

"Listen, Alix, we aren't doing anything to hurt you two, I promise," Sora pleaded, still unable to admit the truth.

Alix backed further away from Sora. Her mind raced, her heart pounded. *What are they hiding? A trap? Did they connect with Wick to trap us here, at Silas's order? Does Xypha know we're here?* Alix reached a hand behind her, feeling the grip of a Plasveld and pulling it from the holster slowly. She did not raise it, but let it hang at her side.

"Tell me the truth."

Sora's eyes welled with tears. "Alix, please."

"Stop." Alix was on the verge of tears, as if she'd already been shot through the chest.

"Sora, don't!" Jo yelled.

But Sora held up a hand to her sister and sighed. "Okay, beneath the floor."

Felix already knew the tech was there and moved a stained, thin rug with his foot to reveal a hatch. Sora and Alix remained locked into a stare: Alix white hot fury; Sora pleading for her to listen. Felix opened the hatch and pulled the black box out of a dark compartment. They had clearly cut it open and knew what was inside, but Felix guessed Sora and Jo didn't actually *know* what they possessed.

"Where did you get this?" he asked.

"A drop ship, the one out there where you killed those engineers," Sora said.

"Why do you have it?"

"I don't know; I was just picking what I could carry, and what seemed useful!"

Alix glanced at Felix, who looked up to her and nodded, judging the explanation to most likely be true. Felix set the box on the workbench and opened it. The contents were all there, and the implant within the smaller box had not been tampered with. This was the source of the second pulse he'd felt. The first was clearly a signal sent *to* the spare implant from the Xypha station.

"You should not have brought this back here," he said.

"Okay, well, tell me why," Sora insisted.

"It is a repair and replacement kit for the Xypha neural implants. Every crewed ship has them, in case something goes wrong," Felix explained.

"An *implant*? Like, they put this big thing inside them?" Jo was in disbelief.

"It attaches to the skull, and small needles probe into the brain. It allows for surveillance, security, communication, health monitoring, the works."

"How did you know it was here?" Sora said to Felix.

"I picked up a signal sent to it. They know you stole it, and now, they know you have it."

"What does that mean?" Jo asked.

"It means this place is no longer safe for us," Alix said, her voice weighed down by disappointment, a crushing sadness.

"For *any* of us," Felix corrected her.

With a boisterous noise, Wick rushed into the shop. He tried to whisper, even though he'd just burst through the door like a frightened ibi. He obviously had been running and now, he bent over at the waist, trying to catch his breath.

"We've got trouble," he gasped. Wick looked up and saw everyone frozen in place, staring at him, at one another. He could feel the tension in the air. He saw a Plasveld in Alix's hand. "Okay," he drew the word out, "What did I miss?"

"Trouble," Alix snapped.

"Well, you better resolve that shit fast. The marshal's here."

"*The marshal?*" Sora yelled.

She and Jo shared a glance but were unable to move, their minds stuck and indecisive. Alix clicked into a driven, commanding tone. She now had a singular focus.

"Okay, here's what we're going to do. Felix, Wick, and I will head out to the orchard. You can tell the marshal we split, headed west. He's looking for us, *not* you two." Alix picked up her belt and spun the Plasveld on her finger, landing it in the empty holster.

"We'll take the implant with us," Felix said. "That way, Xypha will track us, and once we're remote enough, I will destroy it. They'll have no reason to think it was you who stole it."

"No, Alix." Sora laid a gentle hand on Alix's arm.

"There's no time." Alix pulled away from her and wrapped her belt around her waist. She used buckling the belt as an excuse to not look Sora in the eyes.

Sora was overcome with guilt. *If I hadn't taken that box from the ship… if I had known about Alix's past with Xypha…*she thought. Everything fell back on her. She had no idea how to make this right, other than to let Alix decide the best course of action. Sora felt like a child, standing helplessly while her parents tried to clean up her mess.

Alix slung her rucksack over her shoulder. "Tell him we were here, that we left, you got that?" Alix said.

Sora stood in her way, begging for one last solution. She couldn't manage words, only a somber nod. Jo shut the hatch in the floor and covered it again before she rushed to Sora's side, taking her sister's hand.

"We can handle this," Jo said confidently, but her eyes said, *Get out of here.*

Alix looked down at the young girl and smiled. She was made of steel, or at least she was *becoming* steel. It was like looking into a mirror, reflecting her past self in the correct body.

A heavy fist knocked on the door, and Jo and Sora jumped. Alix and the others fled the shop. Sora cleared her throat and waved Jo away, whispering for her to act normal. When Sora opened the door, the marshal stood with his hands hanging on his belt.

Sora tried to smile or look surprised to see him, even confused. She stammered, "Marshal, what's going on?"

"Can I take a look through your shop and the stables? I'm looking for suspicious persons who may have come through."

With a slight hesitation, Sora backed out of the doorway and waved the marshal inside. The old man walked with a limp, hands on his hips. Jo stood frozen by the workbench. His boots on the stone floor became the only sound in the room as he walked around the shaker, the scanner table, and smiled at Jo as he passed by her. Finally, he pointed up the stairs to their apartment.

"That's our apartment," Sora said. "You can head up there, no problem."

At the top of the stairs, the marshal didn't need to enter the room to conduct a search; plus, he didn't want to disturb anything just yet. The apartment looked like a completely normal place for two sisters who stayed together. He started to turn but hesitated, a familiar set of goggles on the table catching his eye. He said nothing. Sora and Jo watched him turn and walk down the stairs gingerly.

"Well, everything is in order," he said. "If you see someone you don't know around here, please alert me."

Sora hung her head, "I know who you're looking for."

"You do?" He stopped scanning the room and looked surprised.

"They were here two nights ago," Sora spit out, like she expected to have to say something else but changed the words at the last second.

"What happened?"

"We didn't know they were in trouble with you, marshal, I swear," Sora pleaded—Jo thought her sister was putting it on a little thick. "They wanted a place to stay, and well, our village is pretty welcoming."

The marshal rubbed his chin, nodding. "Well, nobody was hurt, I see."

"Of course not! They left, heading west. I don't know where they intended to go."

"Well, I'm glad everyone here is safe. If you see them again, maybe don't let them hang around. And tell your elders to send me a transmission." The marshal tipped his hat, scanning the room one final time. "Alright, thank you. Have a pleasant day."

He left and Sora closed the door behind him. She and Jo rushed to one another, whispering. "What do we do now?" Jo demanded.

"I don't know," Sora told her.

They waited a few minutes before they peeked out of the shop and around the stables. The marshal seemed to have headed back to the meeting house or left the village entirely. They ran out to the orchard, and under the purple shade, they searched for Alix and the others.

"Alix!" Sora said in a loud whisper.

"Over here." Alix walked out from behind a tree.

"He's gone."

"Good. It's time we split, too."

"Wait, this is our fault! If we hadn't taken that Xypha thing—"

"It isn't all our fault! Wick brought them here!" Jo reminded Sora.

"Look, don't worry about it." Alix held up her hands. "Either way, we're leaving. The marshal won't bother you any longer."

"Where will you go?" Sora said.

"I don't know yet. I need to get the *Shadow*, so, we may return to Verisport."

"What if I had a suggestion?" Sora said, and Alix waited for her to continue. "Wick, Jo, and I were planning a robbery."

"Sora!" Jo protested.

"You could get plenty of crits to pay off your debt to get your ship back," Sora continued as she ignored her sister.

"There's no paying to get it back anymore, Sora," Alix said. "The marshal is after us. The dockmaster would turn us in immediately, even if I had the crits to pay the debt."

"So what are you going to do?" Sora's eyes were wet and soft as she tried to keep it together, to keep the feeling stuffed down. She had ruined everything.

"I don't know!" Alix growled, tired of the questions.

"I want to come with you."

Jo couldn't believe what her sister was saying. "Are you crazy?"

"No," Sora snapped. "Alix, I know I screwed this up. I want to help you."

"That's very kind." Alix's voice was distant, and her heart had closed. No matter how much Sora tried, Alix could not find it in herself to soften and reach back. She was driven by self-preservation, a will to survive that had been her only thought for so many years. "Let's go get our stirrols, and then we'll head out," Alix said to Felix.

There was nothing else Sora could say or do. It was over; she'd lost. She wanted to burst into tears. Instead, she followed the others back to the shop, wrestling with herself the entire way. Everyone walked in silence, saddled the stirrols in silence.

As Alix tied her rucksack to the stirrol, she realized her goggles were missing. She headed back into the apartment, and as she picked the goggles up from the table, she took a moment to mourn the idea of living this kind of life. She stared at the bed beneath the windows. *Of course it isn't possible,* she told herself.

When she returned to the stables, Sora had her own stirrol saddled up, a defiant look on her face as she tightened the billet strap.

"Sora, what are you doing?" Alix sighed.

"I'm coming with you," she replied without looking at Alix.

"Sora, no. You have to stay here; you have to stay with your sister."

"Jo can take care of this place. You said it yourself, the marshal won't bother us anymore. We're in no danger."

Jo grabbed her sister by the arm. "Sora, this is not your problem! Stay here, please."

"I'm sorry, Jo," Sora knelt and took her sister's hands. "This is a mess of our own making. I need to make it right."

"You always do this! You try to fix things." Jo began to cry. "Some things you can't fix!"

Sora's lip began to quiver, and she gripped her sister's small hands even tighter. "I will be back, I promise."

With that, Sora walked her stirrol out with Felix and Wick. She led the animal by Alix, keeping her eyes straight ahead, her head high. Alix turned to Jo, who wiped her nose on her sleeve, watching her sister leave.

"I'm sorry, Jo," she began. "I won't let anything happen to her. You have my word."

"If you do, I will kill you," Jo said, trying to steel her voice.

Alix smiled, not laughing at the girl, but admiring her. "I know you, kid."

"No, you *don't*."

Alix held out her hand, offering it for Jo to shake. The girl gripped it, and Alix held on tight. "No one will hurt your sister, and if they do, and you want to kill me, your vengeance will be justified. I would welcome it."

She let go of Jo's hand and led her stirrol toward the orchard. She stepped into one stirrup and swung her leg over the other side. She caught up with the others beneath the twilight canopy.

"Alright, we'll ride west to Burreville and destroy the implant there," Alix said. "We can lose them, then head back to Verisport."

"Maybe while we're out there, we can, you know, make a little money?" Wick spoke up.

"Why am I not surprised?" Alix scoffed.

"All I'm saying is the plan was going to land us two hundred thousand crits."

Alix kept her Solar face, but the amount rang in her ears, an almost incomprehensible number. She shook her head and ignored him. She snapped the reins, and her stirrol leapt and galloped out of the orchard, ahead of the others. Alix stared ahead, grit her teeth, trying to push the myriad of voices out of her mind.

* * *

The sun began to descend in the east toward Verisport. The rays of light through the clouds touched the orchard's treetops. The branches swayed with a gust of wind, revealing the different colors on opposite sides of the leaves, dark green with flashes of pink and purple. The marshal checked his pocket watch, shifting in his saddle atop the stirrol. He stood alone on a ridge north of the village orchard, commanding a clear view of the land west of the line of trees. The metal roof of the shop reflected the low sun.

He went over the encounter in his mind—the young girls in the shop, the respectful village elder with a dignified air, Alix's goggles. He knew them well. He'd seen them on Alix's head every day, back when they were still close enough to speak, much less work together. He remembered how she served as his deputy once she became old enough. He could at least give her targets for her rage, which he had tried to soothe. Over the years, it became clear there was no way he could ease that pain.

Finally, he saw shapes exit the orchard. Through a vizscope he saw four riders: Alix, Felix, Wick, and Sora, galloping westward. He put the scope back in his saddlebag and picked up the reins. With a gentle nudge from his heels, he turned the stirrol west and rode along the ridge.

Deep in the night, Alix and the others camped beneath the stars. The flames of a small fire waved and struggled in the wind as everyone sat back against their saddles, quiet. Felix and Alix sat together, and across from them, Wick and Sora slept. Alix inspected one of her Plasvelds, making sure the cylinder was clean, flipping a plasma charge between her fingers. She clicked it into place, spun the weapon on her trigger finger, switched directions with a flick of her finger, and then turned it horizontal with another spin, finishing with it sliding into the holster.

"I can tell when you're anxious," Felix said.

Alix needed to exercise her restless hands, but Felix wasn't wrong. Her mind wouldn't stop, either. The box sat beside Felix, just in her peripheral vision. She hated having it around, knowing that any minute, Xypha drop ships could come out of the night air. They would be sitting ducks. They were heading into Burreville mainly because nobody there wanted to kill them, but the prospect of two hundred thousand crits kept returning to her.

"Are you not?" Alix finally said.

"Sure," Felix shrugged. "I think we're doing the smart thing, for what it's worth."

"Good, because I feel lost."

"We'll fix this."

Felix smiled at her, his eyes bright like stars, the fire reflecting subtly off his face. His huge arm wrapped around her and squeezed her tight. Alix nestled into him and closed her eyes. Even here, exposed in the valley, the marshal looking for them, Xypha able to find them at any moment, and Silas double crossing them, she felt safe in the space between Felix's arm and chest. Alix felt weak and cornered. She *hated* that feeling. She wanted to do something, anything; she *needed* to do something that made her feel in control.

When Sora awoke, the fire had burned out. The cold air nipped at her neck, and a layer of fog hung in the dell where they'd stayed for the night. She could only see a faint glimpse of the sky through the fog. The ground and the saddle for a pillow may have been the most uncomfortable position in which she'd ever slept. She grimaced as she squirmed under the blanket. When she rolled over onto her left side, she saw Alix.

But Alix was unaware that anyone else lay awake. She had her left foot up on the horn of her saddle, her pale thigh bare against the cold. Guilt diverted Sora's eyes for a moment, but curiosity, and the allure of Alix's skin and the muscles beneath, drew them back. Alix prepared a metal syringe barrel, sliding the needle into her thigh and pressing down the plunger. When Alix looked up, the cap of the needle between her teeth, Sora quickly looked away.

"Good morning," Alix said with her teeth clenched around the cap.

"I'm sorry," Sora said, her voice still raspy from sleep. She cleared her throat.

"Don't worry about it." Alix set the cap back on the needle and removed it from the syringe, stashing it in a bag. She pulled up her pants the rest of the way and buttoned them. "Nowhere to get privacy around here anyway."

Sora sat up and reconfigured the blanket around her shoulders, pulling her legs up to her chest. She looked into the cold soot and charred wood at her feet. A small, crumpled metal fragment stuck out, seared black from the flames. Alix sat down beside her, their hips touching.

"Felix crushed it and burned it last night," Alix said about the Xypha implant.

"So they can't find you anymore?"

"Well, this is where the trail will go cold. Hopefully, nobody picks it up again."

"What if they do?" Sora didn't want to turn her head. She just kept staring at the charred remains.

"Then we will make them regret it." Alix's voice was cold and serious.

Sora did not doubt her.

"My parents didn't die from sickness," she said. "Silas and his family have owned our land since even before Sim was born. Men have always come to collect taxes and payments for us being there. Sometimes, they have been violent. I don't know why, but one day, there was a fight, and…" Her voice reduced to a hoarse whisper, and she caught the last words in her throat. "Both of my parents were killed."

"I'm sorry, Sora," Alix said.

"I am so sorry for putting you in danger. If I had known—"

"Don't worry about it. You didn't know. But now, we keep moving forward."

Sora rested her chin on her knees. Even now, she felt distance between them. The words hadn't yet sunken in; it would take time to heal, for the defenses to drop again.

Alix laid her hand on the blanket over Sora's knees then stood and walked back toward her saddle and the stirrols grazing nearby. She hefted the saddle up and slung it over onto the back of her stirrol. It didn't even lift its head from the grass below, its lips reaching out, teeth grabbing and ripping. After cinching the billet straps, she ran her hand gently along the stirrol's neck, holding the bridle and reins in her left hand. The animal finally lifted its head, and she put her hand over its snout, sliding the bridle back over its long ears. The small tuft of white hair at the ends looked just like the swaying panicles on the chis.

Sora was up and about too, still keeping the blanket around her shoulders. Wick finally groaned and farted, rolling his head off the saddle, startling himself awake. Felix sat cross-legged, his hands lying in his lap, eyes closed. He looked like a grey and silver statue.

"What's he doing?" Wick said.

"Keeping you safe," Alix replied, annoyed at the way Wick asked the question, like Felix was some sort of strange animal beyond comprehension.

Wick yawned big and loudly. Felix finally opened his eyes, the orbs lighting up to their usual blue glow. Everyone began packing up; Wick moved in a still groggy stupor as Felix walked up behind Alix and put a hand on her back, kissing her cheek. She stood up on her tiptoes and kissed him back.

They rode out as the sun finally became visible over the hills ahead of them. Clouds hung low on the horizon, creating great beams of light between them. The orange star was thankfully dulled behind the clouds, saving their eyes. They would reach the outskirts of Burreville by the afternoon. Sora remarked at how similar the landscape remained: the chis filling the lower depressions between light, green hills, small tributaries of the river crossing their path. The stirrols splashed through a shallow stretch of a stream, the spray catching the rising sun like diamonds in the air.

Kilometers behind the four riders, the marshal slowly approached their abandoned camp. He studied the ground from the high vantage point of his stirrol, seeing the clear signs of boots and hoofs in the grass. He dismounted and walked around the remains of the fire. The marshal crouched down, unsteady, and held his hand over the remains, feeling only a hint of residual heat in the charred wood. He used a burrey branch to poke around within the remains, turning over a blackened piece of metal. It had been crushed under a rock or boot and tossed in. *This must have been the stolen tech that Otto mentioned, how he knew they were in the village,* he said to himself, afraid to break the silence of the valley around him. *They're hoping to break the trail.*

He stood up straight and looked at the ground again, seeing patterns stamped into the wet grass and dirt around the fire. Climbing back onto his stirrol, his gentle voice commanded the animal to keep walking. The marshal looked at the ground the whole time as he moved west, seeing a faint jumble of hoof prints. The grass was ripped up into small scatterings of dirt, where the four stirrols before him had been spurred into a gallop. *Burreville has to be the only place they'd go.* His eyes finally looked up from the ground, westward. The sun finally climbed high enough to begin burning away the remaining dew. The marshal nudged the stirrol with his heels, snapping the reins until the animal leapt forward and broke into a sprint.

Burreville spread out like a wagon had tipped over and spilled its cargo into the valley. The wood buildings created no coherent pattern, none of them higher than two stories. The town had been a crossroads town nearly since the beginning of Celestine's settlement. It grew in significance as people settled White Sands and served as the last comfortable stopping point for travelers heading west. Ibi herds stood on the hillsides to the north, white against the green. Just outside the clump of buildings, great pens and chutes were all fenced in to gather the ibi and prepare them for sale and slaughter.

The sounds of hammers on nails and boards; men shouting; ibi baying; a cacophony of noises came to meet them as they approached. The smell of manure, ibi, smoke, and filth hit them, but above it all, the smell of greasy breakfast on many a grill and fire made their mouths water.

From their vantage point, Alix and the others looked down on the town. Beside it, a great white ribbon curved up from the south, heading east. The Xypha rail line had a fledgling system of pens and buildings growing beside it, a wide stretch of grass and mud between it and the town proper, from people and animals trampling the ground.

"So, about this robbery..." Alix said, breaking their silence.

Wick looked at her. "What about it?"

"Tell me the plan."

"Oh." He shifted in his saddle. "Well, uh, we were going to rob some of Silas's men after they headed out of town. He collects take from the gambling halls here."

Alix turned her head and narrowed her eyes at Wick. He couldn't meet them. "Silas's men?"

"Yep."

"Silas doesn't have gambling operations in Burreville."

Sora whipped her head around to glare at Wick.

Alix smirked; *he'd lied to her*. Alix shook her head. "So who was the *real* target?"

Wick sighed and rolled his eyes; there was no use trying to keep it up any longer. "Okay, fine. It was Youngard's men."

"So, one of Silas's chief competitors in White Sands?" Felix added.

"Yes, but in my defense, I did really intend to give Sora her cut!"

"I ought to strangle you!" Sora snapped.

"Don't worry—whatever Wick had planned, we're tossing it out the window," Alix said, enjoying the back-and-forth. It was nice to have a punching bag. "I'll come up with something." Let's just get into town, get some rooms, and act like nothing's wrong."

"I could use a nice bath," Wick said, stretching.

"Let's not get carried away," Alix said as they rode down the hill. "We still need to be on our guard."

11

The Standoff

Rain poured in the early evening, and Burreville became a muddy mess. Heavy raindrops pelted the wood roofs, creating a noise that overwhelmed everything else. Alix swiped a long black duster from a man who had laid it over a barrel. When the man turned back from his business unloading a wagon, he'd notice it was long gone. She slipped it on as she walked, flipping the collar just as she stepped off the boardwalk into the rain and muck.

Her boots slipped and splashed in the mud. If the street wasn't so treacherous, she would've run across it to get to the hotel and saloon. Instead, she just endured the sheets of rain that soaked her hair, ribbons of water running down her neck, dripping off her eyelashes and nose. She braved the slippery mud for one quick jump onto the boardwalk and shook the water off the duster. *Fuck me, this sucks*, she said to herself.

Everyone in town sought refuge from the rain, many of them filling The Dirty Blonde saloon that Alix now entered. The room smelled of smoke from a fire burning in a wide fireplace at the back of the room, along with the thick haze of pipe weed. The rain made everyone smell like wet ibi. Alix brushed past men crowding the bar, surveying the room, weaving through the tables and chairs. Instead of finding a table, she leaned against the wall near the front window to the right of the door.

Just outside the window, a man sat in a wooden chair. He leaned the chair back on two legs, resting his shoulders on the outside of the saloon, a beat-up grey hat on his head. Although he pulled the hat low, his eyes still scanned the street, paying close attention to the saloon door to his right. Only a meter and a pane of glass separated him and Alix.

A woman with big blonde hair wearing a red dress with black lace approached Alix. She leaned in close with a smile, her cheeks and lips bright red. "Can I get you a drink, darlin?" she said.

"A double chisik." Alix smiled.

"Comin right up." The woman smiled with her lips slightly puckered.

Alix watched her walk away, the many layers of her dress waving with her hips. "Are we in a rush?" she said to the rest of the crew on their private comms channel.

"Eyes on the prize," Wick's voice said.

"Trust me, I've got my eyes on a prize, alright."

"Knock it off," Sora piped in.

Was that a hint of jealousy? Alix wondered with a smile.

"Skimmer's coming in," Felix said. "Wick, looks like these are your guys."

Just after entering town, Alix scrapped whatever plan Wick had in mind as she positioned everyone strategically. Felix remained on the western edge of town, keeping an eye and sensor out for the guys Wick planned to target. Sora remained out of sight in a hotel across the street, Wick sat outside, waiting to confirm when Youngard's men showed up.

Despite her confidence, picking on Caleb Youngard's business was like grabbing a currclaw by the tail. Youngard was a slick rich man in White Sands who, unlike Silas, dressed in high-end clothing and made himself above the dirty work. But it didn't fool anyone who knew him well. He had climbed the ladder in White Sands with blood-soaked hands. Silas may run things east of Burreville, but Youngard claimed the west. His men would beat, kill, rape, and steal when and where they pleased.

Alix kept a low profile inside to make sure everything went as planned. The woman showed up with a glass of amber chisik. Alix pulled several crits out of her belt and slowly put them into the woman's outstretched hand. They stared into each other's eyes as Alix put one crit after another in her hand. After the last, Alix slid her fingers down the woman's fingers.

"Thanks," Alix said.

The woman blushed, pocketed the crits, and walked away to serve others.

"Skimmer is heading your way," Felix said.

"Wick, I.D. them, but remember, don't let them get a look at your face," Alix said into her glass.

"Don't worry, I know my job: sit over here doing nothing," Sora said sarcastically.

"Your part will come soon enough."

The rain bounced off the glass windshield of a skimmer as it hovered over the mud, creating a gentle rush of air beneath it that rippled the puddles in the street. The rectangular craft was only wide enough for two, and their seats were back near the rear, two engines on either side. Luckily for them, the windshield connected to a retractable roof that formed a bubble.

The skimmer stopped just outside the Dirty Blonde, and the bubble opened long enough for the men to hop over the sides, one of them splashing his black boots in the wet, sloppy street. They were dressed remarkably alike: black dusters, black hats, black boots, and white shirts behind black vests. Wick lifted his head just enough to get a look at them out of the corner of his eye.

"That's the Finkle twins alright," he said.

Alix watched the twins after they swaggered through the doors. "Alright, you and Sora get going. Tag that skimmer."

"Aye, aye, captain."

She saw Wick fall forward in the chair, putting its front legs back on the boardwalk. He lit a cigarette and strolled by the front of the saloon. With his left hand he tossed the match he'd just used into the street. Imperceptibly, he snapped a magnetic signal beacon onto the rear of the skimmer before walking out of view, heading to fulfill his next part of the plan.

"Signal is clear," Felix reported.

Alix watched the twins strut through the crowded saloon. They approached the bar and spoke to the barkeep, who hurried off toward the back of the room. Both men tapped patrons on the shoulders and told them to scram with a jerk of their thumbs, taking the seats left behind. Alix finished the last drink of chisik, warm and calming as it went down. The twins made no effort to watch their backs, having done this errand a hundred times, never with any issues.

The barkeep returned with a black satchel, faded and rough around the bottom corners. He set it on the bar in front of the twins, and words were exchanged between them that Alix couldn't hear. The men didn't even stay for a single drink. One carried the satchel out to the skimmer, the other close behind him. In a few moments, they were gone. Alix walked over and set her empty glass on the bar. She buttoned her duster and headed back outside into the downpour.

By the time the marshal made it into Burreville, he and his stirrol were soaked to the bone. Towering clouds rolled in from the north, dropping sheets of rain over the west valley. It slowed him down, but thankfully, the rain had ended. His stirrol clopped through the mud, down the main street. People were just emerging from their homes and businesses, looking up to check if the rain truly passed. The clouds remained, obscuring the sun, leaving a chill in the air. The marshal could've gotten a room, a bath, and a shave. He was exhausted, wet, and hungry. At the very least, he needed to ask around town if anyone had seen Alix and Felix come through, so he might as well eat while he was at it.

Inside the mostly empty Dirty Blonde saloon, a mustachioed man pushed a broom across the floorboards, moving water, mud, spilled drinks, and spit toward the door. The place had died down since the rain stopped. The marshal sat at the bar and a blonde woman in a red dress smiled at him.

"Can I get you a drink?" she said.

"Coffee, please."

"Sure thing." She set a small metal cup on the bar.

The marshal shook the rain off his hat and set it next to him on the bar. The woman returned with a steaming pot and poured him a warm cup. It worked wonders, and he felt alive again, like his toes were frozen solid but now began to thaw. He set the cup down, and she refilled it immediately, eyeing the silver badge beneath his coat.

"Say, have you seen a couple of folks come through here, one of them a big sentient?" he said.

She thought for a second. "Doesn't ring a bell."

"What about a woman a little taller than you, lean, dark hair, blue eyes?"

"We had a lot of people in and out of here during the rain, mister." She didn't think much for that answer.

"No worries," he said, drinking his coffee.

The place was quiet except for the rhythmic brushing of stiff bristles on wood. About three cups of coffee later, heavy boots thudded, and spurs jingled in through the door. The marshal felt men at his back, and then they appeared in his peripherals. He paid them no mind, but he knew they stared daggers through him. The woman behind the bar set a bottle and three glasses in front of the man to the marshal's left.

"Wet out there, wouldn't you say?" the man to his right said.

"Yes, I would," the marshal replied.

"Ain't seen you around here before."

"Well, I don't make it out here much."

The man to his right leaned on his elbow, looking right down the marshal's neck. But the marshal didn't turn to look at him or the man to his left. He stared ahead, drinking his coffee.

"What's that badge you got there? Ain't no badges in Burreville," the man said, noticing the silver on the marshal's shirt.

"Get lost."

"It's you who must be lost, pal."

The marshal set his cup down one final time and looked up at the man breathing down his neck. He was a tough looking son of a bitch, big and tall, with calloused knuckles. The marshal sighed and shook his head. "I'm just passing through. Go on about your business."

"You are my business. Why don't you tell me why you're in town?"

"I'm just here for the coffee."

With a sudden sweep of his arm, the man slapped the metal cup with the back of his hand. It pinged off glass bottles and clinked its way to the floor. "Now you got no reason to be here."

The marshal reached into his jacket and set crits on the bar to pay for the coffee, plus a little extra for the woman, who nervously watched what was happening. He picked up his hat and set it back on his head, standing and looking up at the man who clearly wanted nothing more than a fight.

"I'm going to head outside," the marshal said.

He walked calmly out the door, and soon, the other men followed. There was no getting out of it now, and the marshal took off his brown, ibi-wool-lined coat and laid it across the saddle of his stirrol. Rolling up his sleeves, he stood in the street, nearly ankle deep in the mud. The other man grinned as he pulled his duster back to reveal the Plasveld at his hip.

The marshal leaned a little to his left as he stood, his prosthetic not as effective as it used to be. His left thumb hooked on his belt as his right hand dangled at his side.

The other man's arm was poised, tense, waiting to strike.

The marshal sucked his teeth, impatient, agitated.

People began watching out windows and creeping out onto the boardwalks. Whispers traveled up and down the street.

Fingers twitched. The man's narrowed eyes keyed in on his target, studying the marshal to see if he had any tics that would give himself away.

The marshal stood like a stone, eyes tired.

Zmmph. Zmpph.

With a heavy splat, the man fell backwards into the mud, two holes smoking in his chest. The marshal turned coolly to the man's companions, Plasveld still in-hand. They stared at the old man in disbelief, their confidence shed, their faces drenched in fear.

"Now get the hell out of here," the marshal said, shooing the men away with the barrel of his Plasveld.

After taking one last look at their dead friend, his weapon still in its holster, they backed away and scurried out of sight. The marshal holstered his Plasveld, put his coat back on, and mounted his stirrol. No one said a word as he rode slowly west out of town.

In the early morning, the Finkle twins piloted their skimmer west, Burreville several kilometers behind them. Framed by the sunrise, they saw a woman ahead on a nearby hilltop, waving.

"There's no way this is going to work," Sora said, waving her arm like an idiot.

"Trust me, these guys are going to stop," Wick assured her through their comms.

"You know them, huh?"

"I know how Youngard's men operate."

"Alright, they're veering your way. Pipe down," Alix said.

"Remind me why *I'm* the bait?" Sora sighed, her tone and mood not matching the increasingly anxious and desperate waving, jumping up and down as if in distress.

"You're prettier than me," Alix said.

"How nice." Sora rolled her eyes, but inside, her heart skipped a beat.

The skimmer slowed, and Sora got a good look at the two men inside. The rainclouds had moved on, and the men rode with the glass top down. Sora breathed heavily from jumping and waving to flag them down; it added to the act of desperation. She ran up to the skimmer, trying to look as panicked, but relieved as possible.

"Thank you, oh thank you!" she gasped.

"Are you alright, ma'am?" the brother nearer to her tipped his hat.

"My husband and I, we were heading to White Sands, but our skimmer broke down just over there." She pointed behind her.

The brothers leered at her, eyes traveling up and down. Sora fought off the urge to become hostile; instead, she smiled, as if the men's hungry eyes flattered her.

"We're on our way to White Sands," the brother piloting the craft said.

"Could you help us with our skimmer?" Sora pleaded.

"Maybe we could fit you in, give you a ride the rest of the way. Then we'll send help back for your husband."

"Do *not* get in that skimmer," Alix insisted.

No shit, Sora thought while outwardly playing coy with the men.

"Please, my husband's just over there," she said, backing away.

The brother in the passenger seat climbed out, closing the distance between him and Sora. He smiled unpleasantly, reaching out a hand for her, but she continued backing away.

"It's okay. We're here to help," he said.

"Alright, follow me," she said, turning.

"Now, hang on a minute." One of the brothers grabbed Sora by the wrist and yanked her back.

She would've spun and punched him in the face, but instead, she tried to pull away, making sure not to show her true strength.

The other brother had jumped out of the skimmer. "We'll help you out, but first, you can help us."

"Move in," Alix said over the comms, urgency in her voice.

Alix lifted her blue handkerchief over her nose as she put her heels into her stirrol, which sprang forward. Felix held his stirrol, which instinctually wanted to follow, instead turning it in a circle. Alix rode up and over the hill in seconds, disappearing to the north. She saw the struggle on the hilltop, pressing the stirrol to move faster, and she regretted the plan almost immediately. Sora's cries for help over the comms struck fear into Alix, making her forget Sora was playing a part.

"Wick, you moving?" Alix said.

"Closing in," he replied.

They approached the scene from opposite directions. Without breaking the stirrol's stride, Alix swung her left leg in front of her, sitting side-saddle then jumping to the ground, drawing her Plasvelds. One of the Finkles saw her, reaching for his plasbolt under his coat.

"Try me," Alix barked, two Plasvelds up from just a few paces away.

The brother lifted his hands.

Wick rode up from the north, plasbolt in-hand, his face covered. The other Finkle had a tight grip on Sora. He would've drawn down, but Sora finally flexed her muscles, ripping her right arm free, throwing a punch solidly in the man's face. Behind her handkerchief, Alix grinned ear-to-ear, no longer fearing for Sora's safety. The Finkle brother stumbled backward, hand to his face.

"Howdy, folks," Wick said behind his mask.

The Finkle brother holding his hands up glared at Alix furiously, already plotting his revenge. The other brother cursed Sora and stuffed a white handkerchief to his bloody nose. Sora stepped confidently beside Alix.

"Toss those bolts to the ground," Alix ordered.

The Finkles reluctantly complied.

"I believe you've got a satchel in that skimmer," Wick said.

"I don't know what you're talking about," the brother without the bloody nose snarled.

"Let's take a look," Alix said.

Sora began searching the skimmer, opening compartments, tossing out junk that wasn't the satchel. She hopped into the passenger seat and looked in the floor, felt under the seat, finding nothing. Leaning over the center to reach under the pilot's seat, she noticed a subtle compartment door in the panel behind the seatbacks.

"There's a panel behind the seats," she called out.

"Open it," Alix demanded.

"You know who we work for," one of the brothers said.

"Does it look like I care? Open it, or I'll make your brother do it."

"He ain't gonna open it neither," the man sneered.

Alix's eyes narrowed. She fired two quick shots, dropping the man to the ground. She cut off the other brother's cries and curses with both Plasvelds now in *his* face.

"Your turn," she said.

Sora's eyes widened as Alix shot the first brother without hesitation. She realized she'd never seen a man killed, much less by someone she knew and cared about. Conflicting feelings ran through her; fear of Alix and the Plasvelds in her hands, the satisfaction of seeing the man die who would have taken her, guilt and shame that she was now involved. She, Wick, and Jo had planned a robbery, but Sora's naïveté prevented her from thinking of the possibility that she or anyone else would kill someone in the process. Now, she doubted herself, thinking of what might have happened had Jo been here, been the one to pull the trigger. Her hands shook, but she hid them in her lap, still in the passenger seat.

"You kill me, and you ain't getting that satchel," the remaining brother boasted, hoping it would save his life.

"We'll get it open," Alix said confidently. "You get to decide if you live to tell your boss about it."

"So, you *do* know? You are in for a storm, lady."

"I *am* the storm. Now, open the fucking panel."

The brother shook his head in disbelief. He thought Alix was a damned fool, but he complied, preferring to live. Sora jumped out of the seat and backed away—from the Finkle brother, from Alix, whose eyes were cold steel, unflinching. Finkle reached into the skimmer and put his left hand over the compartment. A built-in print scanner detected his patterns, and a drawer slid out of the panel, presenting the satchel. He picked it up and turned back to Alix.

"Here it is."

"Hand it to her." Alix tilted her head to Sora.

Finkle didn't look away from Alix but stretched out his arm and let Sora take the satchel from him. She nervously took it, surprised by the weight, and backed away quickly.

"Nice little game you got here," Finkle said. He looked at Sora. "I'll remember your face, darlin'."

Zmmph. Zmmph. Zmmph.

His body flew back into the skimmer, hitting the side and dropping to the grass. Alix spun her Plasvelds and holstered them before she dropped her handkerchief and spit on the man's dead body.

"No, you won't."

Wick finally ran up to the skimmer, holstering his own plasbolts. He knelt down, checking the man's pockets for anything valuable. "I didn't think the plan was to kill both of them."

"Plans change," Alix shrugged.

Felix came riding up, leading Sora's stirrol beside his own. Alix smiled at him. Sora stood, clutching the satchel, staring at the dead man by the skimmer. Her heart hammered in her chest as panic crawled over her skin. *How could they just…*

Alix gently touched Sora's arm. "You okay?"

Sora recoiled, panicked breaths escaping her lungs. She felt unsteady on her feet. The satchel fell to the ground, and Sora nearly followed it. Alix caught her, held her close.

"It's okay, you're safe," Alix murmured.

Sora shook her head, fought against Alix's embrace until Alix let her go. Sora put her hand up to her forehead, tried to slow her breathing. Everyone stared at her with genuine concern, their eyes so different than before—Alix's eyes so different. Alix had somehow flipped a switch, the hard, cold stare of death now gentle and caring. Sora could not process the switch; she couldn't believe the difference from one moment to the next. She ran from them, but she dropped to her knees only a short distance away on the other side of the skimmer.

Sora regained control of her breathing, each breath coming slower than the one before. She drew in deep breaths through her nose, letting the air escape through her tight lips. When she opened her eyes, she stared south across the rolling hills, green and gold in the morning sun, sparkling dew atop the chis. She felt the wind brush against her neck, cooling the sweat running down her back and under her arms. She felt the wet ground with her hands, dew soaking into her pants at the knees.

"Is she alright?" Wick said, pocketing a few hundred crits from the Finkles' dead bodies.

Alix stared across the skimmer at Sora's back. *I went too far. She thinks I'm some sort of monster, no better than these goons.* Whether it was true or not, the thought was now planted, and it wouldn't let go. Alix bent down and picked up the satchel, turning back to Wick.

"Burn the skimmer."

"Seems excessive." Wick shrugged.

"Youngard will figure out they aren't delivering his crits by the end of the day. By tomorrow, he'll have a team of guys out here. I'd rather not leave any sign of who may have been responsible."

Alix crouched down and felt the hull of the skimmer, finding the beacon they had planted there yesterday. She pulled it off and stuffed it into a pouch on her belt. Wick jerked a panel off the engine and reached his hand inside. He pulled a knife out of its sheath at his belt and cut through a hose. The sound of escaping air and the smell of ozone escaped from the open panel. Alix tied the satchel to her saddle and mounted her stirrol. Felix still sat on his stirrol, holding the reins of Sora's mount.

"Sora, we need to go," Alix said, trying to sound sympathetic, but it didn't come out right. She heard herself say the words like she delivered an order.

Sora slowly stood and walked back to them, wiping her eyes. She climbed into the saddle, taking the reins from Felix, whose face was gentle and caring. That comforted Sora, who smiled back, though it only came through as an upturned half of her mouth, and she looked away quickly. Alix brought her stirrol into a steady trot down the hill. Felix followed her, then Sora.

Wick lingered, walking his stirrol a few meters away from the skimmer, and drawing his plasbolt. He closed an eye and shot a single round into the engine. It wasn't so much an explosion, but a wave of flames bursting out and over the engine, then through the interior of the skimmer. He watched it burn for a few seconds before turning and riding away.

Riding across the valley with great speed prevented Alix and Sora from speaking to one another. No one else said a word through the comms channel either. There was no hope of Alix focusing on anything other than the look in Sora's eyes, the way she recoiled in terror from her touch. It made Alix sick to her stomach. Had she become a terrible thing? A force to be reckoned with, whose appearance was frightful, and not only to her enemies? She could never unsee the fear in Sora's eyes, and no amount of fury and focus could burn away the guilt she now felt.

Just a few stirrol lengths behind, Sora stared at Alix's back, her ponytail waving, the duster she'd stolen in Burreville tied down behind the saddle, the satchel bouncing on the left. Each time Sora tried to picture Alix's blue eyes, the confident smile she displayed back home in the shop, it burned away with the sight of Alix's cold, ruthless stare. But Sora remembered what Alix had told her on the hill that night—how she spent her life fighting, doing whatever it took to escape Xypha's grasp. Then, Sora did not imagine Alix killing someone. Now, she admonished her own foolishness. Sora thought she was prepared for this, for revenge, to help her sister and her village be free of Silas's grasp. She was wrong.

Ahead to the east, the marshal sat on his stirrol, one eye scanning the horizon through a vizscope. He saw the four riders coming, Alix at the fore, heading northeast back to Burreville. He lowered the scope and returned it to a saddlebag. He clicked his tongue and gently brought the stirrol up to speed, cutting across to intercept them.

He was well past his time to deliver, but maybe if he brought Alix and Felix in alive to explain themselves, to explain what he believed to be true, that Silas hired them to kill those engineers, it might be enough. It was the only chance he had, the only chance any of them had to maintain some semblance of peace.

Alix was so lost in her thoughts, she barely noticed the man ahead on the trail. The marshal sat calmly on his stirrol, directly in their path. They could've easily bypassed him, but Alix knew it would only delay the inevitable. At least he was alone. Alix reined in her stirrol, the others following suit. The old man's ibi wool collar stood up around his neck, shielding himself from the wind. He chewed on his lip as he waited. Tired, weary eyes looked straight at Alix.

"What the hell are you doing here?" she said.

"Don't ask questions you already know the answer to," the marshal replied.

"Get out of the way."

"Can't do that."

The wind kicked up, blowing at Alix's back, her stirrol's gold mane flowing in front of her face. With her eyes, Alix implored the old man to move, to take off and say he'd never found her. But like an old burrey tree, he was stuck, buried in the valley ground: he would never voluntarily move. *That was always the problem,* she thought.

"So," she said, waiting a beat, "what's your proposal?"

"You killed Xypha engineers, and I suspect Felix did too. Can't speak to your other companions. Maybe they had a hand in it, I don't know."

"They didn't."

The marshal narrowed his eyes; Alix's face was deadly serious. He knew she had an excellent Solar face and wouldn't let any lie show. "If you and Felix come with me..."

"Not a chance," Alix said, raising her voice above the wind.

"Listen! You stand before the council in Verisport and tell them Silas hired you to kill those men."

"And then what? Xypha's just going to let us walk away?"

"It's the best option you got, kid!" he pleaded with her. *Don't make the same mistake. Don't walk away again.*

"You haven't learned a damn thing, have you?" Alix was beside herself. "I told you then, and I'll tell you now: do you have any idea what they'll do to me? To Felix? If they found out who I am? Who *we* are?"

"I won't let that happen."

"You're delusional." Alix shook her head.

Déjà vu swept over them both. Years ago, when Alix told the marshal not to let the Xypha prospectors anywhere near Verisport—or better yet, to kill them the moment they stepped foot on Celestine— he'd reacted the same way. *Be realistic, Alix,* he said. *I can't set aside the law just for you.* Alix writhed in her saddle now, anger bubbling to the surface. She'd left Celestine all those years ago, but not now. Just as she told Felix, she was done running.

The marshal dismounted, his left leg giving way just a little as he hit the ground. He walked toward her, palms out, almost begging her. *Don't do this again, I can't do this again.* Years ago, he begged her to stay, to remain his top deputy. He could keep her safe, and her position would shield her. Law was already brittle in Verisport, in the valley, and he couldn't put a gaping crack into it, no matter how much he loved her.

"Alix, please. I need your help. We can take Silas down together. We can stand up to Xypha, together, but I got to keep the peace."

"Whose peace are you keeping?" her voice dripped with venom. "Whose justice do you seek? *Theirs?*"

"The valley's justice. You'll have to answer for those men you killed, but not to Xypha—to me." He opened his coat, a gesture that sent an unmistakable message.

Alix jumped down from her stirrol as they faced one another. She saw the marshal's hand shaking, his *conviction* shaking. He couldn't do it. He wouldn't draw on her, no matter how far he thought she had fallen.

"Please, Alix. This is your last chance."

She stretched her long fingers, her right hand hovering just above the dark stained wood grip of the Plasveld. There was nowhere else to go, no other words she could muster. He made it clear then and made it clear now: the marshal would put the *idea* of peace and justice in the valley above anyone else, even if that justice was a distorted image of the truth. *What good was peace under Xypha's shadow?* Alix set her jaw, her lip stiff. She could almost feel the Plasveld grip in her hand, envisioning the draw, the shot, the kill.

Then, she thought of Sora. She took a deep breath.

Alix drew her Plasveld.

The marshal hesitated.

Zmmph.

The marshal's stirrol reared on its hind legs, snorted, kicked, and bolted. The plasma shot at its front hoofs left a dark burn in the grass. The wind quickly blew it out, smoke dissipating. Frozen in place, his heart racing, the marshal's face lost all color as his eyes bulged. He had his hand on his Plasveld, but it was still holstered, his hand shaking.

Alix's weapon steamed as she spun it on her finger and holstered it, her upper lip curled in a rage. "I'm not giving you the out you're seeking." She calmly climbed back in the saddle. "You'll get back to town eventually, but know this, if you stand in front of me again, you better be willing to draw. I won't spare your life a second time."

She gently spurred the stirrol forward, riding away from the marshal. He turned to watch her leave, mouth slack. Wick and Sora rode by him, and Felix stopped his stirrol beside the man Alix once looked up to as a father.

"That's the only peace offering you're going to get," Felix said.

"Felix, she *knows* she can't do this. She knows she can't stop what's coming on her own," the marshal said.

"She isn't on her own."

Felix nodded, tipped his hat, and rode past.

12

The Ghost

Alix and the others returned to Verisport under the cover of night. The ride back was cold and silent; everyone was on edge. As they rode east, keeping a distance between them and the south edge of town, the lights of the shipyard lit the flight tower from below. For the first time in years, Alix felt uneasy about seeing the sleek tower—the glow felt ominous. The whole structure looked like the barrel of a plasbolt, the glow of the spinning chambers signifying oncoming death. A shiver ran up her spine.

"You know Jesse well? You sure you trust them?" she said to Sora.

"Yes." Sora was tired of answering that question.

Sora led them to the patchwork metal wall of Jesse's scrapyard. Heaps of twisted metal and trash leaned against the wall, at least providing some concealment as they stood beside a heavy, sliding gate. The gears complained as the door opened, and Jesse stood with a lamp hovering over their shoulder, wearing a grey sweater and a heavy, dirty apron.

"Sora, this is not how we do things," Jesse said as the stirrols walked through the gate.

Sora dismounted and ran to Jesse, throwing her arms around them, grateful to see a familiar face. Alix, Felix, and Wick's faces had become so strange; the violence spooked her more than she realized.

"I'm sorry Jesse, but we didn't really have anywhere to go. I need your help—*we* need your help."

"We?" Jesse looked at the others standing around their stirrols in the dark.

"These are…friends." The word felt like a rock in her throat. "They are trying to fight back—against Silas, against these new Xypha people."

"Whoa, hold it." Jesse held up a hand. "Let's get inside before we talk shop."

They gathered in a large room near the back of the dark and crowded shop. Everything inside was made of scrap metal, from the desk to the chairs to the shelves along the walls. Even the door that hung open unevenly was made of several plates welded together. Jesse went to a pathetic looking coffee maker, preparing to brew a pot.

"What can I do?" they asked.

"My friends need to get into the spaceport discretely," Sora said. Everyone let her speak for the group, since she and Jesse were obviously close.

Jesse looked at Sora and narrowed their eyes as the two seemed to exchange information. The coffee maker rattled, a water tank on top slowly draining. "What's your trouble?"

"My ship is there," Alix spoke up. "You're a scrapper, so I'm guessing you know Silas Purvida."

Jesse spit on the floor at the name.

"He's got it in for us," Alix added.

"What's in it for me?" Jesse crossed their arms and leaned against the table behind them.

"How about ten thousand crits?" Sora said.

Jesse had to shake the disbelief out of their face. "You're joking."

"We're not," Alix said. She produced the satchel and dropped it on the table.

Jesse looked down at it, studying it, skeptical. "Where'd you get that kind of money?" They looked at Sora suspiciously.

"I'd rather not get into that." Sora said, the memory of the ambush and the look on Alix's face haunting her.

"I have a way into the port, but it's blocked up," Jesse said as they turned and poured a cup of coffee. "You give me the crits and clear the path, you can get in."

"Deal," Alix said, extending her hand.

Jesse turned, holding the metal cup in both hands, blowing on the steaming hot liquid. They raised an eyebrow at Alix and looked at her outstretched hand. Jesse had sensed Sora's discomfort; something about these *friends* unnerved her, and Jesse sided with their longtime friend over these people. Taking a sip, Jesse didn't shake Alix's hand, but merely nodded.

"Follow me."

They left the room and led everyone down a dark hallway, then a set of cramped stairs underground. The hoverlamp followed them the whole way, flickering as they entered and moved through the underground room. Jesse stopped, pushed a crate aside in the dim light, and rolled a toolbox off a large steel plate. They bent at the knees to lift the plate.

"Give me a hand," they said to Felix.

Once Felix got a hold of the plate, Jesse realized they didn't need to help him at all, so they backed away as Felix effortlessly moved the plate and leaned it against a cabinet. There was a pitch-black hole in the floor; Jesse swiped on the syncpad on their arm, and a beam of light shone from their wrist into the hole.

"This is a scrapper tunnel."

"A smuggler's tunnel," Wick added.

"You keep this to yourselves. I trust Sora, and if she trusts you, then I guess I do too."

"Where does it lead exactly?" Alix said.

"I don't know where it comes out specifically. Like I said, it's blocked off. But I was told it leads beneath the port."

"There was once a scrapyard off the port, on the north side, when the tower and docks were constructed," Felix said. "It is likely this tunnel leads there. The yard is gone now, covered by more docking bays."

"Leave this end open if you don't mind—just in case we need an exit," Alix said.

"I don't know what kind of trouble you're in with Silas, but if word of this gets around, he'll own my shop by tomorrow evening, or worse," Jesse said.

"Nothing's going to happen to your shop," Alix assured them.

"Don't make promises you can't keep."

Alix gave Jesse a sideways look, pulled her goggles down and adjusted them over her eyes. Felix dropped down into the tunnel first, his heavy feet splashing into a small stream of unknown liquid. The sound echoed down the tunnel. Wick followed him and cursed once his boots hit the liquid.

"Wait," Sora stopped Alix before she could jump down herself. "Be careful."

"We will." Alix smiled as Sora stared into the foreign lenses that covered Alix's eyes.

Alix dropped into the tunnel, and the smell of oil and harsh chemicals overwhelmed her. She covered her mouth, thankful that the goggles at least protected her eyes. She saw Wick in the dark, wrapping a kerchief around his nose and mouth. Felix's eyes glowed bright as he examined their surroundings.

"Almost a kilometer," he said. "The tunnel collapsed, likely sealed on purpose, I'd bet."

"Can we survive long enough to clear it?" Wick asked as he coughed.

"Didn't think we'd need breathers," Alix said.

"The time it will take to get there and clear the obstruction, you should be fine," Felix said.

"Comforting," Wick noted sarcastically.

Felix led the way with Wick behind Alix. Occasionally, they had to avoid rocks and twisted metal jutting out of the water, oil, and who knows what else on the tunnel floor. The tunnel itself was once a giant pipe, running from the port during its early construction period to what was once the outside of town. After a short time, they stopped at a pile of rock and metal blocking the tunnel, and Felix scanned the area around him.

"We're under the northeast area of the port. Clearing the obstruction is not possible. We'll have to cut through the tunnel and ground above us."

"Where's that lead?" Alix said.

"If we cut here," Felix pointed above him but back a few paces from the end of the tunnel, "we can come into a storage hangar."

"I'm sure Jesse has plascutters we can borrow."

"Great. Let's get out of here so I can breathe again," Wick said.

"How long should it take to cut through?" Alix said to Felix, ignoring Wick's complaints.

"We're about one and a half meters below the hangar bay. I could cut through it in a couple of hours."

"Let's head back and get what we need."

They started walking, but Felix stood still, and Alix knew he sensed something. She paused and waited as he looked up, his eyes darting back and forth.

"There are Xypha drop ships in the port."

* * *

Back inside the shop, Sora and Jesse gathered around the table and the coffee maker. Jesse poured Sora a cup as Sora leaned her elbows on the table, head in hands. "You look like shit," Jesse said.

"Thanks," Sora groaned. She eagerly took the cup and savored the warmth. "I don't know, Jess. The past couple days really got away from me."

"What happened?"

Sora recounted the events: finding the dead Xypha engineers, meeting Alix and Felix, going to Burreville, the robbery. The events blurred together, distorting the passage of time. Sora didn't realize she was staring blankly at the wall as she talked, her voice quiet and weary. Her body felt heavy.

"I warned you, Sora. That job you were planning with Wick and Jo…" Jesse said.

"Really not in the mood for an 'I told you so' right now," Sora said, looking sideways at Jesse.

"Sorry." Jesse took a sip of coffee.

Jesse was right, though. Sora's image of herself, or at least the level of toughness she believed she had was shattered. She *wasn't* cut out for this. Before all this, when she and Jo met Wick and began to plot the robbery, it seemed so remote, almost implausible. Maybe she didn't believe they'd ever pull it off, but it gave her and Jo a drive, as if one day, there would be justice for someone like Silas.

"So…you like that girl?" Jesse said.

"Jess! Ugh." Sora dropped her forehead on the table with a thud.

"Come on, it's obvious. Why else would you want to help them? You already got the crits you and Jo wanted for your people."

"Yes, I do, okay? Happy?" Sora said, head still on the table. She looked up and avoided eye contact with Jesse, "She was so confident and magnetic."

"Was?" Jesse raised an eyebrow.

"Then I saw her kill two men."

"Yeah, I guess that'd kill the vibes, huh?"

"She had this rage. Not like it isn't warranted, but—" Sora nearly spilled the whole story to Jesse but caught herself before she betrayed Alix's trust. "It was like she turned into someone else. It scared the hell out of me, Jess."

"People are complicated." Jesse shrugged. "And this world can be dangerous, especially now."

"What do you mean?"

"Xypha drop ships in the port. They showed up a couple days ago. It seems the council finally let them in."

Sora's eyes went wide.

Alix paced frantically. She couldn't think past the fact that Verisport had finally let Xypha in. She thought back to the encounter with the marshal and how he failed. Everyone else sat around the room, following Alix with their eyes, the anxiety radiating off her, seeping into each one of them.

"This makes things incredibly more difficult," Alix thought out loud. "If their drop ships are already docked, that means security is going to be tighter."

"What does that look like?" Sora said.

"I don't know. More of the marshal's men, Xypha personnel, or worse…" Alix's voice trailed off. She didn't even want to go there.

"So what? We've got our way in. We sneak in there, board the ship, and blast out of there," Wick said.

"It'll be much harder for us to *get* to the ship."

"What are they bringing down from that station?" Jesse said.

"Materials, omniite, tools—things people can't normally get around here. They'll line pockets and make a big show of providing all sorts of new things. People will contract with them, and before you know it, they're the only game in town," Alix said.

"I guess that's why Silas is working with them," Jesse said. "That son of a bitch has taken every good scrap from here to Curio."

"He's cozy with the Xypha officer, no doubt," Alix said. "He'll get a big cut of whatever business Xypha takes over."

Alix finally sat down, rubbed her face, and leaned back into an old dusty chair. They would have to fight their way out of the port. Alix thought of all the eventual outcomes. She had no fear of the marshal's men; they were mostly bumbling fools. But with Xypha drop ships, there were worse enemies than facing down some ragged Verisport deputies.

"You've got a plan, right?" Wick said.

Yes, I do. Get my ship or die trying, she thought. Just as she expected, as she said would happen years ago, the marshal lost his grip, and Xypha was now entrenching itself in Verisport. They would run security at the port to protect their ships. Silas and Xypha's forward officer had obviously planned to ice the marshal out, and it dawned on Alix that she had played right into their hands. Killing the engineers was a means to an end, a crisis Xypha could push on the council, demanding justice, knowing the marshal couldn't deliver. *He always wins*, she remembered Wick saying of Silas.

Felix watched Alix, her mind long gone from the room, as she stared into the void. He knew what realization settled on her: it was now or never. The two of them faced possibilities worse than death at Xypha's hands if captured. He knew beyond a doubt that Alix would die before she let them take her.

"I will cut through into the storage hangar," Felix said. "Jesse, do you have plascutters I can borrow? Once inside, I can disable security systems, and the mag-clamps on the *Shadow*."

"How you going to do that?" Wick said.

"Just trust me," Felix was not in the mood for someone casting doubt. "Once the power is out, I'll meet you at the docking bay, and we'll get to the ship together."

He looked at Alix, hoping his plan would spur some kind of movement, feedback, *anything*. She remained detached, elbows on her knees, staring into the distance.

It was early in the morning when Felix had finally cut through the tunnel, up into the floor of the storage hangar above. When he emerged from the tunnel in Jesse's shop, Alix had finally moved. She geared up, double checking her Plasvelds and ammunition, holding a hair tie in her teeth as she brushed her hair back with her hands into a fresh ponytail. Wick tried to hide his nervous fidgeting by spinning the chamber on his plasbolt. Sora and Jesse waited and watched the others.

"Where will you go when you get to your ship?" Sora said, fearing the answer.

"Somewhere remote. Probably put her down in the canyonlands south of here," Alix said through her clenched teeth.

"You're not leaving Celestine?"

"No."

"We have to get my ship; don't forget about that!" Wick said.

"I haven't forgotten," Alix said.

With her hands free, she hugged Sora. "I'm sorry for what's happened," she whispered in Sora's ear.

"Please come back." Sora felt herself shudder, fighting back her tears.

Alix pulled away and nodded with a smile. She flipped a switch to a deadly serious face, turning to Wick, "Let's go."

Felix sat with his legs hanging over the hole in Jesse's floor. Alix crouched onto the balls of her feet beside him, looking down into the darkness.

"You okay?" he said.

"Anxious," she answered.

He leaned over and kissed her, then dropped back into the hole. Alix could see his glowing eyes in the dark as he looked back up from the bottom.

Wick hesitated before following Felix. "This is a stupid plan."

"It's the only plan," Alix said.

"Well, it's still stupid," he sighed and looked at her without a hint of sarcasm or false bravado. "You promise we'll get my ship after this? You're not going to blast off to Corto as soon as you're on board?"

"I promise. Once we have the *Shadow*, we're going to level everything Silas has."

Wick laughed and shook his head before he jumped into the hole. Alix paused and looked back at Sora, biting her bottom lip to keep it from shaking. Alix walked over to her, put an arm around her waist, and kissed her. Sora gripped Alix's face as the tears flowed.

"I'll see you soon," Alix said.

Then, she was gone.

They reached the hole Felix had cut into the tunnel roof. Felix boosted Alix and Wick up in his hands and into the hangar before he jumped effortlessly after them and pulled himself up. All around, the dark hangar was filled with a maze of crates, skimmers, engines, and parts of engines. Even their whispers seemed to echo inside.

"Felix will cut the power cells. Wick, you and I are going this way to the *Shadow*. Remember, the goal is to *not* be seen," Alix said.

Alix remained crouched by the hole in the floor, watching Felix leave out the opposite side of the hangar, disappearing into the darkness. She knew nobody would see him, and his part of the plan would go off without a hitch. She took a deep breath. The *Shadow* sat only meters away, through maintenance passages that ran between the walls of the honeycomb docking bay structure. In the past, she had used them regularly, working for the marshal, working at the docks doing the exact job a skeleton crew performed tonight. Her goggles displayed a wire diagram of the path to her ship—the way home.

The sound of hissing air and steam released from a coolant hose covered the sound of the door opening to the maintenance passage.

Alix stood back to the dark steel wall, Wick on her left, following her lead. He relied on her sight in the dark.

Thankfully, he's kept his mouth shut.

Alix tapped him on the shoulder and crept forward. As they moved, a light on the wall flashed on, and Wick nearly jumped out of his skin. Alix grabbed him by the shirt collar and calmed him down silently. The maintenance passages were lined with motion triggered lights, bright enough to illuminate a few steps ahead, but no more than that, until they reached the next one. Alix knew there was no one in front of them.

After seventy-five paces, they came to another door. Alix adjusted the sight of her goggles and looked through the walls, scanning for any heat signatures on the other side. The coast remained clear, so she gently opened the door, which groaned on its heavy hinges. They followed the passage in between two docking bays, and the corridor angled around to another junction. When the bays converged, the passages ran in multiple directions. They stopped at a heavy door, a junction on the other side. Alix held her left hand behind her, touching Wick's chest, holding him steady and quiet. Another scan through the walls. More empty passages.

There should be somebody working, but maybe they were busy elsewhere? It's getting close to shift changes, anyway.

Alix figured she better not look a gift stirrol in the mouth and opened the door. They had to follow the passage on their left, around one last docking bay until they reached the *Shadow*. At least coming from the maintenance corridors meant she didn't have to enter a code sequence to get into the bay.

Felix moved silently, the sound of his footsteps dampened by the slightest adjustments in internal pressure, the give of his membrane, and the hyper-fluid between it and the hard omniite of his frame. His gaze pierced the dark—every wall and body around him was clear as day. He felt movement, air pressure, the slightest electrical charge in the air. He heard the hiss of fluids, coolant and fuel moving through pipes and hoses, air circulating through vents, hushed voices, footsteps, the clanging of tools over a hundred meters away. At a time like this, he couldn't afford to let anything escape his senses.

The control tower reached far overhead, but Felix attuned his sight to see through the floor, down into the room below ground that housed the power cells and generators. He descended a small stairwell near the base of the tower. At the heavy steel door, he touched the keypad with two fingers, and it opened on his mental command. According to the passive temperature scan in his mind, the room was freezing, but he couldn't feel the bone-chilling cold. Four huge power cells stood in the center of the room. Generators were connected to them through thick, heavy wires along a structure that ran up to the ceiling then down the walls. Hoses went from the cells along the floor, through the walls into another room, where coolant tanks kept the cells at optimal temperatures. Several computers and their blank screens hung on the wall, but he didn't need to touch them to access the entire port's systems.

In mere moments, he remotely passed through the system security and went to work. Nobody could possibly detect his intrusion. There was no computer system on Celestine sophisticated enough, no engineer experienced enough, to compete with his sentient mind, a relic of another millennium, a lost art. Once he had control, he could remotely turn any function on or off in the entire port. The power cells, however, needed to be disabled by hand due to an old backup system. Three huge levers beside the computers had to be switched to disable the backups. He pulled them down, one by one. As soon as he felt the system begin to alert its engineers that something was wrong, he cut the signal.

Now, he was in control.

However, before Felix left the room, he saw something in the port's network, like someone trying to casually watch him from across a street. They weren't watching him; that was impossible. They monitored something else. He mentally moved through the network, one system to another. Then, he found the Xypha signals. Their drop ships in three docking bays were patched into the local communications network, on a frequency that passed only between them. He found the watcher.

Alix's hand dripped with sweat on the lever of the last door, the *Shadow* on the other side. She wanted to burst through and sprint to her ship. She had to wait. Felix would be along any moment. Instead of him approaching from the passage behind them, her left wrist vibrated, and she looked at the syncpad and the silent message from Felix.

GO. NOW.

She didn't question him. She engaged the lever, a heavy clunk, and pushed the door open. The docking bay lay dim, and the *Shadow* loomed like her namesake, dark and cold. Alix could see the mag-clamps on her landing gear. She looked around before she entered a command sequence on her syncpad to open the cargo bay at the stern, facing them. She winced at the sound of the metal grinding and the pressure seals hissing, shooting steam and air as the ramp opened. Lights within the cargo bay flickered on.

She was home.

Before she and Wick could make it the few meters to the ramp, the main door of the docking bay moved, the inner mechanisms breaking the silence. The sound startled her, and then she froze. Looking toward the main door, she saw a line of men. Instinctively, Alix drew her Plasvelds and opened fire. The men at the door returned fire, a crisscross of blue plasma sparking overhead as their shots hit the hull of the *Shadow*. Alix ducked and rolled behind heavy supply crates that offered the only cover between the wall of the docking bay and the ship. Still, the prospect of sprinting the open distance between the crates and the cargo ramp was ill-advised.

"Felix, what the fuck happened?" she shouted into their comms.

"They knew we were coming. Xypha frequency. I've got the controls. I'm on my way."

"Ten men here. Wick and I can hold them off, but we need you."

Alix popped over the top of the supply crate and picked off one of the men who had tried to get around them toward the *Shadow*. She ducked down again, looked to her left, and saw Wick crouched, plasbolts in hand, chambers spinning and alight.

"Felix is on his way!"

"Great. I'm sure we won't be dead before he gets here."

Alix ducked back down behind the crates. *The marshal,* she thought. She hoped she had given them more time when she sent his stirrol running. *He must have gotten back into comms range and alerted his deputies.* Wick fired with her over and around the crates, their plasfire pinning the men back by the main bay doors. Alix couldn't tell from the view through her goggles who exactly the men were, and adjusting the frequency to heat signatures would render her almost blind from the plasma rounds being exchanged. Whether it was the marshal's men, Silas's men, or Xypha didn't matter. They were keeping her on the ground, so they had to be eliminated.

Suddenly, the plasfire stopped, and Alix turned and peeked over the crate. A shroud of smoke and steam obscured the doorway into the docking bay, but she saw through it, to more figures approaching. But these were not the outlines of men; they were thin and moved in perfect unison—her blood ran cold. A line of robotic figures approached the bay door, unconcerned with taking cover. The Xypha Z-16 security drone, or zig, was an omniite machine with a slender profile, a flat faceplate, and a heavy plasma rifle. Alix had seen them patrolling mindlessly back in the Cradle. The heavy footfalls and strange garbled sounds of communication between them seared into her memory. She ducked back behind the crate.

"We've got to get to the ship. *Now.*"

"What the hell are those things?" Wick yelled, barely peeking around the crate.

"Zigs, Xypha drones. If we don't get to the ship now, we're dead."

Wick looked at her in disbelief, his own panic nothing compared to how Alix now felt. Her hands shook, her Plasvelds no longer steady. The zigs' footsteps halted together, and the moment of silence seemed to last an eternity. There was no time to waste. She looked at the loading ramp of the *Shadow,* open and waiting for her. She'd have to run a few meters out in the open, but with enough plasfire, maybe she could make it. Then, she could cover Wick with the ship's defense systems.

"Wick, you've got to cover me!"

"Wait, Alix! Listen, you—"

But she already leapt to her feet and ran, blindly firing to her left. She focused only ahead, only on the loading ramp. *Almost home.*

A plasma round ripped through her stomach.

Another went through her chest.

She stumbled, tripped on the ramp's edge, and fell face-first. The fall kept the last shot from slicing through her head.

Alix looked up through wet and blurry eyes. The inside of the *Shadow*'s cargo bay lit softly ahead—just a few paces. Her skin became pale, and she could barely hold her head up any longer. She moved her mouth as if attempting to speak, but her eyelids fluttered and slowly closed.

Felix raced through the maintenance passageways. He detected the zigs' activation sequence, but there was no point in warning Alix. She had seen them at the same time as he'd felt them powering up. There was no point in waiting, no longer a need for caution. With the mag-clamp controls accessible to him, he unlocked the *Shadow*, but more than that, as he ran, he ripped through every system the port had. Lights, heating, cooling, communications, proximity monitoring, all of it shut down in an instant. Suddenly, a signal shot to him, taking his mind away from the port's systems. It was Alix's vitals, monitored by her syncpad, always feeding into his mind.

The heartbeat slowly faded.

Alix's eyes opened. She couldn't build a rational thought. Her body shivered, and through her drowsy eyes, she could see the smooth metal floor in front of her covered in blood. But it was her own, she realized as she brought her left hand up to her face, seeing her fingers red and wet. Her head lay on her right arm, and she coughed, choking on blood in her throat. The pain passed through her entire body, burning and paralyzing, but she tried to move. Her fingers were numb in her left hand, and she could barely lift her head. With only the strength in her right arm, she crawled, pushing with one leg, tears streaming down her face. She could barely breathe.

She reached the cargo bay. The workbench against the hull on her right seemed kilometers away.

But still, she crawled, pulled, pushed, a smear of blood left on the floor behind her.

Reaching the workbench was a miracle. With one hand, she gripped one of the bench legs and pulled herself with a scream, sitting up against the hull. She looked down at the burnt, black, bloody holes in her body. At least it was her right arm that still worked. Alix pounded on the false panel beneath the workbench, again, and again, and again. She'd lost almost all her strength. Finally, the panel came loose, and she pulled the box from its hiding place.

With her right hand she fumbled with the locks, but managed to flick them open. Inside lay the three metal vials: the nano hyper-fluid. The only thought she could manage was of Felix. The fluid kept him alive, healed any wounds.

In seconds, she'd be dead, right here in her ship.

But instead of lying still and fading, she focused on the memory of Felix—his touch, the soft vibrations of his body comforting her.

There was no other choice.

She lifted one of the vials and flipped the cap off the syringe with her thumb. Her breath came in ragged gasps through one lung, the other obviously painfully collapsed. Her hand shook violently, but with all her focus and will, she steadied it long enough to hold the vial near her abdomen and plunge the syringe into her skin.

The black liquid entered her body with a sharp, searing pain. The fluid and the pain branched out like a newly released river following ancient branching beds. She dropped the tube and her body convulsed. Her mind went blank. Shaking violently, she fell over onto the floor. She screamed in agony. The dark liquid now operated of its own accord, moving through her body, following some unknown and strange programming given to the nanites within it. Through her tissue, bones, and veins, it moved, searching and finding the wound in her chest.

Swirling and surrounding the damaged tissue, the liquid went about its purpose, as if it occupied the body of a sentient. It stemmed the bleeding and bound together the broken tissue inside her, forming a microscopic webbing and a hard molecular structure that slowly grew and covered the hole with a dark layer of hard film, bonding to her skin. Though her mind still reeled, and she remained cold and weak, she no longer shook uncontrollably.

She reached again for another vial.

Wick cowered behind the supply crates, weeping. The lights went out with a loud shock, and the electric buzz faded. The mag clamps swung open, the arms falling away from the *Shadow*'s landing gear. Machinery broke down with a crash, the ground around him vibrating. One of the Z-16 drones, blacker than the dark around it, turned its body around the crate and lowered its plasma rifle. Near the top corner of its blank faceplate, Wick could see a small, square, red light.

This was the end.

Suddenly, a great force of wind rushed by. No one in the docking bay saw what was coming, and the zigs didn't react until it was too late. Felix knew they had no programming or system to detect him when in a cloaked state. He was invisible to all eyes and sensors. He needed no weapons to do the job.

With a powerful hand, he gripped the zig beside Wick beneath its head. He squeezed, and the joint fractured and sparked—the head broke free. All anyone could see was the drone snap and crumple to the ground as the blue and gold sparks from its neck flashed and disappeared. The zigs reacted, turned toward the other, but they had no target. Felix moved between them, from one to another, tearing frames apart. The men at the bay doors looked on in abject horror, pure disbelief. They would have run if they could have comprehended what was happening, what would happen. Metal arms and heads fell and flew through the air by an invisible force.

When Felix eliminated the last zig, he moved to the men at the door. He sent one of them flying, and the man screamed as he slammed into the opposite wall of the wide lane between docking bays. His body cracked and broke against the steel.

The other men opened fire, but they shot wildly into nothing. They couldn't see Felix or hear him, so the lane became a blazing hot disaster. Men shot one another. Felix broke arms, necks, and slammed men against the walls. Some tried to flee, but there was no escape.

Once the last was dead, the lane fell quiet.

Alix lay on her side and held the second vial in her weak hand, the first vial still hanging by the needle in her stomach. She stabbed the second into her shoulder. The pain tore through her again, and she screamed and clenched her jaw, trying to withstand the pain that twisted her limbs and stole her breath. The liquid moved through her, searching, replacing, binding—repairing. Despite the pain, with each passing moment, she felt a kind of strength return to her, though she stared at her bloody fingers, rubbing them together, strangely numb. Her body curled and her muscles seized as she clutched her arms to her chest and convulsed. Her muscles finally relaxed, and she lay on the floor, cold and trembling. She coughed and vomited blood.

Alix put her hand to her forehead and opened her eyes, her sight growing clearer by the second. She saw the alien sight of black liquid, in small lines, passing through her veins in her left arm, beneath her skin, and it no longer carried any pain, but a strange feeling of motion. She closed her fist to stop her hand from trembling and leaned on her other hand, sitting up.

Felix didn't reappear to the naked eye until he bounded up the cargo ramp and came to Alix's side. She smiled and tried to laugh, her breath still weak. Blood covered her face, hands, and the floor around her, the burnt holes in her clothes showing the wounds clearly. Felix immediately saw the hyper-fluid within her, and his eyes widened. One vial remained in the protective case. He put it into his belt and scooped Alix gently off the floor. He couldn't believe it, but somehow, the fluid followed its purpose and held her body together. It stymied the internal bleeding, bonding her damaged organs and tissues together. She reached her hand up and touched his face, blood smearing from her fingers onto his smooth membrane.

"I'm sorry," she whispered.

"Don't do that."

"I was dead either way."

"Come on, let's go."

As Felix got to his feet, he felt a plasbolt on him, like hair standing on the back of a human's neck. He spun and saw only Wick. His hat had come off in the shootout, and his face was pale, mouth hanging open as he saw Alix still alive. He held one plasbolt at them in a trembling hand.

"Wh- What the fuck just happened?"

Felix's eyes narrowed and his lip curled.. The man was in shock, afraid of every whisper and shadow. Felix's mind calculated the speed and precise movements needed to put Alix down and get to Wick before he could fire a shot. The trembling hand put that calculation even more in Felix's favor, but there was something else that caught his attention. Wick's plasbolt was the least of their worries.

"I'm not waiting for you," Felix said.

Wick's eyes searched for something barely visible, like following an ember from a fire up into the wind. He dropped his plasbolt, muttering to himself, rubbing his hand up and over his head. Felix detected the wave of reinforcements, and another squad of zigs approached as quickly as the stiff drones could move. With Alix near death, he couldn't wait around to eliminate them.

Felix pushed past Wick and ran down the ramp toward the maintenance door. Wick tumbled over, losing his balance as Felix went by. He fell to the ground and looked up, clearing his head. Three black orbs bounced through the docking bay door, rolling toward him, toward the ship.

He pushed up off the ground and stumbled, running, falling, scrambling away toward the door.

The orbs behind them exploded. The force ripped through the *Shadow*'s landing gear, blowing open the hull. The ship groaned and tilted, falling to the ground, the gear no longer able to hold its weight. Supply crates went flying, and Wick felt the force of the explosions at his back. It threw him forward, and he hit and rolled on the ground, head over heels. In a panic, he crawled on all fours, reaching the door and breaking into a sprint once inside.

Felix landed in the tunnel, Alix unconscious in his arms. A distant voice screamed like a madman. Felix looked back and saw Wick dive through the hole and splash in the water, oil, and muck. Felix pulled a small metal sphere from his belt.

"Move," he ordered Wick.

Wick crawled through the water as Felix tossed the sphere up. The sphere whistled and then detonated. The tunnel ceiling broke and collapsed, debris falling from the storage hanger as the floor broke apart. The tumbling rocks and metal blocked the tunnel once again, leaving Felix, Alix, and Wick in the dark.

13

The Flame

The marshal saw a looming column of black smoke on the eastern horizon. He spurred his stirrol, covering the final stretch of chis between him and Verisport. When he arrived at the black outer wall of the spaceport, he sent a signal to Cole indicating his presence. The gate to the yard opened for him, and he finally gave his stirrol a break, the animal's nostrils flared and its breathing heavy. Cole came running.

"What the hell happened?" the marshal said.

"You were right, they went for the ship in Bay 12, but—"

"But what?" the marshal snapped at Cole, not having time for worries about protocol, rank, or any other bullshit.

"While you were gone, the council put Otto's men in charge of security here. They have three ships landed, these weird robotic guards, and some guy named Loucks is in charge."

"Did we lose anybody?"

"Half a dozen men. The rest were Xypha guys."

"Who listened to you?"

"Dunn, Rhodes, and Underwood."

"They're the only men we can trust—and I mean the *only* men."

"Yes, sir."

Crews raced around the facility trying to restore order from the bloodbath in the pre-dawn hours. Everything from the power to the fire suppression systems had to be reset. Engineers and operators in the tower worked on no sleep, all-hands on deck, trying to get the network back into shape after Felix had torn everything apart. He had left them blind and powerless. The best they had done so far was get the bare minimum back online. A crew flipped the manual switches to restore emergency power, but it was only meant to operate the most basic functions. No one had been able to activate the fire suppression hoses yet.

Inside Bay 12, the flames continued to burn beneath and within the *Shadow*. If the explosives hadn't been tossed by programmable machines, someone would've accused them of recklessness. But the move was calculated, and it left the *Shadow* in ruins, listed to one side, the hull digging into the metal, rock, and dirt of the docking bay floor. Black smoke poured into the sky, and men stood around watching, clear respirators over their mouths and noses. The marshal and Cole grabbed respirators from an underling as they approached the bay themselves.

"Unbelievable," the marshal whispered.

"Power systems were completely shut down. We got no security footage of what happened. No survivors," Cole said.

Felix, the marshal thought.

The smoke and chemicals in the air burned the marshal's eyes. He rubbed them with his fingers, turning away. When he opened them, a stiff man in a Xypha slipsuit leading three other Xypha men, approached him.

"No one is permitted in here without my authorization." The man's voice was deep and commanding.

"Who the hell are you?" the marshal replied.

"Officer Fenn Loucks. I know who *you* are, Marshal Rayburn. The council has given full authority to the Sovereign Xypha Corporation to oversee safety and security in this spaceport."

The man spoke like his own thoughts had been programmed into him. The marshal sneered. Loucks stood straight, his broad shoulders carrying a large head, made even larger by his opinion of himself. The Xypha neural implant glinted over his left ear, his hair shaved on the sides, short and flat on top.

"Guess we'll be moving along, then," the marshal said, making a sweeping gesture with his hand toward the chaos in the docking bay.

At least the power had been restored enough to operate the lift. Inside his office, the marshal felt safe enough to talk freely. He watched the men below from his window, the black column of smoke nearly obscured his view.

"Get Dunn, Rhodes, and—"

"Underwood," Cole interrupted.

"Get them together—quietly. Set up a separate frequency."

"What are we going to do?" Cole's voice trembled.

"Restore order."

Far out west in the valley, Wesley poured grain down a line for a portion of his ibi flock. The short, puffy-coated animals crammed in to eat their first meal of the day. The sun hung low, and as he turned, he saw a solitary man riding in from the east. He looked over to his right, seeing Anna and the boys feeding the chickens gathered around their ankles. His heart dropped like a stone.

"Anna, take the boys inside," he called.

She looked up to see the rider before she dropped the feed bag from her shoulder and shooed their sons inside. Wesley stood at the corner fencepost of the pen on his left. His ears burned and the sound of his heart in his chest seemed to overtake the baying ibi, and the stirrol's hoofs in the grass as the rider approached. The Thin Man dismounted, straightening his long, black duster. He was freshly dressed, in a dark red shirt, a black vest, black trousers, and boots. He pushed the wide brim of his gray hat back with one finger and smiled.

"Morning, Wes. Let's go inside and have a chat."

Anna and the boys hid somewhere in the quiet house while, in the kitchen, Wes poured himself a glass of water. The Thin Man sat and put his boots up on the table. Wes stared at the man across from him, mind racing as silence hung between them. The Thin Man picked at his fingernails with a pocketknife, unconcerned. He knew no one around the farm posed a danger to him.

"What does Silas want?" Wes finally broke the silence.

The Thin Man put the pocketknife away and stared at Wes, studying his worried face. The farmer was afraid, but outwardly, he looked angry. "The rent's come due, Wes."

"Silas doesn't own this land."

"No, he doesn't, but there's still a debt to be paid."

"Wickford went with you—he paid our father's debt."

"This ain't about your daddy, but your brother..." The Thin Man paused. "Now that is a problem."

"I don't know where he is."

"Yeah, I know." The Thin Man stared a hole through Wes.

"Then what're you here for? If you want to hurt me, just get it over with." Wes tensed, sweat beading on his brow. His hands trembled on the table, so he pressed his palms hard into the surface. He was angry, but there was no escaping this. He thought of his wife, his boys; there was no escape for them, either.

"Your brother's with some people who have caused a lot of trouble. I know you don't know where these people and your brother are, and neither do I. We've got to smoke them out," The Thin Man said.

He let the silence linger, and the Thin Man just waited, seeing if maybe Wes would try to jump him, fight for his life, no matter how futile. But the farmer didn't move, his fate accepted.

The Thin Man dropped his boots off the table and stood, the Plasveld on his left hip shimmering. He didn't draw fast, but slow, deliberate, spinning up the chambers. Wes sat up straight, his face twisting, bracing himself for the shot. The soft whining of the charged Plasveld became the only sound, the room taking on a soft blue glow from the plasbolt.

Wes's eyes watered, staring back at the man who would be his end. Wes begged, prayed, in his mind that Anna and his sons had fled, that they may escape this grim death. The Thin Man let out a heavy sigh. He showed no signs of the weight of the plasbolt wearing on his outstretched arm. He stood tall and imposing, unmoving.

"What are—"

Zmmph.

The room flashed blue. A single plasma round pierced Wes's heart, cutting off his last words. The Thin Man remained still, staring at the dead man in the chair: head tilted back, eyes open, mouth slack. He stood, listening, as footsteps hurried toward the room from elsewhere in the house. The Thin Man made no sound when Anna came frantically around the corner, crying, already knowing what had occurred.

He didn't let her reach Wes's body. Instead, a single shot killed her instantly, her body crumpling to the floor between the kitchen and the table. Still, the Thin Man did not move. More, smaller footsteps—a door opening. He smiled.

Without any flair, he holstered his Plasveld and moved toward the kitchen, stepping over Anna's body. In a storeroom on his right, he found sacks of grain, household tools, cans, jars, and medicine. The fire in the kitchen burned low. An oil lamp sat on the table in the center of the kitchen. He knocked it over, and the glass broke on the stone floor. Another lamp from the storeroom broke on the floor. The thick oil pooled around broken glass.

The Thin Man lit a cigarette. He took a long drag, looked around, and dropped the cigarette into the oil, which caught fire almost immediately. He walked out the front door, pulling his hat back low and tight. He sat in the saddle of the stirrol and turned it to look back at the farmhouse as the fire spread. The ibi in the pen began crowding into one corner, baying wildly, pressing against the fence. Wherever Wes's sons had run off to, the Thin Man didn't care.

He turned the stirrol, riding slowly away from the house.

Behind him, glass shattered and wood cracked. Flaming curtains blew in the wind.

Alix lay on a lumpy mattress in Jesse's room. Sweat soaked her hair and dripped down her face. Felix had stripped the bloody clothes from her body, and she lay only in her underwear and a tank top. Her body shook as a fever burned through her, though she felt ice cold. Felix leaned over her, trying to figure out what to do. Sora paced behind him, chewing on her lip. All morning, they'd tried to keep Alix from dying, but in the most futile ways. She could drink sips of water. They put a cool cloth on her forehead and wiped the sweat from her arms. Felix would have dressed her wounds, but the black, solid matrix formed by the hyper-fluid now in her body took care of that. The wounds didn't bleed, and as Felix peered through her skin, he could see that her collapsed lung was now full, and she breathed steadily, though shallow.

There was nothing else he or anyone could do. Fear gripped Felix as he sat on the bed, trying to comfort Alix, a hand gently holding hers. The only thing he could do was study her. No one had ever mixed the hyper-fluid with human DNA, especially hadn't injected it directly into a human body. Felix assumed the interaction would kill her immediately. He waited and feared that it would come to that. Although the fluid worked for now, he didn't believe it could last. At some point, Alix's body would reject it, or the fluid would reject its human vessel.

He would have wept if he was able.

Felix gently closed the door and saw Sora leaning against the wall beside him. He could see the concern on her face, not to mention hear the pounding heart in her chest. "How are you holding up?" he said.

"Is she going to be okay?" Sora said.

"Not sure." Felix looked down at his feet. "But I'm hopeful. She's stable, at least."

"What is that stuff?"

"It's a fluid consisting of nanorobotics, designed for sentients like me," he said. "I have what you would call veins, just like you, but this is what courses through mine. It regulates temperature, repairs wounds and tears in the membrane, and can repair and remanufacture interior components, other than the omniite skeleton I have."

"All that, huh?" Sora blinked rapidly.

"It was designed and programmed by…" Felix's voice trailed off. "Well, another sentient. I had spare supply, which is what Alix used in the *Shadow*."

"You said it could kill her?"

"I mean, it's a foreign substance in the body. Her immune system could go haywire to oppose it." Felix winced. "Or the hyper-fluid could just…do its job, as it is right now. It has never been put into a human, but the fact that it is performing the same function as it does *within me* indicates the nano-programming can somehow communicate with a natural human biology."

"So, basically, we wait and see if she dies or wakes up." A tear ran down Sora's face.

"All we can do at this point is hope," Felix said, laying a hand on her shoulder.

They hugged one another. Sora wept, her face pressed close to Felix's chest. He stared over her head, through the steel door, at Alix as he silently pleaded for her life.

By the following day, Alix's fever dissipated. When she opened her eyes, the room appeared cloudy, out of focus. Seeing Felix sitting in a chair beside the bed brought a smile to her face, as best as she could manage. Her entire body felt stiff, a little numb, like she didn't have full control of her muscles yet. Felix's body was in sync with her vitals, and he awoke as she began to stir.

"Alix!" He turned and held her hand, smiling. "How do you feel?"

"Like shit," she moaned. Her tongue felt like a wad of cotton in her mouth. "Water," she murmured.

Felix held her head, putting a bottle to her lips. The water poured down her chin and shirt. She fell back on the bed, licking her lips. From head to toe, she began testing her movements, blinking heavily, wiggling her fingers and toes.

"What do you remember?" Felix said.

"Getting shot." Alix took several deep breaths and managed a weak laugh. "Don't look at me like some kind of test subject."

"Sorry," Felix said, embarrassed. "I just can't believe you're okay."

"Am I?" Alix was not so sure.

"You are stable. It was touch and go yesterday. The hyper-fluid has…worked. Remarkably, it followed its programming to repair your wounds just like if you were…well, a sentient."

"I'm sorry, Felix. I know it's precious."

He stopped her. "I'd rather have you alive."

Otto sat in his command center, quite pleased with himself, his chair suspended over the great window, looking down on the planet. Everything had worked out in his favor, although the plan was rather nonlinear, not calculated down to the tiniest variable. The whole thing had been a little too chaotic for him, which is why he needed a man like Silas Purvida. With the marshal in the wind, chasing ghosts of his own past, Otto and Silas managed to secure the spaceport for Xypha business. The marshal's own call to his chief deputy, that a threat was incoming to the port, accelerated things in their favor.

The marshal was absent, but Xypha swooped in, white ships glittering in the sun. The aftermath, however, was less pristine. One of the twelve docking bays lay in ruin, a freighter lying on its side, split open. He looked through live images of crews trying to restore order. A prickly man, Arthur, the dockmaster, argued with Loucks on the surface. Otto felt intense relief that he didn't have to be on the ground himself.

Now, he began calculating and planning the logistics of getting materials from the station to repair the spaceport. All complimentary, of course—for now.

He received a transmission from Silas, who seemed as smug as ever, but there was a hint of joy in his voice. "Otto! I'm eager to get a salvage crew in for that ship."

"Loucks should be able to coordinate that with you," Otto replied, not taking his eyes or attention away from plotting the drop ship routes.

Otto couldn't care less that Silas grew impatient, seeing as Otto now had a middleman between them. Silas would be useful until he wasn't any longer. For now, the man still had the capability to sway opinions that Otto needed to be swayed a certain direction. Silas insisted the fight in the spaceport be bloody and destructive. Otto knew the Z-16s would easily dispatch their prey, but the explosions were an extraneous step. Silas wanted that ship for his own ends, and now, he could have it—if he could fix it.

"Loucks's report has just come in," Otto said.

This diverted his attention. He absorbed the high-level conclusions then drilled down to the painstaking details, data from the Z-16s, which were independent of the virus that had rendered the port's network inoperable. Otto and Silas knew the destroyed ship's pilot had an artificial companion, but there was no data of his presence: no visuals, no electronic readings—nothing. Otto stumbled over that fact. It had to be a mistake, an impossibility. But, based on the damage to the Z-16s, the only conclusion would've been that an artificial destroyed them with its bare hands.

"Anything of interest?" Silas said, impatiently.

Otto ignored him.

No artificial out here could do this kind of damage, he thought. Xypha's data and projections on the frontier indicated that the only artificials would be late models, non-combatants, but holes in the data in front of him screamed something else entirely. He didn't believe it. *It must be some kind of mistake.*

In the evening, Jo sat alone on a stump at the same spot where she and Sora had once looked down on a scene of death. The larger moon was high, its smaller kin lower toward the horizon. Pale blue and purple light covered the valley, shadows behind her beneath the twilight orchard. Her plasrifle lay across her thighs. Sora had been gone with the others for days now, and she'd heard nothing since. Every night, she came here and looked west, hoping to see her sister riding home. Tonight, she saw only the waving chis, wild stirrols moving through, carving lines in the sheaths.

Footsteps approached behind her.

She jumped up and wheeled around, rifle at the ready.

The Thin Man walked toward her, palms up and out. "I'm unarmed."

She narrowed her eyes, kept her rifle level with his face. He appeared out of the darkness, dressed in black, save for his grey hat and dark red shirt. Looking down at his waist, Jo saw that he was, indeed, not carrying a plasbolt—both holsters hung empty.

"Do not take another step," she demanded, and he complied. "What the fuck are you doing here?"

"I came to talk."

"Like hell you did. I've seen you before. You are Silas's goon."

The Thin Man smirked and held out his arms, shrugging his shoulders. "I am."

His calm demeanor struck Jo. She wouldn't have expected a man like him to come without a weapon, much less be so calm about it. Jo assumed the worst, and suspected he had some other kind of leverage.

"You wanted to talk? Well, let's hear it. You got demands?" She kept her rifle at her shoulder and didn't once look away from the sight.

"Nah, I don't have any demands." He had put his arms down and lit a cigarette.

He walked where he wished, toward the edge of the hill, looking up at the moons. Jo backed up to keep distance between them, her rifle still on him. The Thin Man blew a trail of smoke into the cold air and held his cigarette between his thumb and forefinger of his left hand. He let out a deep breath then drew one in, letting the cold air fill his lungs.

Jo subconsciously started to relax.

"Put that rifle down, kid. You ain't about to shoot me," he said.

"I wouldn't bet on it," Jo snipped.

The Thin Man turned his head toward her, still smiling. "You would've done it already."

Jo dropped her shoulders and held the rifle at her waist, proving him right.

"You're not a killer. Not yet, at least," he said.

"Are you looking for my sister? And those other three? They aren't here."

"Yeah, I know they ain't here. I suppose they're somewhere in Verisport, licking their wounds."

Hearing that Sora had returned to Verisport without even stopping by the village or even calling to say where she was headed shook Jo. She looked at the ground, her eyes darting back and forth, trying to think.

"Your sister is alright," he said. "You're going make a call to her, and she'll come running."

"So you want me to be your bait?" Her anger washed over the fear.

The Thin Man shook his head and laughed. He looked out across the valley, taking stock of the whole scene. The cigarette burned low in his fingers. "Bad things are coming, kid. A vengeful fire is going to spread across this valley. That woman and artie your sister is with set it off."

"You're here already. I could just put out the fire right now," Jo said, raising her rifle again, but only as a show.

The Thin Man took one last drag, then put the cigarette out in his right palm. He tossed it to the ground. "I ain't the fire, kid. Just the flame." He sniffed the air, then turned to face her. He tipped his hat and smiled one last time. "You got things to take care of."

Jo furrowed her brow, and then she smelled the smoke in the air. The clear sound of a clanging bell in the village echoed. She looked back, and a faint orange glow like the setting sun, sat above the orchard behind her. Jo ignored the Thin Man, slung her rifle over her shoulder, and ran toward the fire.

The following morning, Alix sat up in bed, legs over the side. Felix, Sora, and Wick stared at her in anticipation. She hated it. "Stop looking at me like that," she said, focusing on her legs.

With all her might, she stood, her legs, back, and hips aching, stiff and weak. Felix gave her a hand to keep her balance, and she let out the breath she'd been holding as she stood. Sora began to smile, hopeful that Alix would be okay.

"The big question now is, what will the hyper-fluid do when your wounds heal?" Felix said.

"Have you ever…gotten it *out* voluntarily?" Sora said.

"Outside of *very* specific circumstances in a medical or laboratory facility? It being within a *human* is completely uncharted territory," Felix recalled.

"Maybe it'll just come out on its own, you know?" Alix raised an eyebrow. They got what she was saying.

"Let's hope not." Felix allowed himself to laugh at that idea.

Alix was going stir-crazy, lying in a bed for days beginning to gnaw at her. She hated it. Felix tried to object, but she had to get up, move around, test her limits. A wave of relief washed over her as she managed to stagger out of the room, back into Jesse's office and through the shop. Through windows, she could see the still-dark morning, the glow of the city against it slowly giving way to the rising sun. She finally let herself think of her ship.

"The *Shadow*?" She looked at Felix.

"The zigs had explosives. We ran, and I don't know what state she's in," he said, holding her a little tighter in case she weakened.

Alix clenched her eyes shut, fighting off a wave of pain—not from the wounds on her body, but the thought that the *Shadow* might be damaged, destroyed, grounded for good, just like her. She slapped away Felix's hand and stood on her own, hand on her head, taking a deep breath.

Sora felt her syncpad vibrate on her forearm. She looked down and saw Jo trying to contact her.

"It's Jo," she said out loud, worried. "I totally forgot to let her know what's going on. She's going to kill me."

"She'll be relieved that you're alright." Alix smiled.

But Alix was wrong. Sora answered the transmission, saw Jo's panic-stricken face, and although she couldn't see the world around Jo, her sister yelled to raise her voice over some kind of chaos.

"Sora! You've got to come home now! There's been a fire."

"What? Are you okay?" Sora began to panic too. Everyone in the room now stared at her, wide-eyed and fearful.

"I'm fine. We've been dealing with it all night, but we need your help. *I* need your help."

"I'll be right there!" Sora looked around the room, tears in her eyes. "I have to go."

Alix spoke without hesitation, "We are coming with you."

Felix disapproved. "You need to take it slow."

"Don't tell me what I need to do," Alix yelled. "We're sticking together."

"Alix, he's right. You can't risk riding out there," Sora pleaded with her.

"Saddle up," Alix replied, defiance in her eyes.

The four of them returned to the stirrols. The animals seemed eager to run again, sensing the urgency of the people throwing saddles on their backs and bridles over their ears. Alix limped and clenched her jaw, keenly aware of her wounds, feeling the alien substance holding them together with her fingers. Her hand trembled, but she pushed that aside, pulled herself up into the saddle, and collected the reins. There was no time to waste.

The crew rode out of Jesse's scrapyard and spurred the stirrols south, through the outskirts of town. Then, they turned northwest, hoofs turning up the grass and dirt as the stirrols stretched their legs.

The marshal looked out from his window, seeing the view of Verisport return. The black smoke faded into white, and the once thick, heavy column thinned and spread out into the wind. Below, fire crews finally had their equipment up and running, white foam spraying, sitting on the *Shadow* and the ground around it in great big globs. His thoughts drifted to Alix, somewhere in the city, he guessed. *Was she wounded or worse? How did they get in unnoticed?*

He activated the window display, darkening his view again, but cycling through data from the incident. There was a sudden cliff where the data dropped off—when Felix destroyed the network. The marshal worked backwards from there. He had no clue what Felix was capable of, and though he didn't see the scene as it had been in the immediate aftermath, the thought of Felix shutting down the entire network and Alix killing every man sent into that docking bay sent a shiver down his spine.

I put a plasbolt in that kid's hand, he thought. *Look where that got me.*

Alix worked in the spaceport before he let her become a deputy. He remembered that scrawny kid, already tougher than the grown men she worked beside. *She knows the layout of this place in detail*, he thought. *She'd find a way to the docking bay without being detected.* He knew that if Felix had destroyed the network before Alix was ready to leave, it would only send the spaceport into a frenzy. It had to be intended to cover their escape.

But the marshal's call to Cole, warning him that Alix would go for the *Shadow* above all else, cornered her in the docking bay. *Otto probably used the warning to land his ships.* He hoped Cole and his men could keep things under control, to keep things civil. He overestimated Cole's abilities.

The marshal couldn't undo the past, but he could preserve the future. Looking through the layout of the port, three great pipes crossing underground offered a clue. They were old, going way back to Verisport's early days, most of them sealed up. He flipped through current surveillance footage of where the pipes intersected or ran under the port. There, a storage hangar where the floor was caved in. He followed that pipe's trajectory out into town, to the eastern edge— beneath scrapyards and industrial facilities.

The marshal tapped his syncpad and opened the private frequency Cole had established for him and the remaining men he trusted. "I found their entry point. Get your guys and meet me in the market. We'll check the east district on foot."

A massive cloud hung over Sora's village. Alix saw it on the horizon from a great distance out, climbing up into the sky, spreading out into a wide cap. Everyone in the village wore cloths over their faces. Soot and ash covered hair, clothes, and skin. Every person in the village took part, and it looked like they'd been through hell in the night.

The eastern edge of the orchard lay in ruins, trees burned down to black stumps, the ground thick with smoldering wood and grass. Sora couldn't tell how far the damage extended, the smoke hung heavy, obscuring her view further into the orchard's remains. She dismounted her stirrol while it still trotted, leaving it in the commons.

Many people washed their faces in the cistern as hoses ran from it out toward the fire. The village used a very unsophisticated method to fight the fire, but it seemed they managed to put it out eventually. She raced across the village toward the barn, shouting Jo's name. A neighbor pointed her toward the trees, and Sora changed her path.

When she found Jo, her sister sat on a harvester, a wagon attached, hauling water. Sora wept as she dropped to her knees in front of Jo, hugging her tightly. Jo barely reacted, still in shock and exhausted. Her hair was dusty grey, her eyes wet and red, face covered with soot, a kerchief down around her neck that she wore all night over her mouth and nose.

"What happened?" Sora said, pulling back from the embrace, but still holding her younger sister's shoulders.

"Silas happened." Jo broke into a coughing fit, her lungs burning from the smoke.

"What do you mean?"

"I mean, one of his men was here. I've seen him before, giving orders to others who stole money from us every month."

"Did you get shots at him?"

Jo deflected a pang of guilt, then shook her head.

"What's the damage like?" Sora looked around.

"Not sure. We saved some, maybe a third? Three died overnight. Lots of people are sick from the smoke."

Alix, Felix, and Wick finally caught up, since Alix couldn't manage to run. She held her hand over the wound in her chest, out of breath. The wound felt like it could burst open, like the black matrix holding it together would decide to give up.

Jo scowled when she saw the three of them. "I thought they'd be gone," she said.

Sora looked over her shoulder and turned back, "No, they're here to help."

"This is all their fault." Jo grew angrier. The words of the Thin Man echoed in her mind as she stood up "This is all *your* fault!" she pointed at Alix.

"Jo, you shouldn't blame them," Sora said.

"Why not? You should have been here!" Jo pushed her sister back and stormed away.

Sora stood dumbfounded as the world all around her fell apart. The villagers' efforts, combined with luck, prevented the fire from spreading to the homes. The black ground beneath her feet showed the edge of where the fire reached. The water tank behind the harvester sat empty. People moved around like hollow shells of themselves. She didn't know what to do.

"Sora, are you alright?" Alix asked, gently touching her arm.

"No," Sora gasped.

"What can we do to help?" Alix embraced her.

They found Sim in the same shape as Jo, broken, exhausted. She directed them to places where people still put out residual flames. The walk to the edge of the burn was longer than they feared. The fire cut a wide swath from the east, eliminating much of the northern edge, sweeping southwest.

Alix quickly found she could hardly stand the air. It burned her lungs, and the work strained her still-weakened body. But she pushed through, her anger fueling the effort. She and Wick dragged hoses, held them as water drenched the land. Felix helped pilot skimmers out to the edge, returning with fresh water. Sora helped those who were already collapsing from exhaustion. Wagons ferried men and women back to their homes; the people were fed, given water to drink, and poured half of it over their faces to wash off the thick soot and dirt.

At the edge of the burn, Alix hauled a hose as men directed water out in a wide arc. She stumbled, tripped, and fell to one knee, catching herself with one hand. She felt a sharp pain and lifted her right hand, seeing a large splinter stabbing into her palm. She pulled it out, blood seeping behind it, but then, she felt the hyper-fluid move within her, agonizingly passing through her body, her veins, straight to her hand. She had no idea there was more left that wasn't holding her together. It gathered in the cut and turned her blood black, before it sealed the wound.

14

Red Right Hand

Many years ago…

Alix carried the coils of a heavy hose over her shoulder. The midday sun burned overhead. The spaceport filled with men's voices, the sighs of ships' engines, the clink and clang of machines and locks and hammers and drivers and the hissing of pressurized air. She dropped the coils on the ground at the base of a coolant pump, locking one end of the hose into the pump. A shadow fell over her, a man blocking out the light.

Alix looked back and closed one eye from the sun to see the marshal looking at her and smiling. Alix returned the smile and stood, wiping her hands on the chest of her grey, standard issue dockworker jumpsuit. The marshal held a box under his arm.

"What's that?" Alix cocked an eyebrow.

"A present," he said. "It's your birthday."

Alix crossed her arms. "We don't even know how old I am."

"Fine. It's the day I found you, remember?"

"Is it?" Alix counted back in her head and on her fingers, as if it was only ten days ago.

The marshal laughed. "You're a young man now, and I know you had been asking for this, but I told you it had to wait—until you were ready."

Alix bristled at the words. *Young man.* She knew the truth, but hadn't worked up the courage to say it to the marshal, yet. She quickly remembered the moment was supposed to be happy and she tried to return to levity.

"Please not *the talk*." Alix rolled her eyes and smirked.

The marshal opened the box.

A pristine Plasveld-7 lay inside. The polished silver steel glistened in the sun. A subtle gold inlay ran down the long barrel, but the cylinder sat empty; no plasma charge had touched it yet. The grip of fine, dark burrey wood bore a carved pattern in a lighter polish.

"Take it," the marshal said, gesturing the box forward.

Alix lifted the Plasveld in her right hand, feeling its weight. She wrapped a long finger around the trigger, ran her fingers down the barrel to feel the inlay. Her face was as bright as the sun and for a moment she forgot about the truth in the back of her mind. She threw her arms around the old man's shoulders, the Plasveld dangling behind the marshal's back.

"I'll teach you after your shift," the marshal whispered, holding Alix proudly.

Now...

Alix sat in the bare cabin where she and Felix had before stayed in Sora's village. On the floor in front of her was the disassembled Plasveld—barrel with gold inlay, bright silver, dark wood grip. A dirty rag, brush, and polish sat next to her on the floor. Slowly, she began reassembling the weapon. From barrel to backstrap, the plasbolt shined as she held it. It weighed the same, but she was stronger now.

She flipped out the cylinder and loaded a blue plasma charge cell before she flicked her wrist and locked the cylinder back in place. She spun the chamber, and the plasbolt began to glow, to *sing*. Alix spun the bolt on her finger, back and forth, turning her wrist to change the spin horizontally, moving between fingers until the grip clapped back in her palm. Her belt lay on the bed, her other Plasveld already cleaned and ready. She slid the gift back into its holster, then wrapped and buckled the belt around her waist. Her goggles hung around her neck, and she tied a red band to hold her hair back.

The others thought she slept, taking her rest while they continued the cleanup effort. A small doubt passed through her mind—a whisper. With a deep breath, she let it pass. Alix headed to the barn, saddled a stirrol, and raced out of the village. The cool air rushed by her ears, watered her eyes. Her body still ached as the stirrol galloped, but she felt strong and focused. The sun set in front of her, leaving a long, thin shadow behind.

Sora played over what she might say in her head. The long, contentious talk with Jo still stung, but Jo was right; Sora needed to stay here, with her people, with her sister. She had a responsibility to help them, especially now. The crits they stole from those men in the valley would help keep the village afloat. Sora could not keep up— with Alix, with the rising tide of violence and revenge.

Before Sora could knock on the cabin wall, she peered into the open doorway and saw the cloth on the floor, the brush, the polish, the dirty rag. But she did not see Alix, nor her things. Fearing the worst, Sora ran.

Felix helped a team of men clear burned and fallen trees, large, dark piles of brush forming. He lifted a burned trunk and tossed it onto a pile with minimal effort.

"Felix!" Sora shouted. She stopped short of him, her face covered in sweat and terror. "Alix is gone," she said between heavy breaths.

The market still buzzed as the lanterns came to life with the setting sun. Ropes crisscrossed over the large square, hover lamps within colorful hanging paper lamps, spreading a beautiful rainbow of light. Alix smelled the coffee, the twilight fruit pastries, the seared ibi legs, roasted kien roots. The sounds of people laughing, shouting, and playing filled her ears. She stood among the crowd, which moved around her like a gentle stream.

With a single step, she started on the path—down the street, around corners, away from the market lights. The city dimmed as fewer lamps hovered about. Fewer people enjoyed the night air. She didn't hesitate as she turned the final corner, walking to the large building at the end of the lane: *The Black Barrel.* Its lights beamed into the shadowed street through large windows. Rowdy shouts, laughter, and music came from the open doors.

She stopped in the center of the street.

"Silas Purvida!" she roared.

Men at the door took notice of her, as did those within earshot inside. Faces appeared in the windows. The boisterous swell began to die down as people asked questions. One of the men in the doorway left, while the other stopped leaning and stood, loose and dangerous.

Alix did not see Silas emerge from the front door. Instead, the doorman returned, standing on the opposite side of the door from his partner. Then came the Thin Man, shadowed by the light behind him. He walked to the edge of the boardwalk beneath the veranda, the spark of his lighter revealing his face in small flashes. He lit a cigarette and lifted his head, staring at Alix.

"Good evening, captain," he said in a formal tone.

Alix set her jaw. The Thin Man saw she would give no reply.

"I must say, I am surprised to see you on two feet. I thought those Xypha drones did their job in the dock." He waited for a reply, but there was none. "Your friends, are they not here with you?"

A long pause.

"Fine, you are here to see Silas, but I am afraid he's indisposed for the evening." The Thin Man took a drag.

Finally, Alix spoke. "Move, or die."

A smile crept across the Thin Man's face, showing his teeth, like an animal bearing its fangs. The fight he wanted was inevitable now.

"I shall move." He held a hand to his chest, bowed and stepped aside.

Behind him, more men came out of the saloon—large men, small men, wide men, thin men, angry men, sneering men, confident men— dead men.

The Thin Man took a drag. "See you inside, captain." He waved to her and walked through the line of men, back into the saloon.

The men formed a line on the boardwalk in front of Alix. They cast a haphazard shadow over her, and she looked from one to another. A dozen now stood between her and the door. As she raised her hands, the men cautiously moved their hands toward their belts, but Alix lifted her hands to her neck, stretched the leather goggles strap, and affixed them over her eyes. Outwardly, the lenses reflected the light from within the saloon, and a soft blue glow took over around the edges. The men now looked at her with a twinge of fear and doubt.

Her hands drifted back down toward her sides.

Her hands passed her chin. The men began to flare out.

Her hands passed her neck. Three men on her right.

Her hands passed her shoulders. Three men on her left.

Her hands passed her breasts. Six men in front of her.

Alix filled her hands faster than any of those who stood against her. *Zmmph, zmmph.* One shot from both Plasvelds killed two of the six ahead. She immediately dropped to one knee. Plasfire from the men on either side of her crossed above her head. One man on her left died. She threw out her arms: *zmmph, zmmph.* A man on each side fell. She tucked, rolled to her right, and finished on one knee. One of the men thought he could grapple her. As soon as he reached in close, she put a plasma bolt through his chest. She let the body fall on top of her: a shield.

Alix extended her left arm from beneath the dead man, her goggles looking straight through him to the last living man who had stood on her right—living no more. She rolled over top the man's body, tilting her head back, her outstretched right arm dead accurate as the last man on her left fell. She continued rolling, plasfire hitting the dirt street around her. She rolled beneath the boardwalk into the dark.

The four men standing above shuffled their feet and fired wildly through the boards. Alix lay on her back, shoulder against the stone foundation, safe from any shots. The men paused to see if they had done the job.

She couldn't extend her arms, so her elbows rested on the soft mud. She saw them through the wood and smoke. *Zmmph, zmmph, zmmph, zmmph.* Each man fell heavily on the wood, and blood poured through the holes, dripping onto Alix's face and shirt. A drop fell onto her left goggle lens. She wiped it with a thumb then rolled out from under the boardwalk.

The doors hung wide open, bright lights inside. She crawled out from under the boardwalk, bearing both Plasvelds. The music stopped, tables overturned, glasses broke. Feet pounded and shuffled on the floor. Women screamed as they ran. Slowly, she walked up the steps, her boots thumping on the boardwalk. She stood at the threshold.

Alix took one step. As her foot touched the floor inside, a searing pain spread through her body. Her blood seemed to boil, and her head felt like a clapper within a bell. Screaming, she put her full hands up by her ears, as if a siren blared only centimeters from her head, and stumbled through the doorway.

Men hiding inside took their chances. Plasfire rained on her, and she took one in the left shoulder. Alix pushed through the pain and rolled to her left, behind overturned tables and the curved corner of the bar. She spat blood onto the floor as the painful vibrations under her skin began to subside. Then, she remembered.

Felix detected a security system at the door when they first came to Silas's place. Then, it had been passive, expecting their arrival. This time, it was coiled to strike. *Did they know? Did they know about the hyper-fluid? No, they expected her and Felix,* she said to herself.

Then, she felt the black blood moving through her body, up her arm, in a wave of pain. She clenched her teeth as it reached her shoulder. She took long breaths, steadying herself, and raised her hands again. She spun around the bar, opening fire on every silhouette of a man she detected.

Another plasma bolt cut through her belly, and she faltered, then killed the man who had hit his mark. Men came in through doors from back rooms, stairwells from lower levels, all trying to stop her. Alix's mind operated on a linear path, like a train barreling down a track. She felt as if her body moved involuntarily, preternaturally seeing the men before they made their moves. Each one was too slow, too off the mark, too gripped with fear.

She killed every last one.

The saloon fell silent. Smoke hung overhead. Wood sizzled from the plasma burns slowly cooling. Alix ejected the plasma cells onto the floor with a metallic ringing. She reloaded, spun the chambers, and headed up the stairs.

Then, she noticed her unsteady balance. Her left foot caught on one of the steps, nearly tripping her. She held the Plasveld in her left hand just a little lower than the one in her right. Her breathing became labored. Leaning on the wall, she lifted her shirt slowly, seeing the black patch covering her wound from the dock. Blood seeped around the edges, and she knocked her head back against the wall.

Fuck, this stuff is giving out, she thought. *I guess there's only so much it can hold together.* Laughter at the grim truth took over.

She continued the climb.

The door to Silas's office was cracked, and a soft, pleasant song drifted out over the silence of death in the saloon. Alix pushed the door open the rest of the way with her foot, scanning the room with her Plasvelds. No Silas.

The Thin Man stood at the wet bar on the far wall. There was no point trying to sneak up on him—he knew she was there. Ice clinked in a glass. Alix saw to her left an old phonograph playing a symphony. The Thin Man turned, a glass of chisik in each hand.

"Well done, captain," he said with a smile.

Alix glared at him through her goggles, but they couldn't hide her furrowed brow. She still held her Plasvelds level. She stood a little heavier on her right leg, her left arm sagged. Her hair had begun to drop out of the red band, blood smeared on her face around her goggles. Stains of blood and booze darkened her shirt.

"Have a seat," he invited, pointing to the plush chairs and couch.

"I'm not here to listen to you talk," she said.

"Then shoot me." He shrugged.

For the first time tonight, she hesitated.

The Thin Man sat in a chair and set one of the glasses on the table for her. Alix used her thumbs to push her goggles back on her head, revealing her cold stare and a red outline where they had been tight to her face.

"You burned Sora's orchard," Alix said.

"That's correct." He took a sip. "It seems tragedy befalls everyone who follows you, a path littered with death and destruction."

"Those were your actions, not mine."

"Actions have reactions."

"Just tell me where Silas is, and I'll come back and kill you later."

"He's gone, I'm afraid. Out of your reach. Please, have a seat. Catch your breath. Have a drink. You'll need it."

"Why?"

"Because afterward, you and I are going to finish this." The Thin Man settled in his chair.

Alix narrowed her eyes as she looked around the room and found no sign of foul play. There were no men left in the saloon coming to kill her. No one at her back. The Thin Man didn't even wear his plasbolts. He made that clear by hanging them on the corner of the couch. Alix waited, then holstered her Plasvelds. She unbuckled the belt and set it on the table as she sat down and picked up the glass of chisik.

"I learned quite a bit about you," the Thin Man continued. "Well, everything *possible* to learn. I really don't care about the mysteries of who you are and where you came from, as Silas and Otto wanted to know. There was just one detail I found fascinating."

"What was that?" Alix said, the chisik warming her throat and chest, her head swooning.

"You became quite the prize fighter on Corto—after your transition, I might add. All the more impressive."

"Spiros was a good teacher."

"Men came to test themselves against you, and all of them left broken and beaten."

"You want to see how you measure up?" Alix scoffed into her glass.

"I have my pride too."

"All *men* do."

"Don't try your Solar face with me."

Alix swallowed the last sip. "Don't pretend you have honor."

"Like you?"

She paused as she set the glass back on the table. "I never claimed to have honor."

The Thin Man smiled and reached into his shirt pocket. He pulled out a stack of crits bound in a casing and set the stack on the table. "Five hundred, I'll wager."

Alix curled her lip and smiled. "You're on."

The Thin Man rolled his sleeves up past his elbows. Alix set her goggles down and pulled her shirt off, revealing a threadbare tank top. The Thin Man got a look at her bloody, black and blue body, the black patchwork of the hyper-fluid holding together many wounds. He didn't know what to make of it, other than it presented advantages for him to exploit.

Alix stretched her neck, her shoulders, while the Thin Man stood, fists up—right foot and fist forward. She remembered he was left-handed. They sized each other up, subtly swaying as they stood apart from one another.

He obviously has the reach, Alix thought.

The Thin Man stepped forward and threw a quick right jab. Alix moved aside easily, knowing the jab was only a test of her reflexes. She smiled, and they circled one another in the space between the chairs and the wet bar. Two more jabs came at her, and Alix leaned away from each one, letting the Thin Man step forward. Finally, he threw a left cross. Alix ducked and put three quick jabs into his gut. He brought an elbow down like a hammer on an anvil.

The blow staggered Alix. She wrapped her arms around the Thin Man's waist, using his balance to steady herself. Another elbow. Alix pushed him back, driving him into the wet bar, glasses and bottles shaking in their racks. The Thin Man grimaced as Alix popped back up, sending a jab into his face, but her left was stymied as he got his hands back up in defense.

Alix backed off, smiling confidently.

"You're not as rusty as I imagined," he said, wiping his mouth with the back of his hand.

"Funny, I expected better from you," she quipped.

The Thin Man returned to his stance, and she let him come to her. They both moved, bobbed, looking for openings. He wasn't impatient.

She leaned, ducked, and stepped back from more of his offense, but the step cost her—he pressed forward, put a foot in as she stepped back, tripping her. Alix fell, crashing through the coffee table.

So that's how it's going to be, she thought.

She quickly stood and put one of the chairs between them, moving around to get into clear space again. He had let her get up, showing her he could have mounted and trapped her. Instead, he let her up and invited her in.

Alix stepped forward, throwing a combination to keep him busy. He deflected and avoided, but now, it was her turn to show him it would not be a simple boxing match. She swept her right leg, putting her shin hard into the inside of his right crus. He screamed and doubled over as Alix grabbed the backs of his shoulders and lifted her knee into his face. His head flew back, and he stumbled on his heels, falling to the floor. She stood, waiting.

Anger started to burn in the Thin Man's eyes as he stood. Blood leaked from his nose, and Alix smirked. He came in with his full weight, tackling her, throwing the silent rules out the window. She put her knee into his stomach and flipped him over her head, sending him crashing through one of the plush chairs. Rolling back onto her feet, she turned, and he flipped the sofa back and against the wall.

Now, his frustration began to drive.

Alix still avoided his every blow, ducked under, put a hook in his ribs with her left, but he snatched her ponytail, jerking her head back as she cried out. With his right hand, he drove his thumb into the black wound of her left shoulder. She screamed in agony as he pressed into the soft, black film formed by the hyper-fluid. He pulled back and hammered fists into the wound. She felt dazed and unable to respond as the pain came in unbearable waves.

Finally, she reached up with her right hand, digging her fingernails across his face, blood and flesh beneath her nails. He let go of her so he could put his hands to his face and backed away. Alix fell to her back, held her shoulder, and tried to stand. She was unsteady; she shook her head and blinked rapidly, putting up her hands again.

The Thin Man's left eye had trouble staying open from the cuts, but he drove forward with full force. They traded blows, neither combatant able to keep all at bay. Alix felt the warm blood running down her left arm from the wound he targeted as her head began to sway.

Alix threw a right, but the Thin Man caught her wrist, flinging her around and throwing her into the wet bar. She crashed into it, her back and elbows shattering cabinets and bottles as glass embedded in her skin. She fell to the floor, bottles and glasses following. She felt chisik soak her hair and clothes, running into her eyes, burning. The Thin Man's heavy breathing came closer as she tried to wipe the liquor from her eyes. Then, she heard the *click, click* of his lighter. Alix opened one burning eye in time to see the flame rush up and over her.

She rolled back and forth, patting the flames off her clothes. The Thin Man hefted her off the floor and slammed her back and head into the wall. He threw his forearm into her face, again and again. Alix couldn't see, but she squeezed her left arm up to stop the next forearm. The dull hit on her arm knocked her sideways along the wall. She tried to steady herself.

The Thin Man grabbed the waist of her pants and threw her across the room, over Silas's desk. Alix spilled headfirst into the floor, crumbled into the space between the desk and the wall. The thudding of his boots approached, and Alix felt his hands on her, dragging her across the office and finally lifting her easily. He threw her horizontally through the office window.

Alix fell, her shoulder slamming into the bar; she bounced and hit the floor, glass falling on her. She lay gasping for air among the bodies she'd strewn across the saloon. As she clawed and felt at her surroundings, her head pounded, her shoulder burned, and her whole body began to weaken. Up on all fours, she crawled slowly toward the bar, reaching up for it to pull herself to her feet.

"Come on, captain," the Thin Man called out. "Is this how your vengeance ends?"

His boots thumped on the stairs, crunched over broken glass. The flames in the office reached out over the ceiling in the saloon, and Alix could feel the heat overhead. She turned and leaned against the bar, her left eye swollen shut, chest heaving. Her fingers groped behind the bar as the Thin Man approached.

Fingers wrapped around Alix's throat, and the Thin Man sneered in her face. Suddenly, she whipped a bottle into his temple, shattering it. He stumbled, falling over a table, putting a hand up to cover his face. Adrenaline fueling her, Alix sprang forward and stabbed the broken bottle neck into his thigh above the knee. She ripped it out, arm pressed firmly across his throat. She adjusted her grip on the bottle and stabbed down, but he held her wrist. They pushed against one another, Alix roaring furiously as she tried to force her arm down.

A sudden, sharp pain in her side stole her breath. She pushed back from him, looking down at the knife in her side. She spat blood down her chest. The flames swirled overhead. Smoke grew thick. Alix ripped the knife out, her blood dripped off the blade. Her head was swimming. She could hardly see at all, now, the world falling into a grey and orange blur. She waited for the hyper-fluid to seal the knife wound but could not feel the liquid moving through her. She pressed her left hand over the open wound, staggering back toward the stairs.

Every shred of strength and awareness Alix had left in her focused on pulling herself up the stairs, limping, bleeding, crying. She fell at the top, looking down the hall toward Silas's office wreathed in flames. The fire spread, licking the office doorframe, touching the balcony floor and up the walls. Like a moth, she crawled toward the flames. She pressed her right shoulder to the wall and screamed as she lifted herself up on her feet. Blood streaked what was once fine, stained wood as she took each agonizing step.

The heat intensified, sweat and blood pouring into her eyes. The smoke clogged her nose and throat, but still, she staggered into the office. Through the slits of her eyes, she looked among the carnage. She tripped and fell over a fragment of a broken chair. Her hands groped around, her fingers and hands burning. Finally, her fingers felt the familiar pattern in the wood, and the backstrap burned her flesh. She tightened her grip and pulled the Plasveld out of her holster.

When she rolled over, she saw the Thin Man at the top of the stairs, bloody and broken, bent over at the waist. She clenched her teeth nearly to the point of breaking and stood, her left hand trying to hold firm over the knife wound. A weak and useless gesture, in reality. She stopped in the doorway and leveled her Plasveld.

The Thin Man held himself up with his right hand on the wall, a plasbolt in his left hand from one of the dead men downstairs. He could barely see Alix's face. The fire framed her body in the doorway, appearing to him like a shadow, a force of will and divine retribution.

He smiled.

They both fired at once.

The Thin Man doubled over onto the floor.

Alix dropped to her knees, the Plasveld slipped from her hand. Despite the overwhelming heat at her back, her body had gone numb. She couldn't hold her eyes open any longer, her mouth slack, drawing ragged breaths. She would not stop.

She could not stop.

With her left hand, she gripped the searing hot knob of a door, turned it, and threw her body into the door. Air rushed in, the fire roaring as it followed her. Alix crawled along the floor toward one of the two windows. Vision faded as coughing overcame her breathing. With weak, bloody fingers, she reached for the window, scraping them on the glass.

Finally, screaming, she stood, staggered back from the window—then she ran and threw herself, shattering the pane of glass, flying through the air.

Beneath the flames, Silas and two men, the only ones left alive who hadn't fled, finished preparations to leave. The sub-level was dark and damp, eerily empty. They tossed bags into a skimmer. Silas checked his syncpad, awaiting a message from Otto. The screen went suddenly black.

Two plasma rounds lit the room around him, killing both men at his sides. Silas spun, gazing into the dark as Wick stepped forward, plasbolt steaming in his hand. The other hand hung at his belt. Silas put up both hands, but instead of fear, he smiled and bargained.

"Ah, Wick, it's you," he said. "I was afraid it was that woman or that monster artie."

"You got nothing to fear from them," Wick said.

"Let's talk—come to an agreement. I'm heading out of here to meet Otto's men. I got no use for your ship, so take her! Our debts are settled."

Wick stared, cold and distant.

"I got a hundred thousand crits here." Silas motioned behind him. "They're yours too."

"That's what you think? Every man's got a price?"

"Every *smart* man."

Wick put two plasma rounds through Silas's chest. The man shook and slumped against the skimmer and fell to the concrete floor. Wick stood there with his plasbolt still pointed down at the dead man. He turned and walked away, toward the *Procella*. He opened the personnel ramp and walked inside, turning left to the cockpit.

Alix lay on a roof across a narrow alley from Silas's compound. The cold air competed with the flames that now reached into the sky from the burning building. She rolled onto her back, gazing into the night sky. The billowing smoke veiled the stars. The only memory her mind could conjure brought her back to the Cradle.

As a child, Alix lay on her back in the prickly, dry grass. The night sky was brilliant, filled with stars, the galaxy stretching across from horizon to horizon. No one stood within a thousand kilometers of her—she lay truly alone. Faint wisps of clouds moved in the night. Alix shivered, feeling the cold tickling at her hair and skin.

She looked further back, tilting her head just enough to see the sky behind her and the faint silvery line crossing perpendicular to the galaxy. She stared up at the shimmering line, still against the motion of the stars as the planet turned. The first step she must take was to find a way up there—to the rings.

On Celestine, a blinding light overhead filled Alix's sight. If she had the strength, she would have lifted her hand to block it out, but her eyes closed. A rush of wind swept around her, and a sound echoed against the rooftops and buildings across the street, drowning out the sound of the flames. Alix felt a strong but gentle hand slide beneath her back. Before she faded, she felt her body being lifted, moved. She turned her head, her eyelids fluttering, gazing into Felix's stark blue eyes.

Then, the world went dark and fell silent.

15

The Path

Late in the morning, fire crews still worked as the Black Barrel lay in utter ruin. A faint skeleton stood where the fire could not burn the omniite frame. The beams would soon fetch a high price from other builders. Marshal Rayburn stood across the street, arms crossed, hat back on his head. Fire skimmers showered the buildings with water while flame-suffocating foam covered everything. Down the street, Cole and his men held back the crowd that gathered.

The buildings on either side of the Black Barrel suffered minimal damage, at least relative to the alternative. They would need to rebuild and repair some things, but that was a far cry from losing everything. In the deep pit of his stomach, the marshal knew. Alix showed up, and unleashed hell. She killed a dozen men outside, their bodies within black bags lying in the street. Then she went inside and killed who knows how many more before the place burned to the ground. The fire burned so tall and so intense, the black smoke made the dawn difficult to perceive. Checking his syncpad, the marshal saw that it was near noon, and he had not slept or eaten.

He walked down the boardwalk and met Cole by the crowd. "Keep charge of things here. Don't let any scrappers in for that omni unless they got paperwork."

"Yes, sir."

"I'm going back to the east quarter, check that last lead."

Across town, the marshal stood outside a scrapyard. The scrapper's shop lay open to the street, its metal retractable walls lifted for the day. The machines, sparks, and unbearable noise assailed his ears. He shouted, louder and louder, until the person standing over the guts of a skimmer turned off their plascutters. A metal panel fell away with a loud bang.

Jesse saw the marshal through their protective mask. They flipped it up, pulled it off, then slicked back their hair from their face. The marshal waved politely, limping deeper into the shop.

"What can I do for you, marshal?" Jesse said.

"What's your name?"

"Jesse, this is my shop. Totally legal," they said, the last words stressed and drawn out as Jesse picked up the heavy metal panel and dropped it loudly on a pallet with other flat metal panels.

"I'm not here about your business. I have some questions for you about…other matters."

"Like what?"

The marshal sighed. "Well, I'll just say it—let's not pretend like there isn't a hole in your floor back there." Jesse tried to hide their surprise at his knowledge. "And let's not pretend like you didn't help a woman and a sentient get into the shipyard through that hole."

"You're going to take me in for that?" Jesse tried to keep moving, to avoid letting the stress overtake their hands.

"No."

Jesse stopped. "What is it you want?"

"I want to know what happened *after* they came back."

Jesse shrugged and leaned against the skimmer frame. "The woman was wounded. They patched her up here, and then left."

"You don't know where they went?"

"Look, I didn't know those two at all."

"Then why did you help them?"

Jesse cocked their head to the side. "Ten thousand crits."

"Was there anybody else with them?"

"Just those two, and another man." As Jesse said it, they turned and picked up a rag from the frame. Better to not let the marshal see their face as they lied. Jesse began wiping their hands.

The marshal thought for a few moments, rubbing his fingers over his unshaven face. Of course, he suspected Jesse of lying. *They knew more than they let on, and perhaps there was a deeper connection to Wick or Sora,* he thought. However, he believed them when they said they didn't know Alix and Felix. Either way, it would be a good idea to leave someone he trusted to keep an eye on the place.

"Well, you let me know if the woman and sentient return or get in touch with you."

Jesse simply nodded.

"Thanks for your help." The marshal tipped his hat, and walked away.

Alix squeezed her eyes and blinked them opened, straining to see the dark metal around her. The burning and itching in her eyes rushed back as her mind adjusted to being awake. She squeezed her eyes shut, opened them again, and blinked rapidly—but her vision would not clear. Trying to move an arm failed; all she could manage was to move a few fingers and toes. Even that was painful. She lifted her head, which felt like a two-ton stone, and saw her body beneath a grey blanket. When she couldn't hold her head up anymore, she fell back to the pillow, gasping for air.

She opened her mouth, but no words came out.

Felix opened the metal hatch, excited. He wore the biggest, stupidest grin Alix had ever seen on his face. She wished she could make her face smile back.

"You're awake!" he said.

He knelt by the cot, touching her arm beneath the blanket, staring into her eyes. The soft blue of his swirling eyes soothed her, even though she saw them as if through a morning fog. For a moment, her mind believed they were on the *Shadow*, but then she remembered. A tear ran down her face, and Felix gently caught it with a finger and kissed her forehead.

"You're okay," he promised. "You've been out for days. We're on Wick's ship, in the canyonlands."

Still, she could not form words, her lips moving slow and haphazardly.

"You've suffered a great deal. You were almost dead when we picked you up off that roof," Felix continued. "The burns will heal okay, I think. I managed to set a few broken bones. The hyper-fluid is still working on your earlier wounds. You really pushed it to the breaking point."

Alix felt like the fire of that night still burned in her chest. She coughed, which sent waves of pain through her entire body.

"I don't *think* you'll have permanent lung damage from the smoke, but it will take time before you get back to one hundred percent." He ran his fingers across her brow, keeping the hair from her face.

Days passed before Alix could sit up for any length of time. Even more came and went before she could speak. Each day ran together in her mind: the dark room on Wick's ship, Felix coming in and out to check on her, give her water, some simple food, then more sleep. So much sleep. Nightmares plagued her day and night. At least her voice returned enough to scream herself awake.

Felix cared for her well, but eventually, restlessness took hold. They took walks as her strength returned. Alix's left arm hung in a sling, her face still black and blue. The *Procella* sat on the rim of a canyon where a river once curved sharply, creating a rounded jut of stone like a natural landing pad. The bands of rock down into the canyon matched the light of the setting sun: orange, purple, blood red. Felix and Alix sat together a few meters from the ship, looking out over the desolate land. Alix's thoughts wandered to Sora, who she hadn't spoken to since before she left the farmstead.

Alix remembered the *Shadow* in disrepair; thoughts of Sora became the orchard on fire, and still, as she looked into the brilliant sky, she thought of the Xypha station orbiting overhead. She caught a lump in her throat, wiped a tear from her face. Alix set her jaw. Silas was dead. The Thin Man was dead. All his people were dead. But Xypha remained up there.

"Sora?" Alix could barely get the word out.

"We haven't been in touch since we left the village," Felix said. "She would have come with Wick and I, but she needed to stay to help her sister, and her people."

Alix nodded, fighting back tears.

The sun dropped low in the east where the sky exploded with orange and pink hues. Golden beams of light reached through purple clouds. The desert wind whistled in the canyon below. Alix rubbed her boot in the dark red soil.

Then, she thought of home—the Cradle. A dead world where thick brown clouds blocked the sunset. Grey days faded into black nights; heavy, oppressive heat scorched every stone. She realized the name was a misnomer: it had not been a cradle, but a forge.

Otto stared at his vizscreen, disgusted. Silas was dead. He tapped his fingers on his desk. Silas commanded several weak council members, and Otto could easily continue that arrangement. Those men cared about *wealth,* or at least the illusion of it. There was certainly no problem continuing the flow of crits to those council members, but an even greater opportunity presented itself. The vizscreen showed Silas's landholdings across the valley. The man owned a great band of farms and empty land west of Verisport. With no heirs, Silas had no plan to pass along his holdings, so the Verisport authorities would surely portion the lands for sale. He swirled a glass of wine. Silas being dead was the best outcome he could have hoped for.

A transmission alerted on Otto's vizscreen, and Fenn Loucks appeared before him. "Sir, I have something you should see."

"What is it, Loucks?" Otto's mind was calculating, planning for the future, and he resented the interruption.

"Final analysis of the scene at the docks."

"I thought we'd been over this?"

"Sorry, sir, I did not want to bother you with this unless the results were confirmed."

"Am I going to hear what it is any time soon?"

Loucks cleared his throat, "On your screen now, sir."

Otto studied the new data in front of him—a blood sample. "This is impossible."

"I thought the same, but I checked it multiple times. Without security footage, I am unsure which individual it belongs to, but it was found near that ship."

"One of the attackers."

"Yes sir."

"So someone escaped the Cradle. How fascinating."

"That is Xypha property, sir. Should we call in a seeker?"

"No." Otto cut him off. "We need to focus on Silas's lands in town and in the valley. I would like to acquire them."

"Without Silas, how do you plan to keep pressure on the council?"

"Greed is a powerful tool. We've just cut out the middle man." Otto thought for a moment, swirling his glass, looking beyond Loucks on the vizscreen. "Get your people to Silas's compound. If his data survived the fire, it could be very valuable to us. Let's start there."

"Yes, sir." Loucks disappeared from the screen.

Sora reached blindly for a wrench on the shop floor, her hand groped just out from underneath the shaker. She felt the wrench in her fingers, but not on the floor. Jo handed it to her, and Sora smiled, no one seeing her face as she took the wrench and continued working. She grunted as she tightened the last nut, then pushed her creeper out from under the machine. Sora put her feet on the floor so the creeper wouldn't roll away from her as she sat up.

"All done?" Jo said.

"Finally." Sora let out an exaggerated huff.

Their happiness about finishing the repairs on the shaker came with a cloud of mourning. They fixed an essential piece of their harvesting machinery, now with two-thirds fewer trees to harvest from. Sora had been trying to ease the tension between her and her sister for weeks. She still felt as if she'd lost some of Jo's trust, that perhaps there was something between them that could not be repaired. It would only grow, slowly, almost imperceptibly, until a gap lay between them that neither could cross.

They walked together in the evening. Instead of passing beneath the boughs of twilight trees, they walked amid a blackened, scarred land. The sisters came to the usual spot where Sora sat in the wet grass, looking up at the stars. She leaned back on her hands while Jo laid her head in Sora's lap. The moons hung bright in the deep, purple sky. The sisters sat amid the silence until the stars moved from one place to another.

"You miss her, don't you?" Jo said.

Sora's heart sank. "I do."

"I'm glad she killed those men. They deserved it," Jo said. A moment of silence, then, "Do you know where she is?"

"No, I haven't spoken to her. She hasn't spoken to me."

"Why don't you?" Jo's eyes searched the stars.

"Because I want to stay here with you." Sora gently stroked her sister's hair. "I mean, look what happened when I left."

"You should at least try."

The words stung Sora like a cold wind. Jo's voice was quiet and hollow as Sora kept her face turned up to the sky so Jo couldn't see the pain in her eyes. She wanted to reach out to Alix, but guilt held her back. She needed to stay with Jo, but she could not keep her mind nor her heart from thinking of Alix. The distance between Sora and Jo would only worsen, like a stream carving a canyon over millennia.

The usual crowds of people walked by the marshal's table at his favorite café in the market square. Remains of his breakfast were scattered on a plate in front of him, fork and knife crossed over. The marshal sat back in his chair, sipping a cup of coffee, watching the people going about their business. A moment of peace made him smile.

"This seat taken?" a familiar voice said.

When the marshal turned his head, Alix stood across from him. The marshal squinted in the late morning sun to get a better look at her. A faded purple poncho hung over her shoulders, a small tight braid running over and behind her ear. Her face still carried bruises around her eyes and cuts almost healed from broken glass. No goggles hung around her neck or sat upon her head—he could see no bolts at her waist.

Alix sat before the marshal could reply. The poncho concealed the sling in which her left arm still hung. Seeing her at the table, a woman approached and asked if Alix desired food or drink.

"Just a coffee."

"What are you doing here?" the marshal said.

Alix huffed, "We used to have breakfast all the time."

"I wonder why that changed." The marshal took a sip of coffee.

"You tell me."

"You changed."

Alix nodded, contemplating the statement, which felt more like an accusation. The woman returned and filled a fine white ceramic mug with coffee. Alix smiled at her, the sun kissing her cheeks. She savored the coffee; it tasted far superior to the dregs of Wick's galley on the *Procella*.

"I came back here as myself. I'm sorry that was a problem for you," she said.

The marshal looked past her. "Did you come here to argue?"

"No, actually. I just came here to warn you."

That got him to look at her, and it put his hackles up. "You're warning *me*?"

"Yes, because if you get between me and Xypha, you won't live to see this place return to the way you wish it was."

"Don't threaten me *boy*." The marshal's eyes flashed.

Alix smirked and looked down at the table, at the dark coffee against the white cup upon the white tablecloth. "How long have you wanted to get that one out? Is that why you pulled me out of that box? The childless marshal needed a *boy* to carry on his legacy."

"And what's wrong with my legacy?"

"Xypha thought they could dictate who and what I was going to be too."

"Is that what you thought I was doing?" The marshal shook his head. "So what is it *you* are choosing to be? A killer?"

Alix stared at him. Nothing she said could have cut more than the knowing smile on her face. The marshal was not a parent in pain. He was an order being upended, angered that someone would dare choose to see the world differently.

"Look, I didn't choose this path—you did," he said.

"You would just let Xypha in here, to take this planet and burn it? Your home?"

"There are ways to go about things, Alix. There is an order to things, and it is my responsibility to keep that order. If Xypha enters that order, then so be it. I cannot keep them off this planet. But I can maintain the peace and safety of the people in this valley."

Alix sat back, scratching the cup with her finger. "You'll fail."

"I told you not to threaten me."

Alix finished the cup of coffee. With a heavy sigh, she stood and looked down at the marshal—that man who pulled her out of a box and put a bolt in her hand. Now he dared to tell her not to use it. There was no point in talking any further.

"That wasn't a threat. It was the truth. Goodbye, marshal." She walked through the tables of the café and then disappeared into the crowded square.

The marshal sat alone, a few deep breaths pushed the anger down as he sipped at the last bit of coffee in his cup. The syncpad on his arm vibrated as he reached into his pocket to pay and tip the woman. He drew his hand out of his pocket and looked at the pad—a transmission from Cole. The marshal rolled his eyes and swiped the pad.

"What is it?" he said.

"Scrappers coming in to get that ship from the dock. *Her* ship." Cole's voice shook at hearing the marshal's tone.

"That's for Loucks to handle." It was the truth, if Xypha wanted to have jurisdiction over the dockyard, then it was one less problem for him to deal with.

"I thought you'd want to know. The paperwork is that scrapper I've been keeping an eye on."

The paperwork appeared on his syncpad, and the marshal clenched his teeth, curling his upper lip. *So that's why Alix was in town,* he thought. *Did Loucks know Jesse was the one who let Alix into the docks?* The marshal ran his finger over the rim of the coffee cup. The ship couldn't fly; *wouldn't* fly for months. The places Alix could take the *Shadow* for the repairs she needed were limited.

"Sir?" Cole said.

"Just leave them be. We'll keep an eye on the scrapper's shop."

Dockworkers in grey jumpsuits surrounded the *Shadow*. A salvage hauler hovered above, descending slowly. One of the workers gave a sign with bright batons for the pilot to hold their position. The call came in to the hauler to drop its cables. Six cables ejected from the underside of the ship, lowering until the dockworkers on the ground snatched the heavy hooks on their ends. The hauler pilot held the ship steady, adjusting the gusts of wind and electromagnetic energy in small amounts. One by one, the dockworkers secured the cables to the *Shadow*'s hull, where they'd spent the days before welding eyes to it for this exact purpose.

The pilot in the hauler received another transmission, confirmation that the two ships were secured. The cables tightened, and the hauler descended lower before the pilot pushed the throttle down, the engines screaming, the entire ship vibrating. The *Shadow* was heavy, almost twice the size of the hauler. The men on the ground covered their faces and shielded their eyes as dirt whipped up from the docking bay floor.

At last, the *Shadow* began to rise. The hauler lifted it off the ground at an agonizing, slow pace. The *Shadow* groaned as the landing gear broke and fell away from where it had listed to one side. Sudden breaks in the damaged gear caused the ship to sway, and the hauler pilot tightened their grip on the sticks to counteract the movement. The *Shadow* rose above the docking bay walls in a cruel, ironic flight. Alix fought off the tears as she watched from the hauler's open side door.

"You're all clear, Jess," she said.

Jesse focused so much on hefting the ship off the ground and not crashing it or their hauler into the flight tower that they didn't even reply to Alix. The hauler rotated in air, turning south. As the open door panned by the flight tower, Alix stared into the windows she knew were the marshal's office. She wasn't sure if he looked back at her.

The hauler moved forward, hovering over the town below. Jesse's skill impressed Alix; the way they muscled the sticks, moved their feet to keep the ship level. Flying the hauler while moving a ship of the *Shadow*'s size was like flying a brick with a mountain attached. Alix sat on the floor, holding cargo netting with her right hand as they moved over Verisport. She looked over the chis sea in the distance, somewhere within it, Sora's village.

"Coordinates are in, Jess," Felix's voice said over a shared comms channel.

"It'll take me a while to get this rig up there," Jesse replied.

"Just make sure you don't drop it," Wick cut in.

"If you thought you could fly this thing, why didn't you volunteer?" Jesse shouted back at him over the roar of the engines and the howling wind. "Oh, that's right—you *can't* fly this thing."

"I can fly anything! Besides, I'm on my way to Corto," Wick protested.

"Shut up," Alix groaned, looking up at Jesse's back in the pilot's chair. "Wick, don't forget everything on that list."

"Yeah, yeah, I'll get your groceries and medicine, don't worry."

His attitude made Alix smile before she thought how alarming *that* felt.

Finally, the hauler passed Verisport, the green below fading to brown, then the burnt orange of the desert highlands. Twisting canyons went by beneath Alix's feet as she relaxed, trusting in Jesse's skill. Alix put her shoulder into the hull, arm on her knee on the edge of the open door. To her right, a thin, linear cloud split the sun in two, its rays fanning out above and below. She tilted her head to look along the hull. Far ahead, the sun touched snowcapped mountains.

Sora sat at her workbench, sipping a hot cup of coffee. Her next challenge sat behind her: one of the fire suppression drones that malfunctioned during the orchard fire. A digital scan of the large, globular machine stared back at her on a vizscreen. She manipulated the three-dimensional scan with one keystroke, looking for internal mechanical issues—*click—click—click*.

"I'm looking for a good mechanic." The voice was hoarse and quiet.

Sora spun around on the stool, eyes bright and hopeful. Alix leaned on the drone, face bruised, arm in a sling. Her sly smile spread across her face as Sora fought off her own smile, pursed her lips, and crossed her arms.

"You have crits?"

Alix shook her head. "Not really. I gave them all away."

Sora ran across the room and wrapped her arms around Alix. Tears welled in Sora's eyes as she squeezed, and Alix grimaced and laughed, pain ricocheting through her limbs.

"Hey, easy, easy," Alix said.

"Oh, shit, sorry!" Sora pulled back and threw her hands up over her mouth.

"It's okay."

They both laughed as Alix used her good arm to touch Sora's face. Sora smiled before Alix drew her in for a long, slow kiss. Sora touched her forehead to Alix's after their lips separated.

"You going to stick around for a while?" Sora said.

"Well, I need a good mechanic to fix my ship."

Sora stepped back, playfully defiant. "So I should take my time?"

Alix turned up a smile. "I'm not leaving, Sora. The fight is here."

The words balanced in Sora's mind on a point between relief and dread. "Is that the only reason you're staying?"

"Sora, that's not what I meant," Alix sighed. "This is a thing I have to do, and I can't do it alone."

"I'm not a killer, Alix," Sora said.

"That's what I like about you." Alix took Sora's hands. "I would never ask you to do that."

"Well, then I'm your girl." Sora's mouth scrunched as she tried to hide the smile when she realized what she said. "But, be warned, I'm expensive!"

Alix raised an eyebrow, grinning. She pulled Sora in for a hug as best she could with only one good arm. Sora leaned back and explored Alix's face with her lips. She found each scar and cut that still healed before Alix pressed her lips tightly to Sora's. Their tongues touched, rolled, and intertwined, and for a moment, they were the only two people on Celestine.